hide
with
me

hide with me

a novel

sorboni banerjee

RAZORBILL

RAZORBILL

An Imprint of Penguin Random House LLC
Penguin.com

RAZORBILL & colophon is a registered trademark of Penguin Random House LLC.

First published in the United States of America by Razorbill,
an imprint of Penguin Random House LLC, 2018

Copyright © 2018 by Sorboni Banerjee

LIBRARY OF CONGRESS CATALOGING-IN-PUBLICATION DATA
Names: Banerjee, Sorboni, author.
Title: Hide with me / Sorboni Banerjee.
Description: [New York] : Razorbill, 2018. | Summary: Cade, seventeen, yearns to leave the
border town of Tanner, Texas, and when a mysterious girl appears, broken and bleeding, on his
family farm the two begin to plan their escape, unaware that a cartel boss wants the girl back.
Identifiers: LCCN 2018013403 | ISBN 9780451478351 (hardback)
Subjects: | CYAC: Runaways—Fiction. | Friendship—Fiction. | Foster children—Fiction.
| Farm life—Texas—Fiction. | Texas—Fiction.
Classification: LCC PZ7.1.B3645 Hid 2018 | DDC [Fic]—dc23
LC record available at https://lccn.loc.gov/2018013403

ISBN: 9780451478351

Printed in the United States of America

1 3 5 7 9 10 8 6 4 2

Interior design by Corina Lupp

To my mother for the love of reading,
my father for the art of storytelling,
and my little brother for being my first audience.

THE BOY

The girl was like a train.

When I was a kid, trains still ran on the old tracks behind our farm, and when they came by the whole house shook. At first it was a roar so loud it had layers, deep rumble to high-pitched screech, and you couldn't talk or even really think. Then you got used to it. Maybe I shook with the walls. Maybe my brain was just loud. But the train would pass, and the only sign that it had rattled by was the picture frames on the walls left slightly crooked. And after a while, the slanted lines looked normal.

The girl was like that. Finding her shook the walls of everything. Rattled, crooked, loud—that's the world that starts looking normal when a girl derails and takes you and the town with her.

When I found the girl, she should have been dead.

"What the hell?"

My dog's left paw was red, and so was his nose. I thought he'd killed a rabbit, which would have been a miracle, because my dog

Hunter is not a hunter at all. When rabbits dash out at him in the fields he jumps, four legs off the ground, and then has to run in a circle to calm down.

But that day he was whining in a real funny way, kind of like when he's hiding a bone—excited or freaked out, I can never really tell. I touched the fur under his snout, and my fingers came back all sticky red too. Hunter ran a few steps ahead into the rows of corn, then turned around, waiting to see if I was coming.

It was late evening, after football practice, and I was walking the edges of the farm, like I do. Like it'll somehow make stuff start growing. And that'll somehow make my dad forget I'm the only one around to beat on because nothing ever does.

"What? What is it?" I grumbled at Hunter, and then I saw what.

In the shadows of the cornstalks was a girl. Her blond hair was streaked with something dark red. Blood. It crusted over her swollen-shut eye. Her other eye, bright blue, was open wide, all scared. Her skin had gone gray, no color in her lips, pale neck quivering with her short breaths.

I stood there for a minute like she wasn't real. She looked like a car wreck. A movie. Like someone beat the crap out of her.

Her hand reached toward me, muddy fingers curled like she wanted to hold on to something. I dropped to my knees beside her.

"Good lord, what happened to you?" I asked quiet.

She opened her mouth, but a dry sound came out, air and pain, no words.

"I'll run to the house and call an ambulance."

The girl grabbed my wrist. *No*, her open eye screamed at me.

"I'll come right back. I don't have my phone with me."

Her fingers dug in. Desperate grip. Terrified eye. That's when I saw it wasn't only her head all busted. Her shirt was soaked in blood across the middle.

"Who did this to you?" I asked. People don't get hurt like that by accident.

The girl whimpered and tried to bring her knees up to her chest, curl up and hide, kind of. But it hurt her too much, and she gasped and clutched at her stomach.

"I'm calling 9-1-1," I told her.

"No!"

Her voice was raspy. But even though it was a ragged whisper, it hit me like a scream. She said it in a way that told me she would rather die here in the field than get taken to a hospital.

"You really need a doctor."

She shook her head.

"How am I supposed to help you then?"

"Hide me."

THE GIRL

When the boy found me, I thought it was snowing.

It doesn't snow really in Texas. But I was cold like it was. And I was thinking about how sometimes when it snowed back north, it was like the flakes were coming from the ground instead of the sky, the icy wind swirling them around so you couldn't tell which direction it started from.

It was only light though, little triangles of amber and white filtered through the corn stalks, twinkling like snow, or stars.

When his dog licked my face I wondered what it must feel like to be a deer, shot and dying and not understanding why or how. One minute the deer is looking for food, breathing warm air, listening to the little noises only animals can hear, and then she is on the ground, panting in time with her heartbeat, fast and panicked, then slower and slower till it's dark.

By the time the boy tried to take me to the hospital, I had already decided it was better to die than to be found. But when I said, *Please, no*, his gray eyes flashed like he saw something he understood.

"I'll take you somewhere safe, okay?" he said.

I shook my head. There was nowhere safe.

"It's empty. Nobody even knows it's still here."

His dog had inched closer, and his tail was wagging. He looked at me like he was sorry I was hurting. I like dogs.

"I'm going to try an' pick you up," the boy told me.

He slid one arm behind my back, the other under my knees, but the second he tried to lift me I made a noise that made him lower me right back down.

"Sorry! Shoot. Sorry." He ran his hands through his light brown hair and held on to his forehead because he didn't know what to do. He had serious eyes, like a soldier, but the light smattering of freckles across his slightly sunburned nose made him look kind of like a little boy at the same time.

"I'm going to try again," he said, and that time I held my breath and closed my eyes so tightly I saw colors.

Every step he took I could feel in the slash across my stomach, where my shoulder hung, the eye that would not open.

"Faster," I told him. What if someone saw us?

"I'm trying to take it easy on you."

"Don't," I said. No one does.

THE BOY

There was only one place to take her. She said she wanted to hide. I knew about hiding. On the farthest edge of the farm, hidden behind a tangle of brush, was a small, old cow barn. There hadn't been cows in it in forever. Maybe the people way before us had some. We could barely afford to grow corn, let alone buy cattle.

"We're here," I told her.

I was trying so hard not to hurt her while we walked, and she was trying so hard not to show that I was.

I kicked the creaky barn door open as gently as I could and laid her down on a mattress in the darkest corner. She looked nervously from side to side.

"It's okay. I sleep out here sometimes."

Her brow furrowed like she didn't understand.

"This is where I come when I want to be by myself," I told her. "No one knows about it."

Her shoulders relaxed a little bit.

"Can I see how bad you're hurt?" I asked.

The girl didn't nod or say yes, but she didn't stop me either as I reached for the edge of her shirt. I couldn't stop the sharp intake of my breath when I saw the cut. It went from her stomach sideways around and up to her ribs.

"Is that who you're hiding from?" I asked her. "The person who did this?"

She didn't answer, so I knew I was right.

That's probably when I should have called the police. If I didn't hate the police.

It's definitely when I should have said this is too big for me.

But I didn't.

Because she looked at me like I was going to save the world. So I wanted to.

Instead I told her I was going to go and get her some medicine.

"I know a place I can steal some penicillin or something so you don't get all infected."

I also knew she needed stitches and something for her eye, but I wasn't going to tell her that.

"Water. Medicine. Blankets. All that kind of stuff," I told her. "That's what I'm going to get for you. And you need to stay right here."

I took another look at the gaping cut before pulling her shirt back down. It peeled open in a crescent, and I could see all these different colors and textures, light pink to white to blood. The part where the knife went in was bruised purplish black, like someone tried to kill her and messed up.

THE GIRL

Everything I was carrying, I lost. Maybe I lost it in the fight outside the car or when I was hiding in the storm drain by the highway. It might have been later in the woods, when I was running, running. I thought I would never let go of the bag, that my fist was locked around it. But somehow it was gone, and I didn't know how. I couldn't see anything right in my head, after the knife.

"She's in here."

I heard voices outside the barn. The boy lied. He brought someone. I tried to roll over, get up, get away, but my body was shaking and heavy.

"Hey." The boy came in and kneeled next to me. "Don't be mad. It's my friend."

I tried to throw his hand off my arm. This is what I got for trusting anyone. But instead I threw up, which made me almost pass out from the pain that shot across my abdomen.

"Whoa." The boy backed up as it splattered over his shoe. "Did you aim for me on purpose? Look, I know you're pissed I told someone. But you need help."

I glared at him with my one open eye as I tried to catch my breath. I hated that he was right.

"Okay," he called out. "I told her you're with me. Come on in."

Another boy hesitantly stepped into the barn. He seemed younger, with round brown cheeks and big dark eyes.

"I didn't even know this was out here." He looked around at the cracked beams and dusty old cow stalls. His eyes landed on me.

"Hi," he said softly. "My name's Mateo. What's yours?"

I didn't say a word.

"Oh," said the first boy. "I never said who I was. I'm Cade. Mattey's dad is a vet. We took a bunch of stuff from his office."

Animal medicine? I looked at them like they were crazy.

"Okay, fine," the boy—Cade—said. "You don't like this idea? Hospital then—where you should be anyway."

I shook my head violently no.

"Then it's either me, some fishing line, and a bottle of bourbon, or him." Cade laid it out bluntly. "At least *he* kind of knows what he's doing."

"I help out my father all the time," Mateo said. I scrutinized his face. He looked trustworthy.

"We have to clean you up before we start," he added.

Cade saw the question form on my face. *Start what?*

"Mattey is going to stitch you up," Cade told me.

Were they out of their minds? This *kid* was going to play doctor?

"No way," I choked out.

"Yeah," Cade said firmly. "You said no hospital. You think that cut is gonna heal itself? This is your only other option."

My face pounded, my heart beat like heavy breaths in my ears.

"Hey," Cade said. "You got this far. You clearly don't want to die."

THE WOLF CUB

I could have died of hunger at certain low points in the beginning. And now those who hunger for revenge, or my place at the top, are dying to kill me. The bullets barely change.

I've only done what had to be done. My father always said, "*Quién con lobos anda, a aullar se enseña.*" When among wolves, we must howl.

Survival is an instinct. And I've survived like a wolf in the forest since I was a little boy on the streets, taking everything I could when I could. When their hunt is successful, wolves do not eat in moderation. Deer, elk, moose—they devour everything before them. There is no concept of "later," because in the wild that expectation does not exist.

I read that a long time ago, in the old city library where I used to hide.

Many times when I was hiding, I was laughing, because I had run so easily from the sweaty, huffing shopkeepers I would rob or the lazy police pretending to help them.

But the day I found the wolf book, I was not.

I was tucked in the dim aisles, waiting out three stone-faced men looking to collect what they said we owed. They had me by the throat in the middle of the crowded market. But I was lucky. A bus hit a taxi. Everyone shouted, pushed, and in the confusion, I slipped away. I took every alley I knew, leaped across dumpsters. I balanced on the very edge of the wall behind a banker's big house, deftly avoiding the shards of glass they'd imbedded in the cement to prevent thieves. That was the fastest way I'd found to reach the sill across the way and slide through the broken window, my fail-safe secret passage into the library, a belly of safety no one thought to search.

I hid in the far upstairs corner behind the biggest shelves until my heart stopped pounding and I could breathe in the musty air without gasping. I stayed there until the light changed outside and the whole room turned dusty amber. When I eventually focused on the books in front of me I saw they were all about animals. I pulled down a thick book filled with beautiful photographs of predators. As the sun went down and my stomach growled, I read that a hungry wolf can eat twenty pounds of meat in a single meal. Twenty pounds. That's like a man eating one hundred plates of carne asada.

I would not live like that, like a starving animal. I decided to believe in more. I got what I wanted because I demanded more, deserved it. Cars, boats, infinity pools, beautiful girls, and beautiful books, my own private library full. And two actual pet wolves. Mente and Corazón. Mind and Heart.

Wolves live and hunt in packs. It takes a pack to bring down prey. Yet there is no pack without a leader. I got my name, Lobenzo, the Wolf Cub, because at eighteen I was the youngest boss but also the most ferocious.

A wolf has forty-two teeth, each specialized for tearing or stabbing flesh, shearing bones.

I always offered the choice.

Be one of my teeth.

Or be crushed by them.

CADE

I knew the girl thought it was a mistake telling Mattey. But I trust him like he's me. I've known him my whole life.

I also knew Mattey thought it was a mistake trying to help her by ourselves. God knows what this girl was hiding, but I'd be damned if I was the one who was going to turn her in. I don't tell people's secrets. They are secrets for a reason.

"Holy . . ." Mattey's voice trailed away and his eyes went wide when he saw the cut. Of course they did. He's a gentle kid, likes to draw pictures, watch his dad work. I think I'd only ever heard him swear like that maybe once before, when there was a huge brush fire right across the freeway from our houses.

Mattey shook his head. "Uh, yeah. Because calling *me* instead of 9-1-1 was a good idea how?"

I turned to reassure the girl. "He can fix it."

Her cheeks were caved in, and her ribs quivering under her skin made me think of when a bird hits a window.

"Right, Mattey?" I asked.

"You didn't tell me it was this bad." Mattey tried to collect himself.

"I mean, I guess the good news, from what I can see, is that no organs look damaged. The cut's long, but not deep. I think . . . we can take care of it?"

He said it like he had to convince himself more than us.

Mattey drizzled iodine across the wound to clean it, the bright rust color making it look even more gruesome. Hunter came over and put his head on the girl's feet, and for a second she almost relaxed. But when Mattey started dabbing at the edges of the cut to clean it, she reached out in a panic. I grabbed her hand, and she clenched so hard my fingers went white.

"Have you ever done this before?" she whispered to Mattey.

"Sure," he said, staring with extreme focus as he started the stitches.

"On a person?"

Mattey glanced over at me. "Um, yeah, actually, a few times. Not this bad. But . . ."

I cut him off. "It ain't his first rodeo, okay?"

"Okay," she said with a long, shaky breath.

The girl's face twisted in a grimace at the pressure of her skin being pulled back together. As the needle went in, a tiny whimper came out. Then, when he connected it to the other side, she let out a loud cry.

"Shh! Here, have some of this." I grabbed the bourbon I'd snuck from the house and tipped it to her lips. She sputtered at first but then managed to swallow.

"Sorry," Mattey said. "I should have brought some numbing stuff, but I didn't know what was what in a hurry like that with no one noticing."

The girl had made herself go still as stone.

"Cade, I need your help," Mattey told me, and I pinched her skin together so he could connect it with the stitches.

"Not too tight," he told me with authority, "or you can damage the tissue."

I knew then that he really could do it. It was messy. But it was working.

THE GIRL

Rip. Seethe. Teeth clamped together. The stitches weren't as bad as the stabbing. Hiding was better than running. But my mouth went raw from gritting my jaw, and for those moments, healing seemed worse than hurting.

Mateo was leaning so close over me I could feel his warm breath go in and out. He was working hard. I watched Cade watching us and read in his face that he thought his friend was doing a good job. It was the only gauge I had. Cade wiped off my forehead and put some ice on my throbbing eye. He gave me more booze. I counted time with my inhale, exhale, as that needle went in, out, in.

And then, finally, Mateo sank down to sit on the ground. "You're done."

"How does it feel?" Cade asked.

"Awful. Better."

"I think you're going to be okay," Mateo said proudly.

I tried to settle into the burn, the steady heat of the pain.

"Now what?" Cade asked him.

"She rests," Mateo answered. Then he pointed back at me. "You rest. I mean it."

"Wow. You did it," Cade said.

"I still think she needs more help," Mateo tried again.

"I know."

"For real."

"Yep."

They looked at each other for a minute.

"This is stupid. We're being stupid," Mateo protested.

"Yep," Cade said again.

"Then . . . ?" Mateo threw his arms up in the air.

"Thank you," I interrupted softly, and they both turned and stared at me like they weren't sure I was really there and this had actually happened.

"You're welcome," Cade said to me.

"And you're crazy," Mateo said to him.

"Come on, Mattey," Cade softly said. "You're not going to tell. Right . . . right?"

"Do I *ever* tell?" Mateo answered him and then turned his attention back to me. "You really don't want to go to the hospital?"

"Really," I said.

"Can I ask why?"

"No."

"Ugh." Mateo made a frustrated noise and pulled at his own hair.

"It'll be fine," Cade said. "You stitched her up good."

"I hope?" Mateo responded, and turned to me with an agitated sigh. "I guess you're lucky Cade found you. And you're even luckier I do what he asks."

"Look, I think she should see a real doctor too," Cade defended himself. "But clearly that's not something she's willing to do."

I caught a funny look in his eye. This guy knew about being hurt. He knew about hiding things.

Mateo pressed his lips together. "Someone *attacked* her. I think we should tell the police."

"No police," Cade snapped. "They're all corrupt."

"Gunner's mom isn't."

"Whatever. The sheriff still works with the rest of them," Cade grumbled. "Anyway, thanks, Mattey. For everything. You're the best."

Mateo wasn't winning this one.

"Fine . . . for now. Please, though, call me if you change your mind about all this and need help," he said, like he was really hoping we would. "I'll come back in the morning to check on you, okay?"

Mateo looked back and forth from me to Cade.

"This is not smart," he said one more time.

"If she's worse tomorrow, we'll figure something out," Cade said.

Mateo nodded uncertainly before darting out the old door. The light in the barn was almost gone. It cut through the slats of wood in milky gray thorns. That last bite of gleaming before day ends always seems to whisper sadness. Everything that happened. Everything that didn't.

"Okay, Jane Doe," Cade sighed. "You gonna tell me anything about anything or just hide in my barn till whenever?"

Till whenever the soonest was I could leave . . . or was I far enough away? How long does a person have to run before it's safe? My eyes

18

felt like they were smoking. My throat, past choked. The fight that welled, that got me here, was dry.

"Who messed you up like this?"

Why was he asking again? He had to know I wouldn't say.

CADE

I hated to leave Jane Doe by herself, but I had to get back to my house and check in before all hell broke loose. I left her with blankets, some crackers, water, and painkillers. I needed to be in bed when my dad checked or it would get ugly.

Thank God for Mattey. I don't know what I would have done about the girl otherwise. He always bailed me out. I reached up and touched a bumpy scar at my hairline. That was the very first time he'd stitched me up. He'd gotten better.

As I stepped lightly up onto our busted front porch, I glanced back at the cornfields, wondering where the creep who did this to the girl was. Far away? Or somewhere nearby?

Turning the front knob as quietly as I could, I snuck into the house. I made it all the way to the top of the stairs when my dad woke up from his chair.

"Boy? That you?"

"Yeah, Dad," I said without stopping, hoping he wouldn't get up, but his footsteps lumbered behind me.

"Where the heck you been?"

"Went for a run."

He took one look at me and had me up against the wall. "Bull. You get in a fight?"

"No."

"Tough guy now, starting trouble?"

"I didn't get in a fight."

"Why you bloody then?" he slurred.

I looked down at my shirt, stained from carrying the girl.

"Hunter killed a rabbit and rolled in it. I got some on me."

My dad looked at me suspiciously.

"Was that before or after you drank my whiskey?"

"I didn't drink your whiskey." I pushed his hand off my throat and tried to duck out from under his arm.

"Let me smell your breath."

He got up close to me and lightly slapped at my cheek. And then again. Over and over.

"Come on, boy, lemme smell your breath."

"I didn't drink it."

I tried to sound unaffected, but my adrenaline was starting to kick up.

"Where is it then? Huh? Where's my bottle?"

I'd left it in the barn.

"Damned if I know what you do with your booze."

"Don't mouth off at me."

My father gave me a look of disgust and took a step closer. He towered over me.

"I'm not mouthing off. I don't know where it is. That's all I'm saying."

My father frowned and blew out a sour sigh.

"You must have drunk it," I took a risk and said.

He stared at me, eyes all distant and squinty.

"Yeah. Maybe."

Good. He was calming down.

"I'll look around for you, okay, Dad?"

"Okay. You do that." He let his arms drop to his sides and backed away. "You know I'm just lookin' out for you. Don't mess up your chances, Cade. You get kicked off the football team, that's it for you. You're worth nothin'."

Even after he left the room, my body stayed tense. I sat on the edge of my bed, clenched my fists and my jaw till my fingers and my head ached. "Lookin' out" used to mean showing me how to change the oil in my truck, gut a fish, start a charcoal grill. It was teaching me to tell time, tell a joke, tell the truth. It was throwing a football around out back.

He used to come to every one of my games. At dinner we'd talk about how to run the plays better, rolling our eyes as my mom insisted I was already perfect. She somehow always had food stuck in her hair or to her shirt from the frenzy of what she considered cooking. My dad would tell her it was good, and then when her back was turned, he would make a gagging face. There was never a question that we'd eat what was on our plates. Didn't mean we couldn't laugh about it. There are only so many things you can make with ground round and potatoes, chicken thighs and rice. When we had beans the majority of the week, I knew we were almost out of money till the next harvest.

We'd been eating a lot of beans lately.

How can you turn someone back into who they used to be? No twelve-step program can help a person who won't even step off their own property. My dad hadn't been into town in two years. Not since my mom left.

I looked at my crooked bedroom door.

Inside, the walls were cracked, the paint peeling.

Outside, the corn was dying. A girl was hiding.

I couldn't do anything about the weather or the soil. I didn't choose my mother or my father. There was no guarantee I would get a scholarship to play college ball. All I could do was try my dang hardest to be the best. My only way out. I fell asleep thinking of the girl's bright blue eyes when I told her I would help.

Keeping a promise is one of the only things someone can control.

JANE DOE

Thunder gnawed its hungry noises in the distance. I lay on top of the sleeping bag, listening to the rain come down harder and harder outside, and finally dared run my hand ever so lightly along my stitches—the little pieces of thread holding me together. I couldn't believe that kid actually did it. Mateo. Or Mattey, Cade called him.

Cade. Who was this guy? Would he waste his time on a stranger if he knew anything about anywhere I'd been? I popped some more painkillers and wondered how many were too many. My stomach churned. Maybe I would throw up again. The barn was hot and still. I was caught in a giant, sour exhale. Old air. Everything good about it used up. My eye pounded as if it had its own pulse, and the sewn-up slash across my middle lit up in little points of pain—match heads on my skin. But I welcomed the pain. It said, *You hurt because you're here. You are alive. You got away.*

Raff didn't.

Alone, out in the barn, I couldn't help but think of him. His face, touch, voice—it rolled in with the thunder.

I met Raff because of my last foster mom, Jessie.

Before Jessie, it was:

The Richardsons, who opted out of being a foster family when the stipend wasn't as high as they had hoped.

Mr. and Mrs. Genova, who wanted to start the process of foster-to-adopt until they found out they could have their own kids after all and didn't want a baby and a teenager.

The young couple Lisa and Chris, who left to teach sustainable farming in Chad.

And, of course, the group home where I first stayed when they said my aunt Nikki was unfit.

The longest I ever stayed in one place was when my mom first left me with her.

The second longest was with Jessie and Tae.

Jessie was a hot mess, but we got along. I would cook and keep track of the bills for heat and electricity and stuff. But when Tae got a pretty big insurance payment from some sort of work accident, things started to get weird. They'd always smoked pot, but now that Tae had money, he could get harder drugs. It was a couple of months after that when I met his nephew Raff. Raff was Filipino too, with the cut jaw of a model, dark, sexy eyes, and a grin that made you think about his lips for the rest of the day.

One night when Jessie and Tae did a bunch of lines and were getting too PDA-ish, Raff rolled his eyes at me and said, *Wanna get out of here?* And we did. We grabbed a case of beer and drove Tae's car out to the oil fields. By the time I had drunk two, I was laughing. Raff gave me another one, and I said it was hot in the car. He cranked the heat higher to mess with me and told me to take off my sweatshirt, so I did. Steam clouded the inside of the windshield while drips of rain raced down the outside of the glass.

The oil pumps tilted down and up in the distance like long-necked dinosaurs eating then looking around. Raff traced the strap of my tank top and told me I was too hot for my own good. I said, *Prove it*. He said if I wasn't so sweet and innocent maybe he would. *Maybe I'm not*, I told him. *Prove it*, he said back to me. And I climbed on his lap in the car and pressed against him like I'd seen people do.

That's when the police rapped on the window and told us to get a move on. I was mortified, but Raff thought it was funny. When we got back, Jessie had passed out on the floor, a bottle of someone else's prescription painkillers resting in her hand. Tae was sprawled on the couch, clearly hungover. There were open cans and empty takeout containers everywhere.

"I'm so sick of living like this," I mumbled.

That was the night Raff decided we needed to get out of there and asked, *Want to run away to Mexico?* I thought he was kidding. But he had friends there, connections, he promised. He'd lived near the border for a while and spoke Spanish well. He knew how to make money—a lot of money. It's not like I didn't know what he meant. I'm not naive. Starting over has a price.

We went.

And for eleven sunny months, we were rock stars.

Then Raff got shot through the head.

CADE

Once we were tied in the fourth quarter against Griffin Heights, and I scrambled for a first down and had this long run, but right at the thirty-yard line I dove forward and lost the ball when I hit the ground. It bounced right into the hands of their safety. I woke up the day after all embarrassed before I even remembered how come.

Sometimes when you start out in the morning, in the first flicker awake, there's no good or bad yet. Then . . . a feeling hits you . . . then the reason for it. That's how it was the day after finding the girl.

I'd set my phone alarm twice on vibrate under my pillow, to check on her during the night, and snuck out to the barn and back in the pouring rain. Both times, there she was, breathing all ragged, the outline of her body blurry in the gray light like maybe I was dreaming. It wasn't till I got up for real the next morning that what was going on started to layer itself on me.

As soon as my ears woke up and started hearing the corners of the room, a sort of panic hit me—a you-gotta-figure-this-out-fast feeling. And then *What the heck are you thinking?* was what I was thinking. *There is a* girl *hidden in your barn.* But for some reason the only thing I could figure out to do was make her some food. I threw on some clothes and headed down to the kitchen. Eggs from our chickens. That's what I would bring her. She looked like she hadn't eaten in weeks, all angles and shadows.

"Come on, Hunter," I said softly, but he must have already gone out the dog door somewhere. I covered the plate with an old dishtowel and slid out while my father was still passed out.

I picked my way through the already drying mud. The parched dirt was sucking up the puddles so fast you'd hardly know it had even rained last night if not for the drops of water beaded on the tall grass.

I rapped lightly on the barn door. "It's me, Cade."

No sound from inside. For all I knew she'd run off. Or . . . hadn't even made it through the night. What if there was a dead person in my barn? I pushed the door open with my foot.

The girl was lying on her back, one arm over her busted eye, the other over my dog. When the heck did he come out here? Her chest rose and fell steadily. I didn't want to wake her up, but the second Hunter smelled the food he left guard duty and barreled over to me. The girl let out a small whimper as she stirred, mumbling something that sounded like *hell* . . . or *tell. I won't tell*?

"Hey. You're okay. Hey there, Jane Doe. It's me, um . . . Cade. Brought you some eggs. How ya doin'?"

She was silent for a second, taking stock of where she was.

"Hurts," she whispered, all groggy.

"Yeah. I'll bet. Mattey said to check that nothing looks like it's got puss or is all puckered like."

"And here I was thinking maybe I was hungry."

"Ha. Sorry." I leaned over and helped her sit up.

Jane Doe let out a cry, even as I supported her back. Her shirt was damp with sweat. She couldn't lift her arms to feed herself, so I scooped up a forkful and held it to her mouth. She only had three tiny bites.

"No more."

"How 'bout some water?"

"No thanks."

"You need water."

"I'm okay."

"Drink a little."

She gave in and took a sip. "Hey . . ."

"Yeah?"

"You didn't happen to find a bag, did you? Near where you found me?" she asked.

"No. But it's not like I was looking."

"I dropped my bag . . . somewhere. It, um, has all my stuff."

"I have football practice," I told her as I guided her back to lying down.

She looked at me like she didn't know why she should care.

"But that's it. Other than that, I can help you out. I'll take a couple laps through the corn when I get back to see if I can't find it. What color is it?"

"Black. Nothing special."

The girl's left eye was open a tiny slit compared to before. And she squinted her other eye at me. "Why are you helping me so much?"

"Why not? God made me stumble on you for a reason, right?"

She gave me a patronizing half smile. "Aw. You believe in God."

JANE

While Cade was doing his football stuff, Mateo came over. He brought more pain pills and some clothes. He looked politely over his shoulder while helping peel off my bloody T-shirt and put on a fresh one. It smelled like clean laundry in someone's house, a real house with food cooking and the TV on and people laughing.

"Whose are these?" I asked.

"My sisters'. I have four. They'll blame each other . . . if they even notice they're missing at all."

"That's a lot of sisters."

"Big family." Mateo smiled shyly and shrugged.

"You need something in your stomach," he said, opening a thermos and unrolling some tinfoil. "Will you eat some of this? It's my mom's chicken soup and a few homemade tortillas. It's what I always eat after I'm sick."

"I can try."

My body kept shifting from on fire to a deep and steady aching. The cut was a sinkhole, swallowing me like a pretty little neighborhood full of trees and cars and people pushing baby carriages.

"What about you?" Mateo asked. "Do you have any sisters or brothers?"

"Nice try."

He looked confused for a second. "Oh. I get it. You don't have to talk about you. It's okay. I mean, you're obviously hiding. I hope . . . I hope you're very far away from whoever is after you?"

He was still fishing for information. All I said back was "Me too."

"I know what Cade said. But are you *sure* you don't want to go to police?"

"I'm sure."

"I'm going to ask you every day," Mateo said.

"The answer will be the same."

"That's fine. At least I'll know I tried."

I didn't say anything in response. The food was sitting okay. The tortillas were good. I took one more.

Mateo pulled out a pad of paper and some pencils.

"What are you doing?"

"I like to draw. If you're not going to talk to me, I'll sketch."

I noticed he had dried paint stuck to the back of his hand and the edge of his T-shirt.

"You're an artist?"

"Something like that. Someday."

"Can I see what you're drawing?"

Mateo flipped the pad around. There were two lines.

"Ha ha, very funny. Show me something you didn't just start."

He smirked at me but flipped back a few pages to show me a sketch of a city street. The bold lines popped, and the people's faces pulled me in. The drawing had an energy to it, like you got dropped into it mid-motion, mid-thought.

"That can't be around here," I said.

Mateo tapped his head. "It's from in here. I draw what I daydream. It's like a promise to myself. I want to go to art school in New York City. NYU. Maybe the Pratt Institute in Brooklyn."

"Sounds like you have it all mapped out. How old are you anyway?" I asked.

"Just turned fifteen. I'm going to be a sophomore. We live right down the road from Cade, so I've known him forever. He's a senior. How old are *you*? Oh, I mean, never mind. Sorry."

This kid was too sweet, like 1950s television shows, hair-slicked-to-the-side sweet. And Cade's dog acted like Lassie, staying right by my side. I ran my fingers along the furry ridge of its back.

"What's the dog's name?"

"Hunter. Our old neighbor Savannah Maddison's dog had puppies a couple years ago, and she gave Cade one. I wanted one so bad too, but my mom said her kids were her wild pack of *perritos*. She didn't have the time or money to take care of anything more." Mateo rolled his eyes. "I would have helped."

"So you're Mexican, huh?" I asked.

"Yeah. Half this town is." Mateo gave me a funny look. "Why?"

"Because I hate Mexico," I said, cracking up at his shocked expression.

Mateo was about to hand me a bottle of water, but he pulled his arm back.

"That's a pretty messed-up thing to say to a Mexican."

"Especially one who saves your life with cow meds." I motioned for him to give me the drink, trying to soften what I'd said with a smile. Or at least what I hoped was a smile. I had no idea what my face looked like. My swollen cheekbone felt like there was sand grating in it. He didn't smile back.

"Relax, Mateo. I was only kidding."

"You sure?" he asked.

"Let's just say that country isn't exactly on my bucket list to visit any time soon because of some . . . stuff . . . that happened. Some choices I made. How's that?"

Mateo pointed to my cut. "So this . . . happened. And now you hate all of Mexico?"

"No, Mateo. That was a bad joke," I said, then quieter: "I only hate myself."

CADE

"The US damn government of A may want to ban two-a-days, but don't think I won't still try an' kill you," Coach yelled. His face got purple shouting at us in this heat.

The football field was the only bright green patch around, with the city water restrictions because of the drought. You might not be allowed to water your cornfield, but the football field was a different story. You didn't mess with that.

"There's hot, and then there's this." My buddy Gunner looked like he'd run under a hose. "These up-downs make me puke in my mouth."

"*You* make me puke in my mouth," yelled one of the twins, laughing at his own joke.

I had to look back to see whether it was Taylor or Justin. Taylor had lighter eyebrows. It was the only way to sometimes tell them apart. Today I couldn't tell.

"Fajardo makes me puke in my mouth," said the other twin.

"How did I get dragged into this?" Fajardo complained. His round face was raining sweat.

"'Cause you're fat," Gunner panted as we jogged in place.

Fajardo just laughed.

"Less talking, more working," Coach Hollis yelled.

There was a collective grunt as we dropped to the ground, then used a push-up to launch ourselves back up to standing, then did it all again. Up-downs. Coach blew the whistle. And again.

"Ugh. You'd never even know it rained last night." Gunner kept complaining even after we were all heading to the locker room. "It's hotter than Haiti."

"Hades. It's hotter than Hades," I said.

"I always thought it was Haiti."

"Nah," I laughed. "You're a dumbass. It's Hades, like hell."

"Whatever. It's hotter 'n hell then. How's that?" Gunner answered.

"I don't mind the double workouts," I said.

"*Go* to hell," Taylor or Justin chimed in. "How's that?"

My helmet came off my head with a nasty sucking noise over my ears. Soaked.

"Yeah, you ain't right in the head if you like this twice in a row," Fajardo added, looking at me like I was nuts.

"Says who? You? Some of us are trying to start," I said with a laugh.

Fajardo grinned and shrugged. He knew he didn't care like I did. "Some of us are smart. It's too miserable out. Why kill ourselves?"

"I heard this is the hottest summer we ever had. Like, record-breaking," Gunner said. "Crops are shit."

"Our crops are always shit."

Gunner frowned at me that way he does when he thinks I'm being too negative. When he pulled off his helmet, his thick, curly hair stuck up, making it hard to take him seriously. But Gunner was trying to be serious. He started to say something, then stopped, waiting for everyone else to head to the showers.

"What?" I demanded.

He pointed to my feet. "Dude, you can't play in taped-up shoes."

"Done it before."

"Not varsity ball, man. You'll hurt yourself."

"I'll pick up a new pair after I clean a few more pools," I tried to brush him off.

Gunner hemmed and hawed for a second, then said, "When school starts . . . maybe, um, apply for the free-lunch thing? That could save you a couple extra bucks, right?"

I shook my head no, with an insulted snort.

"It's for, like, anybody who needs it," Gunner stumbled along.

"Really?" I challenged. "Have *you* ever used it?"

"No, but it's not like money hasn't ever been tight for my parents before. A sheriff and a trucker don't exactly make bank."

"You don't get it."

"Come on, Cade. Y'all aren't the only ones in Tanner scrambling. I mean, my mom's a black woman trying to boss around a bunch of white dudes. And you know my dad came in on a work visa, and we thought for a while he'd never get his green card. My aunt had to front our mortgage sometimes. It's okay to ask for help."

"What is this?" I glared at him. "Some sort of intervention?"

Gunner looked down. "I *told* my mom you'd get mad if I brought it up."

I made myself take a beat. I knew he meant well. "Farms are weird. You never know how they're going to do."

"Yeah," Gunner said. "You heard from your mom at all?"

"No. It is what it is," I mumbled. "Who cares?"

"You do."

"I can't. What's it gonna get me?" I was done talking about this.

Gunner gave up and retreated to the showers. The faucets screeched and hissed. We sounded like we were in a factory assembly line. I closed my eyes and let the water slide over my face. Sometimes it feels like maybe I never even had a mom. Other times I forget she left and think that when I go home she'll be right there, tromping dirt from the fields into the kitchen. Leaving a trail of pots and pans behind. Wrestling on the floor with Hunter. *Forget it*, she used to say about the messes she made. *Live life in the moment. We can worry about the cleanup later. If we do it all together it won't feel like chores.*

I wonder what she thinks about this mess.

Now that there is no more "together," who is supposed to clean up?

On the way home I stopped at the Walmart. I had some cash on me from cleaning Mama Travis's pool. It was enough for a not-totally-crappy plastic fan, toothbrush, toothpaste, and some soap and shampoo. I picked a purple bottle with fruit and flowers on it that must be like how Hawaii smells.

"Aye," the cashier said. It was her version of *hello*. She pointed to the shampoo and laughed.

"What's up, Lola?" I grinned at her. "Ha ha yourself. Stop making fun of me. The shampoo's not for me."

"Mmm."

"Yeah, yeah. You think you're so funny."

I always tried to act normal around Lola after what happened to her. It wasn't like the Javiers were those kind of people. Normal family. Lola grew up here with us our whole life . . . but a guy she started dating after she graduated got all mixed up in running drugs. When they broke up, some cartel guys sliced up Lola's tongue so she couldn't say what she knew. Frickin' awful. But just cuz she couldn't talk didn't mean her brain wasn't the same, right? Her voice was stuck inside. So I always made sure to chat with her when I shopped here.

"Bye, girl, see ya next time. Your sister's back from Afghanistan for good now, right? Tell her I say hey."

I shoved the change into my pocket, walked across the parking lot, and started my truck. Less than a quarter tank of gas. Great. I hadn't realized that. I looked down at the plastic bag in the passenger seat and wondered if I should return the fan to have enough to fill up the truck.

Who was my next pool cleaning? The Kahns. But not till next Saturday. But I had Dr. Garcia too, so it would be okay. I could use some of this week's food money for gas. We had some frozen venison left. If I made stew, we could eat that a bunch of nights. I could probably stretch the box of flapjack batter for breakfast too.

The light turned red at the intersection with the Bootjack and Chevrolet. Someday I would buy myself a nice pair of boots. Square toe. Solid. And I'd climb up into my brand-new pickup. Gunmetal gray. That's the color.

A new billboard caught my eye. Luxury canal homes from the three hundreds. Three hundred *thousand* dollars? To live in Tanner. I couldn't believe anyone wanted to stay here, let alone move here, for *any* kinda money, forget that kinda money.

Factories were doing well lately though. As I headed out of town, I glanced over at the manufacturing plants that sat along the river that divided us from Mexico. Weird to think there's a whole other country just behind some brush and buildings. The smokestacks chugged like they were panting from running too many laps.

A car ahead of me abruptly slowed, breaking my stream of thought. The driver rolled down a window to check in with someone pulled over on the side of the road.

Everything all right?" she called out to a man standing outside his SUV. "Car overheat?"

"Nah, sweetheart. All good. Just stopped to take a leak," the guy said.

"All right then." She laughed and offered me a little wave of apology for the holdup.

I waved back that it was fine but found myself shooting a few extra looks in the rearview mirror to make sure the guy drove away.

When I pulled up at the house, I poked my head inside for a quick second.

"Dad, I'm home. I'm gonna go check the corn."

No answer.

I searched around for my pocketknife to cut open the packaging on the fan. As usual, the drawers were overflowing with crap, and I had no idea where anything was. I grabbed a long chopping knife from the block by the stove instead and headed out to the barn.

As I rounded the last bend, I came to an abrupt halt. Something was wrong.

The door of the barn was wide open. And no one was inside.

JANE

I heard someone approach the barn from the other side of the bushes.

I froze and grabbed Mateo's arm, but he called out before I could stop him. "We're right back here."

Cade emerged from around the corner, Hunter bounding next to him. My whole body slumped in relief to see it was only him. I patted Hunter's head, rubbing my fingers down the bridge of his nose. He licked my fingers and wagged his tail.

"Everything all good here?" Cade asked.

"Yeah," I answered. "Is something wrong?"

"I got worried because the barn was empty," Cade said. "Where were you?"

"She had to . . ." Mateo was embarrassed.

I spared him. "The barn toilet wasn't working."

"The barn doesn't have a toilet," Cade said.

"Exactly."

"Was that a joke, Jane Doe?"

"Maybe."

My knees abruptly felt weak. This was the longest walk I'd taken since Mattey stitched me up. Cade came around to support the other side of me, and the boys guided me back inside the barn. Once I was lying back down, a slow smile crept onto Cade's face.

"Whoo, girl. I thought whoever sliced you up was back for more. And here you were just taking care of business," he said, laughing.

I made a face at him. I mean, whatever. So I had to go to the bathroom.

"Hospitals have real bathrooms," Mateo pointedly remarked. "And real doctors."

"I like this doctor," I answered.

Mateo let out a little snort to signify his continued protest while fussing with the pillows and towels around me. Cade tossed a shopping bag down.

"What's all that?" I asked.

"I thought you might want to get cleaned up a little," Cade said. "I, uh, got you some shampoo. And a fan."

"Well, thanks, Lancelot."

"Who?"

"Knight in shining armor. You didn't have to do that."

"This place'll suffocate you."

"Where are you going to plug it in?" I asked.

"It's batteries. Don't you worry, li'l lady," Cade said, fumbling with the plastic casing on it.

Mateo blobbed a huge squirt of antibiotic ointment over my cut. I shifted my gaze back and forth between them. What was in it for either of them? Why help me?

"That looks way better already." Cade pointed to the Frankenstein crisscrosses lacing me up.

"Where is your spleen?" I asked.

"Your spleen is fine," Mateo answered, gently laying my shirt back over the cut.

"What about kidneys?"

"Also fine." Mateo looked at his watch and scrunched up his face. "I'm sorry, guys, but this *doctor* has to get home before his mama starts looking for him."

"I got it from here," Cade said. "Thanks again, man."

"I'll come back tomorrow," Mateo said.

"You don't have to," I interjected. "I'm going to head out soon."

Cade rolled his eyes. "Says the girl who can't even take a crap without help."

"For the record, Mateo only helped me get outside."

"Yeah, she pooped on her own," Mateo added and then turned about eight shades of red. "Sorry. Bye. Feel better. Call me if you need anything. Okay. Yeah."

Cade let out a snort of laughter at Mateo as he hurried out the door, but it was short-lived. His forehead had a worried furrow.

"So how *is* the cut?" he asked after a beat.

"Still stitched up," I said. "So there's that."

"Hurts bad, huh?" Cade's eyes landed on my shirt. Little spots of red had already seeped into it from the spots between the stitches.

"You don't even know."

I pulled the fabric away from my skin, letting a little air in so it wouldn't catch. I didn't know how to explain everything to this normal high school guy who for some reason was doing things like buying me shampoo and bringing me breakfast.

Cade, I wanted to say, *there are people out there who only care about money and power. They will shoot a person like we kill a bug against a window, smeared and in pieces on the glass with no second thought. Something is missing inside them. You can look and look into their eyes, trying to find a way to show your life counts and they shouldn't take it. But all that's there is the dark flash of a pupil, no different than a shark or an alligator.*

"I'm going to get out of here as soon as I can. I don't want to cause any problems for you. You've already done enough . . . more than enough."

"One day at a time, Jane Doe, okay? When you're healed up enough to travel, we'll figure it out," Cade said.

"Any luck finding my bag?" I asked.

"It's definitely not in the fields, far as I can tell. Haven't really gone into the woods."

Cade reached into the shopping bag and pulled out a knife to cut off the plastic around the fan. All of a sudden, I was shaking. The blade flashed, and I saw *that* face. It was like I could feel it happening all over again, how he grabbed the back of my head and slammed it into the side of the car. His fingers over my mouth, trying to keep me from breathing. How he wrapped his arm around my throat and pressed, and I kicked, hit, threw my weight against him. And then the tear of the blade through my skin.

CADE

Total freak-out. When I went to cut the plastic backing, Jane Doe started shaking and sucking in air like a freshwater drumfish when you pull it off the hook. I dropped the knife as quickly as I could and put my hands up to show her.

"It's gone. Look, no knife. It's all right."

She pulled her knees to her chest, crying out in pain at the sudden pressure on her cut. Her hyperventilating got thicker.

"It's okay," I said. "I was only opening the fan."

She gave me a little nod, her breath still coming out in short catches. I reached out and took her hand.

"Let's just lie here, okay?" I helped guide her down. "Close your eyes, maybe?"

She shook her head no.

"Okay, leave them open and look at me. You're safe in the barn."

Jane took a giant inhale and managed to calm her breath, but she was still trembling.

"Jeez, girl."

She wiped hard at her eyes, looking pissed she had allowed even a tear to slide out. I had started subconsciously rubbing the inside of her wrist with my thumb. It seemed to calm her down, so I kept doing it.

She needed to get out of her head. I should say something, anything, just to distract her. I started rambling about football to her. Not that she probably cared, but I didn't know what else to talk about. I told her how practice starts now even though it's still summer vacation, and about Coach Hollis, how Gunner and I call him Coach Holler, or Coach A-hole. I said Gunner always makes fun of me and calls me out on everything, but it's what makes me like him. I talked about how in a town this small, scoring touchdowns makes you feel like you're frickin' Superman or the president, and they give you free ice cream sundaes at the diner when you go there after, and we eat them like we're little kids, all happy about the whipped cream and caramel syrup. We have big rallies, I told her. Even the mayor shakes your hand.

"Do you score all the touchdowns?" she asked after just lying there, listening for a long time.

"Well, hey, look who's back," I said, disentangling my fingers from her grip. "Do I score all the touchdowns? All the amazing ones."

"So you're the star quarterback. Big man on campus. Hanging here with me . . . while I lose it."

"Not gonna lie: That was intense. How about I get the fan going . . . later?"

"Uh, yeah, probably a good idea."

Jane's cheeks were pale, and little lines of sweat ran down her forehead and neck. She lay there staring at the ceiling. Hunter stayed by her side, and she reached over and took his paw in her hand.

"Did you say you got me shampoo?" she asked, lightly touching the ends of her hair. Her voice was deliberately crisp, like she was announcing she had turned the corner and was going to be okay now.

"Yes."

"I still can't really lift my arms up to my head."

I looked at her. She looked at me.

"Um, I guess I'll do it for you?" I said.

I helped Jane sit back up and then stand. There was a hose back by the old stalls. I propped her against one of the half walls and loosened the squeaky faucet until a nice steady stream of cool water came out. It felt good in the heat, and I splashed some over my own face.

"Okay, tilt your head."

Jane was leaning heavily against the stall wall. She adjusted her weight to balance better, and when she dropped her head back I could see a big raw patch on the side. My head had looked like that plenty. It was gonna sting. I aimed the water away from the sore spot, but it still ran pink from the dried blood. I squirted a huge blob of shampoo into my hands and lightly patted it onto her head.

"You have to mush it around," she mumbled. "I want to be clean."

She winced as the shampoo hit the raw, scraped place, but I could tell she wanted me to keep going. It felt weird, washing someone else's hair. Like with me, I dig in and mess the suds around really fast and call it a day, but she had all this hair.

"I don't know what to do with the long part."

She let out a little laugh at me and immediately winced and placed a hand over the cut.

"Bring my hair up on top of my head and kind of scratch with your fingers," she directed. "Thank you. This water feels nice. I'm so hot and thirsty."

"Here—open." I aimed some of the cold water into her mouth.

Jane closed her eyes and let it run down her chin, down the curve of her neck, soaking the front of her shirt. Her left eye was less swollen, even though the lid and skin around it was still bruised.

"I've been beat up, but never this bad," I said.

"I'm not going to talk about it."

"Settle down, Jane Doe. I didn't ask."

"Why not?"

"Because it's your business . . . why you're running," I said. "But I do need to ask: Is whoever attacked you still looking for you?"

Jane Doe hesitated. That equaled yes.

"Would they know where you are?" I asked.

"*I* don't know where I am."

"You're in Tanner."

"Really? I'm farther than I thought," she said.

"Where are you trying to go?" I asked.

"North."

I got the last of the shampoo out of her hair and dabbed at her head with a towel. "How far north we talkin'?"

"Canada," Jane said.

"If you wanna get out of the country, Mexico's right here," I pointed out.

"That's the problem," she answered.

"What do you mean?"

"I got caught up in something."

"What kind of something?"

"It had to do with drugs. Kind of." Jane didn't offer up a real answer. Of course she didn't.

"Look, if I'm going to help you, you gotta tell me *something*. I don't need to know all of it—hell, I don't *want* to know it. But give me something here."

Jane paused. "There are some guys . . . who are worried about what I might know."

"What you *might* know?" I pressed.

"What I *do* know."

The uneasiness that had been nagging me ever since the ride home from practice came back around full throttle.

"And do any of these guys who are worried about what you know drive a black SUV?" I asked.

Jane froze.

"I saw someone on the side of the road," I said. "White T-shirt. Dark jeans. Long, scraggly hair. Big sunglasses."

With each description I gave, Jane got paler. She sank to the wet, gritty floor of the barn.

"He's going to find us."

JANE

My shoulders caved in. My chin tucked down. I shrank against the side of the stall. If Cade saw who I thought he saw, I needed to already be gone.

"Listen." Cade put his hands up in a warning. "If you're some kind of drug-running mule, I'll call the cops right now. I don't care if they're two-faced. Y'all can rot with the cartels together."

Everything I could cry over but don't, then this? This is what makes it happen? Tears spilled over and ran down my face.

"I'm not that," I whispered.

Cade kept his eyes fixed on mine as if daring me to lie to him.

"I'm not running drugs," I said. "But . . . my boyfriend, he knew people who did that sort of stuff."

"Your *boyfriend*? Well, where the hell is *he* right now?"

"Dead."

Silence hit and held.

I hadn't said any of it out loud yet. And when I did, it came out in a monotone. "He got killed. I ran."

"Ran from where?"

"I told you: Mexico."

"You said that Mexico was the problem. You didn't say you were *there*." Cade was trying to put the pieces together.

"I lived there."

"And the guy that stabbed you?"

"He's from the US but goes back and forth."

"Why is he after you?"

"Lots of reasons."

"Can you give me at least one?"

"I had all of my boyfriend's money. He wanted it."

"How much?"

"A *lot*," I said.

"Where is it?"

"In the bag I lost."

Cade shook his head in frustration. "Mattey's right. We gotta go to the sheriff. It's Gunner's mom. She'll know what to do."

"No! I'm not eighteen yet," I told him, holding myself back. Something about Cade's sincere gray eyes made me want to tell him too much. I couldn't say anything that would put him in danger.

Sun and blood, I wanted to say. *Where it starts and where it ends.*

The sun was Raff, loud music, speeding in his sports car or motorcycle. The nights were me, dancing outside under the little lanterns with the swirls of smoke, tobacco, pot. I laughed when Raff showed me the guns he'd bought. I thought he just wanted to look badass. And he did, especially holding the big black one, the AK, AR whatever— no shirt, all the muscles in his arms and abs, like a guy in an action movie.

In Playa Lavilla, the resort town where we lived, I was in a bikini all the time. Bare feet. Salty hair. Raff said all his friends were jealous. They'd say things in Spanish that made him say, "Back off, she's mine." I liked them before I knew what they did. No—even after I knew what they did. They had dark eyes and lazy, suggestive smiles. I was safe with Raff's crew, always a hand on my back, an eye on the door. We had tables and bottles at the clubs, and we partied at condos on the beach. We had anything we ever wanted. But more than that, we had each other. Raff would pull me in close, extend his arm, and snap a picture of us on his phone, our faces pressed together, saying, *We'll want to remember this. All of it.*

I'd never been the best thing to anyone. But to Raff, I was. How he looked at me, how he touched me, talked about me—it made me forget social workers, foster parents, my mom shooting up somewhere, hungry, hollow. Being with Raff made the edges smoother. Maybe there was something to like about myself.

The blood was how it ended. The blood was now.

Now I was just another seventeen-year-old runaway.

Seventeen meant back in state custody, as if none of this last year happened. Raff's blood never spilled out of his head, fast and silent. I wouldn't know anything about the ice picks. Or the gasoline. Or what happened to Raff's friends and their girlfriends.

No, I needed to keep going, somewhere new, far away. An island. A gray one with cliffs and rain and the needy echo of seals and gulls, the kind of island where old wooden ships had wrecked in some other century's winter storms.

"Cade . . . ," I began. "If you take me to the police, I'll get put back in foster care. Once I'm in the system, anyone can track me down. They'll come after me."

"Over one bag of money? Come on, Jane, I'm not stupid. What is this really about?"

I could barely breathe from the pain of the cut. This boy was my only chance. My hands were shaking as I thought about the possibility of being hunted . . . forever. I had to tell him something more, something that would make him help me get out of here.

"I know how they smuggle their drugs."

I saw the information register.

I hated to ask.

I *had* to ask.

"Can you maybe . . . drive me as far north as you can and then let me go from there?"

"So, what?" Cade said. "So you can go find another messed-up boyfriend and wind up half dead again?"

My face flashed hot.

"What do you care?" I defended myself.

"I saved you."

"I didn't ask you to."

"You're asking now."

CADE

Jane Doe was only half right. She might not have asked me to save her. But she did ask me to hide her. And I'd agreed. Even though I knew better. I'm from Tanner, Texas. We have a mayor and police, but everyone knows who really runs this town. I don't live under a rock. I read the news. I go to school.

"If I don't, what will happen?" I asked.

"I don't know," she whispered.

I wasn't going to get her backstory. There was no time for it. If I was going to drive Jane Doe, it was now or never. The reality sank in. If I didn't, and they found her, killed her, it would be on me. A death. Her life. And if they found her, they could find me.

"Fine," I said.

Jane squinted at me.

"Let's get moving. That guy was over by Maddison Electric, which isn't far at all. We need to get a move on."

"To the police station." Her voice was flat.

My mind was racing. "I'm not sure yet. Let's just head to the truck, and we can figure it out from there."

I scooped up the clothes Mattey brought her and a blanket in one arm, then held out the other for her. She hesitantly took it. After about ten super slow steps down the path from the barn she started panting so loud she sounded like Hunter. Another couple of minutes and her knees were buckling and she was half bent over. This was not going to work. I picked her up along with all the stuff.

Sweat dripped down my back even though the sun was starting to get low in the sky. Jane's body curled into my chest as I trudged forward. Her hot breath fell on my neck. I had never touched anything so broken. Maybe the kitten that Mattey's sister Jojo tried to save from a coyote when we were kids. Their dad had to put it to sleep. Right before we buried it, Jojo said the cat needed a name, and I was left holding it, thinking about how soft it still was, while she tried to come up with one so that she would know who to say a prayer for.

"Hold it right there."

The voice came from the dark green shadows of the cornfield behind us. Hunter let out a low growl. Jane's fingers dug into my arms. I started to turn around. A gun cocked, the noise like a quick clash of teeth. It said, *Don't move. Stop. Now.*

I stopped.

"Get on the ground."

I lowered Jane robotically down, beyond careful, heart pounding.

"Facedown. Both of you."

I got down on my stomach next to her, cheeks in the dirt, eyes locked on each other. Hunter's growling intensified and then erupted into a gnashing bark.

"Hunter, no!" I hissed at him, but it was too late.

There was an awful *pop-pop* and a yelp that felt like it ripped me in half.

Jane screamed.

A heavy boot ground into my back.

Then a knee.

A hand wrenched into Jane's hair, mashing her face into the dirt.

And the cold barrel of the gun that shot my dog pressed against my head.

JANE

Ivan smelled. Even out here in the fields it smelled like being locked in the car with him. Cologne, cigarettes, and a strange basement mustiness.

"You still wanna try to run, huh?" Ivan yanked my shirt up to reveal the jagged, raw wound. "I will rip you right back open, one stitch at a time until you can't stand it anymore. I will make you talk."

His left hand covered my face, and his right kept a gun pressed to Cade's.

"Don't move, or I'll blow a hole in the boy's head," Ivan growled.

His voice came in like it was being funneled through a tiny opening. I was where I'd learned to go to get away from reality. If Ivan blew a hole in Cade's head, if he slowly twisted a blade through my body, I would already be gone.

"The police are on their way," Cade said into the dirt. Stupid. Stupid. Why was he talking?

"Bull." Ivan called his bluff.

But Cade didn't stop. "I'm telling you, I found this girl in my corn and called them."

A flash of metal glinted in the blanket Cade had dropped beside us. The knife.

From trying to open the fan.

My eyes met Cade's, connecting in a silent plan.

"I was taking her to my house," Cade continued. "Can't you hear the sirens?"

Cade was emphatic. It was convincing. Ivan straightened up on one knee enough to scan the path and fields. The second he took his eyes off us, I rolled to grab the knife from the folds of the blanket, and without a second thought, I rammed it into him. I didn't aim. I pushed it against him wherever I could reach. It caught on his skin and then plunged into his shoulder. Ivan let out a roar and dropped the gun. His back arched, and he grabbed frantically at the knife.

"Run!" Cade shouted, diving for the gun. He and Ivan were a tangle of arms and legs, punching and grunting.

I scrambled on all fours toward the corn. Back to the lines and the shadows. I clutched my side and forced myself to my feet, taking off in an uneven lope to hide. I ducked through to the next row, then the next. Someone was running alongside me on the other side of the stalks, bursts of heavy breathing, swoosh of leaves, feet hitting the ground. Louder. Closer. And then he broke through the line of corn in front of me.

Cade.

I collapsed against him. He guided us to the ground.

"Shh, shh, shh. Get low. He's right behind us. He got the gun back," he whispered.

The stab wound throbbed. My middle felt like it was missing. Only my head and feet were mine. Crawl. Just keep crawling. Every rustle of the leaves, I expected to be Ivan.

"We need to get to my house."

Cade navigated the maze, glancing behind him and keeping us moving toward the edge of the field.

"Can you hold on to me?" Cade asked.

I nodded, and he knelt down so I could climb onto his back. The second I had a solid grip, he took off running toward the house as fast as he could.

That's when the shots rang out.

CADE

POP-POP behind us.

The man had figured his way out of the corn and was firing off rounds, even though he was still too far away to hit us.

My house didn't seem to get any closer even as I threw every cell of my body forward, racing toward protection. This was the breakaway run of my life. No end zone ever felt so far. Carrying Jane was too slow. I had to buy us time. I ducked behind our tractor.

"Keep going toward the house!" I ordered, lowering Jane to the ground.

"What about you?"

"Get in there. Lock the doors. Call 9-1-1."

"But . . ."

"Go!"

I picked up a bushel of corn and rolled it loudly out to the left, hoping the man would follow the sound. I took off to the right, to try and circle around the back of my house. But he was already coming around the corner, between me and the back door, scanning the yard and field for us.

I snuck behind the chicken coop and scrambled toward my truck to hide, climbing up into the back, lying flat. The clouds slowly expanded and contracted overhead like I was caught in slow motion. I fought the urge to sit up and survey where he was, praying Jane had made it somewhere inside to hide. Footsteps crunched on the gravel. My whole body stiffened.

"Nice try."

The guy was peering down at me. His sunglasses had fallen off, and one of his eyes was swollen shut from a puncture ripped in the lid.

How I'd rolled him off me I have no idea. He was frickin' huge, with a neck as wide as his head. The top of his shoulder was splattered red from the knife going in, but he seemed to barely feel it.

"Where is she?" he demanded, reaching into the truck and grabbing my T-shirt like a noose. He pulled it so tight around my neck I could barely breathe, then he yanked me out of the truck.

"Don't play games with me, bro."

The man jammed the gun to my head and marched me to the front door, throwing it open. "Get down."

I dropped to the floor.

"Come out, come out, wherever you are," he called in a mocking singsong tone. "I have your boyfriend. If you don't come with me, I'm going to shoot him. Tick tock."

He had no reason to keep me alive other than to bait Jane. Every nerve ending braced. I heard his gun cock. My teeth clenched. My whole body tensed for the bullet I knew was aimed my way. *Please, God, no . . .*

There was a click and swoosh, the *cha-chuck* of a shotgun, and then a deafening boom and thud. I turned my head to see the man crumple beside me, blood pooling out around him.

His face was in line with my face on the floor.

His mouth was open. His eyes were open. And he was dead.

As the room came into focus around him, I homed in on the feet standing beside his body.

My father's.

JANE

I heard the gunfire through the fog of being half passed out under the porch and stifled a scream. *Cade!* I tried to roll out from under the front porch where I was hiding, but my legs were lead, bolting me to the dirt. The same free fall of blankness that flooded through me when Raff was killed seeped through my body again. Face, brain, heart. Negative space. A wave of nausea swept over me, and a sob choked in my throat.

Move. Do something.

I rolled onto my side and was about to haul myself out when I heard voices by the door, then footsteps overhead.

I froze.

"Let's wait out here for the police," a man said.

I didn't recognize who was talking.

But I did know the next voice.

"They said they're on the way," Cade said.

I let out a giant breath. He was okay. He sounded like he was straining to speak. But he was okay.

My mouth opened to call out to him, but I caught myself. *Wait it out*, I told myself, *right where you are, under the porch*. All of this, the barn, no real doctor, risking Cade's life—it would be for nothing if the police scooped me up. No, I had to stay hidden. I took a shallow breath and lay as still as I could under the sagging planks of wood, with the wet leaves and empty bottles tossed beneath. Their glass reflected blue, red, blue, catching the colors from the police cars as they pulled up flashing in the driveway, sirens screaming. Police descended on the house.

"Go on in, boys. Check it out. . . . What happened, Danny?" a woman's gruff voice asked.

"All I know is some guy had a gun aimed at my kid. And I took care of him."

Oh, it was Cade's *father*. He shot Ivan! I struggled to hear the conversation.

"So it was self-defense?" the woman asked.

"A man's house is his castle," Cade's father responded. "Helluva lot of cops you got. This really necessary?"

The bottoms of everybody's shoes were outlined by the yellow light from the front door that cut through the slats of wood over my head. Officers kept walking back and forth, up and down the creaky stairs, investigators with white plastic over their feet. Bits of dirt came through the floor and fell onto my face. I didn't move.

The woman's voice was muffled, but it sounded like she was asking Cade's father again what exactly happened. He was standing directly above me, talking louder than everyone, his words a little slurred.

"Like I told you: I heard a scuffle in the front room. I came in from the kitchen. Saw this guy with a gun pulled on my boy."

"Well, you stick to that and we'll be fine."

"What do ya mean, stick to that? It's what happened," Cade's father demanded.

"Look, people don't break into houses for no reason. It's still a murder scene."

Murder scene. Ivan was *dead*. I flashed numb with relief.

Cade's father sounded annoyed at the questions. "Come on, Connie . . . sorry, I mean *Sheriff*. You know we got nothing."

"I don't know what you do or don't have," the sheriff said. "Cade, anything *you* want to tell me?"

I cringed, but Cade didn't miss a beat.

"I have no idea what he'd want with us, Sheriff Healey," Cade said.

Sheriff Healey. His buddy Gunner's mom. I was trying to place who was who.

"Okay. Okay," she conceded. "Why don't you go inside and get a drink of water, Cade?"

"I'm not thirsty."

"Then go get me some."

"Uh . . . sure." I heard Cade walk inside.

As soon as he was gone, the sheriff lowered her voice so much I could barely make out what she was saying. "Danny, you're not getting mixed up in any of this cartel business, are you?"

"Are you out of your mind?"

"Am I? You don't come into town anymore. The farm's been struggling. You've got to be running out of cash. Promise me you're not looking for . . . different . . . ways to get out of the hole."

"Connie . . ." Cade's dad's voice went ragged with warning. "You know what I think about those people. How could you even begin to suggest that I . . . after . . . she . . ."

"You're right. You're right. I'm sorry," she backed down fast.

The sheriff sighed and sat down heavily on the steps, just inches above me. If for any reason she felt compelled to look in the spaces between the steps, there I would be. I closed my eyes like that would somehow help me be invisible.

"Can't blame me for asking, Danny. I don't know where your head is, you know? We used to see each other all the time at the boys' games. We used to *talk*. But this is the first time I've even been out here to your farm in, what, a couple of years? More. I remember coming over for barbeques every other weekend."

"Want me to fire up the grill?" Cade's father said bitterly.

The sheriff clicked back into business mode when he refused to engage, standing up with a grunt. "I'm heading back in to check things out. I'll do my best to get that body out of here ASAP for you. I'm going to grab Cade to walk us through everything. . . . And Danny? Get Tom's guys to do the cleanup. They're the best."

Cade was inside with the police for a long time—long enough that I think I drifted out of consciousness for a few minutes here and there. I touched my shirt over the throbbing cut. It was soaked in blood again. What if I passed out under here and died? No one would find me until my decomposing body smelled too bad to miss. It would be a news story. Girl's body found stuffed under front steps.

Cade's father went in, and out, and in, and then came back and sat on the steps. I heard the crack of a can being opened, and he sighed along with its release of air before taking a long sip.

Finally Cade came back outside. He sank down on the step beside his dad.

"You all right?" his father asked.

"I guess. You?" Cade said.

"I'd be better without this damn circus. They need to haul that piece of garbage to the morgue and be done with it. What'd Connie wanna know in there anyway?"

"Where I first saw him. Anything he said to me. What he might have been looking for."

"Come lookin' for anything to steal, you ain't finding it here," Cade's dad said.

They sat in silence for a while. His father opened another can of beer.

"Don't say I never did anything for you, kid. I think that guy woulda popped ya . . ."

Cade didn't answer.

"Guess I'll go ahead and call up Tommy Mack to clean this mess up once the cops clear," his dad grumbled. "All these damn people in my house."

"I'm gonna go look for Hunter. He, uh, ran off with all this craziness." Cade tried to make it sound casual. The yellow circle of a flashlight flickered overhead as he took off toward the barn.

Through the gaps in the stairs, I watched a piece of plastic yellow crime tape flutter down to the ground behind him. It settled like a ribbon from a birthday present.

CADE

Jane. Hunter. I had to find them. They had to be all right.

Dead eyes. All I kept seeing, as the flashlight cut through the darkness, was that man crumpled on the floor. It could have been me. If my dad hadn't gotten there right then, I'd be on the floor instead, with a face that still looked like a face but had no life inside.

When I got to the far edges of the fields where everything went down, I started walking slower, dreading what I was going to find. The little beam of light barely illuminated anything at all, and I tripped on something soft and motionless. My dog? I crouched down. No. Jane's blanket. I felt around on the ground until I found the knife. I would need to get rid of it.

Everything that happened was a blur—my dad rushing over, pulling me to my feet, getting me out of the house, everything he kept asking that I could only answer with "I don't know." Gunner's mom and the whole sheriff's department showing up. They crawled around, picking up things in their blue gloves while I stood there all sweaty-palmed in the doorway waiting for them to stumble on something that told them I was helping someone hide and that's why we'd been targeted.

My heart had been beating so hard, and I kept opening my mouth to tell Gunner's mom everything, and then closing it again.

Jane was scared to go back into foster care. I'd told her I would hide her. The guy was dead. Threat over. Jane Doe could heal up in my barn and head north like she said she wanted, and it would be like none of this ever happened.

I walked in circles calling for Hunter, shining the flashlight on the same empty places. The urgency turned into a quiet heaviness as I scanned the path to the barn.

You're not going to find either of them, I told myself.

I had texted my mom a while back, that Hunter ate rat poison by accident and was dying. I thought that would make her come home. Not forever, obviously. But at least for a day, an hour, at all. She called Mattey's dad at the vet's office instead of me. When he got confused and told her he didn't have Hunter with him, she knew that it wasn't true, because the first thing I would have done was rush him to Dr. Morales. I would never let anything happen to that dog. And now look.

I'd wound my way back to the barn.

I pushed the door slowly open and crossed the airless room, dropping the blanket at my feet. I found myself staring at the knife in my hand. That guy's blood all over it. And to think all I'd wanted to do with it was open a fan. Suddenly that's what I *had* to do, like it would somehow bring me back to that point and none of this would have happened.

I grabbed that fan off the floor and finished hacking it open with the dirty blade. I stabbed at the casing until the plastic was in shreds. When there was nothing more to chop up, I snapped the fan cover in place, shoved in the batteries, and turned it on, aiming the breeze right at my face. I collapsed on the edge of my sleeping bag with an elbow over my eyes, listening to the hum against the thick quiet of the night. I swallowed the lump in my throat.

The last time I almost cried was the first time my dad went all alcoholic on me, right after my mom left. I didn't understand then that I couldn't get through to him once he'd reached that point. He was shouting that I broke the tractor. It wouldn't start. What did I do to it? I tried to show him what was wrong, and he got so pissed he threw the wrench at me. It hit me right above the eye.

That's not when I almost cried though.

It was after Mattey's dad sewed me up as a favor. Because he believed me when I said a metal ladder fell on me. He believed me that we just couldn't afford the ER. He never thought to ask if my dad did it to me. Because why would he think Danny Evans would do something like that to his own kid? Everyone knew Danny Evans was a good man, a hard worker, salt of the earth.

Almost crying feels like choking.

I would never say what really happened then, and again and again, because that would ruin everything left to ruin. They'd take me away. No family. No Tanner High. No football. If my dad got in trouble, I'd be completely alone. And the thing was, some days he was just fine, funny even, like he used to be. Smartass. Tough. The kind of guy you wanna grow up and be like, comfortable in your own skin. Salt of the earth. Hard worker. Good man. Believe it.

"Cade?"

Jane's whisper broke through the darkness of the barn, soft and small. My heart leapt, and I spun around.

"I found him," she said. "I found Hunter. He's alive."

JANE

I hadn't planned on finding Hunter. I'd planned on running. Everything kept going in and out of focus. It wasn't as bad as in the cornfield. Yet. If I kept bleeding like this, it would be.

I waited until the last of the police cars left and Cade's father retreated inside his house. The cleanup crew couldn't come until the morning. That meant Cade's living room would be soaked in Ivan's blood all night. He didn't deserve this. Neither did Mateo. Maybe I could find some women's center or something, pretend I was a domestic violence victim. No, they would take me to a hospital. To stay invisible, I needed Mateo to stitch me back up again. And then I would go. And their lives could be normal again.

I crawled out from under the porch and made my way across the dead lawn toward the bushes. That's when I heard the whine. Hunter.

Seeing the dog hurt made me stop hurting.

We crawled toward each other and met on our bellies, bleeding and panting. I took his paws in my hands and then grabbed his furry head while he licked my face. No way was I leaving him there. What if Cade never found him?

"I'm coming back for you. Don't you move," I whispered.

I forced myself to stand, then limped in the direction of the fields and the barn.

I wasn't sure at first that Cade was inside, but then I heard the whir of the little fan. When I told him about Hunter he got up and rushed toward me, taking my shoulders in his hands.

"How bad is he?"

"He's whimpering but alert, and he can move. I'll show you where," I said. "Are *you* okay?"

"Are *you*?" Cade slid an arm around me to prop me up, and I found myself burying my face in his chest and just holding on.

"I didn't know who got shot. When I heard the noise inside . . ." I trailed off.

"The guy. He's dead," Cade said into my hair.

"I know. I . . . was . . . under the . . . the porch . . . the whole time." I was having trouble even talking.

"Wow, you can barely stand up. I need to get you and Hunter to Mattey."

Cade helped me sit down on the floor, flipped the flashlight back on, and shined it around the barn until he found what he was looking for.

"Let's get you up in this wheelbarrow," he told me. "I can't carry you both."

Cade pushed me as fast as he could in the dark. I aimed the flashlight and told him which way to go to find his dog. Hunter started whining the second he heard Cade's voice, and Cade ran over and grabbed his furry face. He spoke low to him—*Hey, buddy, it will be okay*—murmuring over and over as he wadded a blanket against the gunshot wound.

"It looks like it only got him in the shoulder," Cade said as he lifted his dog in next to me in the wheelbarrow. "I'm hoping, anyway."

He left us at the edge of the yard and peered in the windows of his house to make sure his dad was asleep before starting up the truck. I held Hunter on my lap as we sped down the road, carefully watching the rise and fall of his uneven breathing. Cade handed me his phone to dial, so he could keep one hand on the wheel and rest the other on Hunter's head, lightly stroking his ears. I put it on speaker.

"Cade? What's wrong?" Mateo answered in a half-asleep muddle.

"It's bad. Hunter got shot. Can you meet me at the office?"

"Wait, what? What do you mean, *shot*? How? Where's Jane?"

"She's with me. Just please . . . meet us there. I'll tell you everything."

Mateo showed up in the empty parking lot on his bike in his pajama pants. They had cowboy hats and bucking broncos on them that in some other reality would have made me laugh. He came around the passenger side and gently scooped up Hunter, balancing him against his body as he unlocked the door of his dad's veterinarian office. It shared a plaza with a pawn shop and little café called Mama's Empanadas. Coupon fliers from the grocery store across the street had blown against the cinder-block walls, collecting with discarded paper napkins and a couple of cigarette butts.

Cade helped me slide out of the truck and wrapped a sturdy arm around me as we hurried inside.

Mateo flipped the switch, and the lights snapped on with a fluorescent buzz.

"Oh man," he said as the unforgiving light hit. "You look awful."

He took a step toward me, but I shook my head.

72

"Hunter first," I said.

"What the heck happened?" Mateo asked.

I let Cade tell him, while Mateo poked around the hole torn in Hunter, who lay there in that way dogs do when they trust that you are going to help them. Mateo put down the probe, mouth dropping open as Cade talked.

"Your dad *killed* a guy?"

Cade nodded.

"And Sheriff Healey believed you about everything."

"Yep."

Mateo made an O shape with his mouth and blew out all his air to calm down as he tried to concentrate on Hunter. Bloody gauze piled up on the table. Cade rested a hand on Hunter's back, keeping him from thrashing around. Hunter was whining the saddest whine, and Cade pressed his forehead against his dog's, softly reassuring him.

"Two holes!" Mateo suddenly exclaimed.

Concerned, Cade leaned forward.

"No, that's a good thing. See, the bullet went in here . . . and *out* right up here. It's a clean sweep." Mateo grinned victoriously. "Big man upstairs must be looking out. Jane, you and Hunter are so lucky no major organs got damaged."

"Yeah," I echoed. "Lucky."

To be shot or stabbed, running and scared . . . it can all fall under "lucky" as long as you're not dead.

CADE

"I should have my own reality show!"

Mattey was beyond pleased with himself. With good reason. I shook my head at him.

"Unbelievable, man."

Hunter was sleeping on his good side, a square of fur shaved off with only a couple of little *x*'s stitched on the patch of bare skin like a game of tic-tac-toe.

The bathroom door clicked open and Jane stepped out, supporting herself against the wall. She looked a million times better, but I still reached out to guide her to a chair.

Jane rested a hand gently over the new stitches on her stomach.

"Makes a difference doing it here, huh?" I said.

"Numbing spray"—she shot me a tired, barely there smile—"is pretty key."

"I feel better about it now," Mattey added. "I was worried the barn was dirty and it was going to get infected."

"Now you tell me." Jane gave him a mock scowl.

Mattey brushed it off, still on a high from being the amazing kid doctor. He rummaged through the front desk and found some chips and candy.

"Anyone else hungry?" he said through a mouthful, spinning on the receptionist's stool.

"Actually, I might be," Jane said. She sank down onto one of the waiting room chairs, nibbling a chip. I grabbed a cup of water for her to sip and then sat back down on the floor with Hunter where he was sleeping. I left my hand right on his rib cage so I could feel the reassuring rise and fall of his breath.

"So . . . uh . . . now what?" Mattey asked.

"Um . . . ," I said. "I guess I'm going to take Jane north once she's up for it."

"Where north?" Mattey turned to Jane.

Jane shrugged. "I was thinking Maine?"

"Why Maine?"

"Closest to Canada I can get without a passport," she said.

"Have you ever been to Maine?" he asked.

"My mom went there once. She said there were puffins. And lighthouses."

"Is that where she lives?" Mattey asked.

"No."

"Where is she?"

"I have no idea."

Mattey looked baffled. "Do you know *anyone* there?"

"No."

Jane glanced over at me for help deciphering his intentions.

"What are you thinking, Mattey?" I asked.

"I mean, the guy after you is dead, right, Jane?" Mattey said.

"Right," Jane cautiously agreed.

"So," Mattey said, "why not just stay?"

"Here?" Jane shook her head no.

"What's she gonna do?" I had to agree with her. "Keep living in my barn? Start school with us?"

"Yeah, I don't think that's a good idea." Jane let out a little laugh at the notion.

"It's a great idea," Mattey insisted. "Would anyone think to look for you at our high school? I dunno, dye your hair or something. My sister would do it for you. Say you're Cade's cousin."

Jane frowned, not buying it. "Why in the world would I stay here?"

"Because *we're* here," Mattey answered simply. "Who else do you have?"

JANE

Who else do you have?

Back at the barn with Cade, Mateo's question stayed in my head. It filled me up. It emptied me completely.

There were only two people who ever mattered to me. And I didn't have them anymore.

Raff was dead. And my mom might as well be. I hadn't seen her since I was four.

When you are four, there is no one better than your mother. All I ever needed was the touch of her soft hand playing with my hair, her wiry arm around me in a sideways hold, my face resting on her rib cage while she sang me to sleep. She was gone so much that when she was home and mine, all mine, it was pure magic, the shimmer of a fairy. We would dance, twirling with our arms over our heads. She showed me first position, second, how to pirouette. She told me she should have been a ballerina; maybe someday, when I was a big girl, I could be.

I didn't notice the marionette angles of her body, the caved-in sockets around her eyes so obvious to me now in the one picture of us I'd kept. I had no idea what the white "sugar" was that she put in pipes.

I thought everyone had to take their medicine through needles in their arms.

And I certainly couldn't comprehend that it was better for her to leave me with someone else, like she said. I cried so hard that day my little world pulsed in and out, dizzy, sick.

A four-year-old only understands that her mother is gone. The reasons why didn't matter. They still don't.

So when Mattey said *stay*, a warmth settled somewhere in my chest. Tanner, Texas. Hiding in plain sight. It could be the smartest or worst move of my life.

I reached out and ran my fingers over Hunter's soft snout. His nostrils twitched, and he gave me the smallest of licks hello. Cade gently stroked Hunter's velvety ears. We lay there, on our backs, Hunter between us. The barn smelled to me like old paperback books. The fan sounded like pages turning. Moonlight through the loose wall slats boxed us in with pale lines that intersected the octagon glow of a hurricane lamp. A reverse cage. Inside was the good place to be. The bars were there to keep the world away.

"Are you okay?" Cade asked.

"Nothing like cat pills to take the edge off."

"That's actually just aspirin I swiped from my dad." Cade smirked at me. "But I can ask for some cat pills if you prefer. The new stitches feel better?"

"It's good to be stitched up again."

"That guy busted them open, huh?"

"Yes."

"What was his name?"

"Ivan."

"Ivan who?"

"I have no idea."

"What's *your* name?"

I shook my head no.

"Come on . . . don't you think I deserve to know *something* about you?"

Cade propped himself up on an elbow so he could see my face and tugged at my wrist. I pulled my hand away.

Cade scrutinized me. His gray eyes narrowed. "Jeez, girl. How many skeletons do you have in your closet?"

How little could I tell him to make him still feel like I was giving him something?

"Honestly, Cade, the less you know, the better. For real. I don't want to be that other person anymore. Can't I just stay Jane?"

My words came out in a torrent, and I could see Cade's resolve soften at my urging.

"All right, relax," he said. "*Jane* it is."

But really, how *could* Jane be it? It couldn't be that easy to . . . become someone else.

"I'm sorry I got you mixed up in all this," I said.

"What? Almost getting me shot by a hitman? Eh, that's nothing."

"It's not a joke."

"I know, I know. It's how I deal with things," Cade said.

"It's not fair to you." I got quiet for a bit, thinking it over. "I can't stay."

"I mean, for a while, you gotta," Cade said, pointing to all the bruises on my face, my black eye, the scab crusted at my hairline. "You're a mess. You get on a bus looking like this, someone's for sure calling the police."

"I know. Also, I don't have a dollar on me, unless we find my bag," I said. "But Mattey's idea . . ."

"Mattey is a fixer," Cade said. "He stitched up your cut, and now he wants to fix the rest of you."

"And he thinks me staying here will do that?"

"Sure. He's happy here. So he thinks you would be too. That's how Mattey works."

"You're not happy here."

"I've got one more year, and then I'm hoping I get picked up to play ball and get the hell out. That's what keeps me happy."

"Well, I guess that means my lease to live in your barn would only be good for one year then." I let out a sarcastic laugh and immediately winced. "Can I have some of that whiskey from before?"

"What hurts?"

"Everything."

Cade handed me the bottle.

"Do you want some?" I asked.

"No, thanks. I don't drink."

"Why?"

"Because my father does," he said.

"Too much?"

"Way too much."

"Has he always?"

"My mom . . . left." Cade's answer was stilted, like he didn't usually talk about this. "That's when it got real bad."

"She didn't take you with her?" I asked. My stomach twisted for him.

"She said my dad needed me more."

"An excuse," I softly said.

Cade scanned my face and then nodded in agreement. "Sounds like maybe you get it."

"Maybe a little."

"I think he'd like it better if I were gone too. I remind him she's not here."

"He saved your life today."

"Lucky he's a good shot even when he's hammered," Cade responded flatly.

I put the bottle down.

"You don't have to stop," Cade said.

"I don't mind."

"Seriously, have some."

"I'll be fine."

The fan buzzed soft and steady between us, a cool breath on my face, his, back again.

"Let's say I *did* stay," I said. "How would your dad not find me?"

Cade snorted. "That's the least of your worries. He never comes out this way. I don't think he even remembers this barn is here."

"What if people ask him about a niece staying with him he doesn't know he has?"

"What people? He's too embarrassed to go into town," Cade blurted out and then abruptly stopped.

He got up and started pacing. He stopped by the door and kicked at it, lightly, over and over until a piece of the dried-out wood came loose with a clatter.

"Everyone knows he got ditched by my mom for a dirty cop," he finally mumbled. "Some jerk who got rich taking cartel bribes. Prince frickin' charming."

It made perfect sense now, his reaction to me, Raff, Ivan. *Y'all can rot with the cartels together.*

Cade reached down and picked up the broken slat. He pushed down with either hand until it snapped in half. It separated easily into giant splinters that he began to peel into smaller and smaller slivers.

"Meantime, him and me? We're still right here . . . living the dream. Look at this dump."

Sharpness. The wood. His voice. It was jagged with the reality he hid from everyone. As he paced in and out of the cage of light, the lines cast made Cade look covered in cracks.

"A dump of a home is still a home," I said.

"Is it?"

"You're letting it be home for *me*. For now." I took a deep breath. "Look, if you really mean what you say about me staying, I think . . . I think I will. But only until I'm better. And hopefully I'll find my money."

"Right. Your money," Cade said, judgment in his tone.

My eyes met his. "You know, Cade, there's more to knowing a person than what they've done."

"Yeah? Well, it doesn't seem like you want to talk about yourself very much."

"I'm not going to talk *about* me, but I'll talk *to* you."

"About what then?"

"Anything else."

CADE

Anything else was colors, food, movies, football. And it filled the sweltering evenings as Jane and Hunter healed up in the barn. Mattey was with us a lot. And he kept Jane company while I had football practice. He would bring his charcoal pencils and sketch pad and draw while they talked, sometimes skylines where he imagined living someday, sometimes the people right in front of him. Mattey's world.

But most of the time it was just Jane and me together.

"What's your favorite color?" I asked.

She told me light green, like leaves when they're new. I said mine was blue. She wanted to know what kind of blue, and I'd never really thought about it before. Maybe like the sky over the corn when it's growing. Or kinda like a pair of old jeans. The sort of blue that is familiar. She wondered if that meant I liked things predictable. I laughed because even if I did, finding her in the field was the end of that.

We talked and we walked, following the fence lines and scouring the woods between the barn and the freeway. It became a routine to end each day with a search for her money.

At first, she wouldn't answer any of my questions.

"When do you last remember having the bag?"

"I don't."

"How did you get away from Ivan?"

"I just did."

Then she answered them a little bit.

"When do you last remember having the bag?"

"After Ivan attacked me."

"How did you get away?"

"I fought back."

And then, one day, we thought we found it.

We spotted a bag in the brush. Jane flew toward it, snatched it up, but quickly realized it wasn't hers. Something about the false hope though, the surge and the crash—it broke down her guard a little. After that, her answers started to have real information, information that threw me no matter how many times I heard her say it.

"When do you last remember having the bag?" I asked, like I asked every time, thinking that eventually something had to click for her.

"The woods. . . . I tried to make a break for it. When Ivan slowed down, I jumped out of the car. But he caught up to me in the woods."

"How did you get away?"

"I had a fork. From the McDonalds at the bus station right before he found me. Plastic . . ."

I glanced over at her. I remembered Ivan's swollen eye. She didn't meet my gaze. I couldn't picture Jane hurting anyone, but I guess when it comes down to it . . .

"Are you *sure* you grabbed the bag?" I continued my list of questions.

"Yes."

"You didn't drop it near his car?"

"No."

"Did you have it in the woods?"

"Yes."

"Did you have it in the cornfield?"

"I don't think so."

"So you lost the bag somewhere between the interstate and my farm?" I asked.

"Right."

We had reached the storm drain where she'd hidden.

I scrambled down into it for her. Again. The dirty cement cylinder had some trash in it, a few plants growing in the cracks, and a dead fish that must've washed in from the river nearby. Mattey and I used to race paper boats in the spillover streams after it rained, running alongside them till they got sucked through the drain and disappeared under the road. I always wanted to see where they went, but Mattey was scared to cross the interstate. His parents told him he'd get run over if he tried.

No bag of money.

"When do we give up?" I asked after I crawled up the muddy embankment, brushing myself off.

"You don't strike me as someone who gives up," Jane said.

"I'm not."

"Me neither."

"I know."

"So tomorrow . . ."

"We'll look again."

We walked in comfortable silence back to the barn. I scooped up my football from where I'd tossed it by an old fence post and arced it back at Jane.

"Go long!"

She missed.

"You suck," I teased.

She scooped up the ball and chucked it hard at me. "Football sucks."

"I love it." I easily jumped out of the way.

"What do you love so much?"

"Everything. You get to wake up and do the thing you want to do. And I'm out there with my best friends, like Gunner and Fajardo and the twins."

"That's it? It's just fun?"

"We all need to have fun somewhere, right? It's also the only thing I feel in charge of. I can actually see the results of the work I put in. I like that."

"How old were you when you started?"

"Six, seven, maybe? I played Pop Warner football. I was a scrawny little squirt."

"Really?" Jane squinted at me. "What are you on now, steroids?"

"Why would you say that?" I felt slightly embarrassed.

"Shut up. You know you're built. You work out, like, twenty-four seven."

"Whatever. I was tiny when I started out. I remember once the biggest kid on one of the teams we played knocked me down and my shoe ripped. The sole flapped right off. And I was so mad because I knew we couldn't afford new ones."

"What did you do?"

"Same thing I do now: duct tape."

"Whatever it takes," Jane said.

"Whatever it takes," I echoed.

With so much resting on the luck of being scouted, my chances for success seemed barely better than Jane's odds of finding that bag of money. Paper boats swallowed up.

Back at the barn, we sat down with our backs against the wall and watched the orange square of sunlight from the door disappear.

"What day is it?" Jane asked.

"You don't know?"

"I've been living in a *barn*, are you surprised?"

That made me laugh, which made Jane crack up too, and suddenly we were laughing so hard we were leaning against each other. It was crazy. All of this was nuts.

"What the heck are we doing anyway?" I asked her.

"I have no idea," she said. "I should have left already."

"You're not going to start school with us? Don't break Mattey's heart."

"Mattey's heart?"

"He's the one who wants you to stay."

"Not you?" she teased.

"Girl, you gotta do what you need to do. I'm not going to tell you what that is."

"Trust me, the offer's tempting," Jane said softly. "But I still feel like your dad will catch on. And then what?"

"Like I told you, A, he never comes out here. I hide in this barn whenever he goes on a bender—hasn't found me yet. And B, he hasn't left the farm in a couple of *years*."

"He's, like, a total recluse then?" Jane asked.

"Honestly, the most human contact he's had in forever was when the police came here after he shot Ivan."

Jane nodded, absorbing the information. "I need to be certain there are no more Ivans coming after me. You can't be in the middle of this."

"Aren't I already?" I pointed out.

Jane's gaze went distant. "We have time to figure it out, I guess."

But time was flying.

Summer was winding down. August was sitting, sweaty, on top of Tanner, and the start of school was only a couple of weeks away.

As each day passed I found myself hurrying home a little faster after football practice to bring Jane some of our dinner and shoot the shit with her. I mean, whatever, it wasn't like *that*. But it was nice having someone to talk to. Real nice. I hadn't liked anything about coming home at the end of a day since my mom left. But now, it was like we were our own little family or something.

"How are you always here?" Jane asked me one day when we were all hanging out. "Don't you have a girlfriend?"

"He's got *girls*, not girl*friends*," Mattey told her.

"Player?" Jane raised an eyebrow.

"Nah." I tried to shrug them off.

A girlfriend would want to come over. A girlfriend would ask too many questions about black eyes and bruises. It sucked, but I could never let someone get close like that. I had to be Cade the quarterback, too obsessed with winning games to deal.

"I'm too busy with football," I lied.

"*Plaay*-yer," Mattey mouthed next to me.

"Shut up." I put him in a headlock.

Sometimes when Mattey would visit, he'd bring Jane things he swiped from his sisters: new razors, deodorant, girl stuff. Then one Saturday when I was cleaning pools, Mama Travis told me she was clearing out their garage and I could have anything I wanted from the pile by the door. And jackpot! There it was, one of those little camping toilets. You woulda thought I brought Jane a car, she was so excited to be able to stop squatting in the bushes.

That day I also scored a card table, two folding chairs, and flowered curtains, which we hung on the stall with the mattress. I tied them back with rope from some old cattle harnesses.

"Wow. Look at you, the interior decorator. It kind of makes it like a canopy bed." Jane surveyed my work.

"*Zee barn* is the most sought-after hotel of Tann-air," I said with a fake French accent. "Actually, it might be nicer out here than in the house, if I'm being honest."

"Really? That's kind of sad," Jane said. "Also never do that accent again. Because *that* is truly tragic."

"Well, we do at least have real furniture in the farmhouse, so there's that," I laughed. "It's just so run-down, and my dad never cleans. But I'm out of here soon. I hope."

"I'm sure colleges will be fighting over you."

"You've never even seen me play. How do you know?"

Just a feeling, she told me, but she guessed she'd have to come to a game to be sure.

"Wee *wee*," I said in the bad accent again to bug her, and she smacked me on the shoulder.

"I've never done anything normal like that, you know," she said. "A football game."

"You and your boyfriend never did things together?"

She shot me a look like *don't go there*.

"What's your favorite kid movie?" she asked, changing the subject.

Hers was *The Little Mermaid*. Because the mermaid is willing to give up everything she ever wanted to save the life of the one she loved. Mine was *Robin Hood*. Steal from the rich to give to the poor.

"You seem older than you are," I said. It was her eyes. A hard edge to the bright blue.

"I feel older than I am," she answered.

"So I really can't ask about your boyfriend?" I asked.

"Can I ask about your mom?"

"No."

"Well, same," she said. "No."

I did anyway. All she would tell me is that even though he got mixed up in dealing drugs he wasn't a bad guy.

"Do you miss him?"

"I found him dead."

Shit. I shut up.

"Anything else?" she asked coldly.

"No."

Anything else was anything else. And then there was everything. Which was nothing we could talk about.

JANE

Dead and pretty.

Hair is dead, but we think it's nice. There's always more pushing its way out of our heads, and we make sure it's clean and shiny. That's what I was thinking about as Mateo's sister cut mine. Hair hanging in a dead sheet down my neck. Attached to a body, with no nerve endings, the only way to know it's being cut is the dry sound of the scissors. I watched the inches fall onto the well-worn lime-and-yellow braided rug. Sunlight streamed in the window of the crowded bedroom. Their colorful house smelled like so many things at once: laundry soap and banana bread, sizzling garlic and onions, lemon cleaner, vanilla candles. Their life in layers, coming, going, cooking, sleeping, laughing. I was just one more moving part, no big deal, securely lost in the mayhem of their morning.

"I don't know why you want to change your hair." Jojo pursed her lips. "I mean, I get wanting a new look, but you look good now."

She thought I looked good? It had been a month and a half since Cade found me, and this was the first time we dared introduce me to Jojo as his cousin. I glanced nervously up at Cade, where he was

91

lounging on the top bunk of the bed in the corner, absently swinging his leg off the edge. I still couldn't believe we were going through with this. How many late nights of second-guessing and here we were, moving forward with Mateo's crazy idea.

I still had a rawness across my stomach, especially if I tried to sit without rolling onto my side and pushing myself up on an elbow. I ran my fingers along my bare arms. Cade had rigged up a shower for me using an old barrel, hose, and sprinkler head. My skin felt like someone else's—smooth and soft, clean in a way it hadn't been in so long. All the hand-me-down furniture Cade was collecting was making the barn look more like a house than a cowshed. As one day ran into the next, we kind of started assuming I really was going to stay.

Jojo continued to chatter as she worked on my hair.

"Oh, and P.S., if moving in with Cade is better off than where you were in California, I feel sorry for you. I mean, it's not like we're rolling in it over here. But have you *seen* the farm lately?"

"Jojo!" Mateo barked at her from the corner, where he was doodling on a notebook cover, elbow resting on a pile of half-dressed Barbie dolls and laundry that got folded but never put away.

"What? Am I not allowed to say it? His dad sucks. Cade . . . your dad sucks."

Cade let out a little snort of agreement over in the corner of the room. He was thumbing through one of Jojo's magazines. "You're allowed. He does."

"See, Mattey? What I said." Jojo surveyed the box of dye Mattey had scooped up for me. "Ugh. Jane, welcome to boring."

"Tanner's not *that* bad," Mateo chimed in.

"Oh, I meant this. What's with this blah brown?" Jojo made a face before tossing her own sheet of long hair around like a shampoo commercial. "If you're gonna go there, go there. Let's do sleek black, like mine!"

"Is this one really that ugly?" I asked, taking the box from her. The girl in the picture didn't look so bad.

Mateo defended his choice. "Don't listen to Jojo. It's not a blah brown. It's burnt umber with streaks of sienna in it."

"Are those paint colors?" I asked him.

"Yes—" Mateo started to say.

"If you wanted to paint the color of *dirt*," Jojo butted in. She made the sign of the cross. "R.I.P., beautiful hair."

"Burnt umber and sienna are only the color of dirt if the sun is shining on it in the morning," Mateo said.

Jojo and Cade looked at each other, paused, and burst out laughing.

"Listen to Michelangelo," Jojo teased.

Mateo shook a finger at her. "Someday when I have a big art show and you want to come . . ."

"What? I won't be invited?" Jojo laughed. "Please. No party is fun without me. Go steal Sophia's dye. She has a better color. Swap it out."

"She'll be mad."

"She's always mad." Jojo laughed. "Blame it on me."

Mateo scooted down the hall and brought back a different dye.

"That's what I'm talking about! That other one will wash you out. This one will bring out your eyes. Back to work," Jojo said, squirting the cool dye into my hair. "Hey, Cade, whatcha reading?"

Cade held up the magazine. "I'm learning about what girls think guys want in bed."

"Ew!" Jojo said.

"It's *your* magazine!" Cade protested.

"Yeah, but it's *you* reading it. So, is it true?" Jojo asked.

"Is what true?"

"The stuff it says guys like. Is it true?"

Cade squinted. "Uh, sure. Some of it."

"Like what?" Jojo asked.

"Yeah, Cade, like what?" Mateo teased.

"I don't wanna talk about that kinda stuff in front of my *cousin*."

Cade tried on the word for size and shot a look over at me that was almost a little smug, like he was telling me, *Yes, we could pull this off.* Mateo's eyes were still a little nervous, waiting for Jojo to somehow catch on, but she was buying it 100 percent, and why shouldn't she?

Maybe this was going to be easier than I imagined.

Ivan was dead. How would anyone know that he had found me here before Cade's dad shot him? No one from Playa Lavilla should think to look in this dingy little town. Still . . . there was a gnawing. It was the same sort of doubt that wormed in back when I realized Raff was smuggling drugs.

People know when they are doing something that holds too many consequences. But I had to eke out some sort of existence now, right?

"So, what else do I need to know about you, Jane?" Jojo asked. "You lived in Cali your whole life?"

"Uh, yes."

"San Diego is supposed to have the best weather in the universe!"

"Yeah, it's nice."

"And your parents got divorced, so you're like, *See ya, I'm gonna move in with my cousin?*"

"It was more complicated than that. I got myself kicked out of school. I needed a fresh start." I recited the story Cade and I concocted.

"You? A juvenile delinquent?" Jojo let out a belly laugh. "You're, like, a cute little girl. You're like Mattey."

"Hey!" Mateo protested. "Really? A little *girl*?"

"Totally. Jane, you seem like a complete rule-follower."

"Yeah, you'd think that, wouldn't you?" Cade said.

Mateo squinted at him as if to tell him to shut up. But Jojo remained clueless.

"Come on!" She led me into the bathroom and tilted me over the sink to wash my hair.

"Aw, hell yeah," she yelled once she started blow-drying it and seeing the results. "I am seriously missing my calling if I don't become a stylist."

"You want to be a hairdresser?" I asked.

"No. Not at all. I'm just saying I'm good at it. I want to be the president."

"Ha ha."

"What ha ha? I'm serious. I want to be the first Mexican American and/or woman president. Preferably both. Or at least a senator. I mean, I guess I could start out as the governor if I *had* to."

"I'm pretty sure you'd have to start out lower than that," I said. "Like mayor, maybe. County commissioner. Board of education."

"Ugh! I say I want to be president of the United States of America and you make me president of the *school board*?" Jojo huffed melodramatically. "A lot of faith you have. Thanks a lot! You didn't ask how I was going to get there. You asked what I wanted to *be*."

"I meant realistically."

"Dreams won't ever be real if you don't dream big," Jojo said.

"That's my theory anyway. Don't you have a pipe dream, the thing that would make you happiest?"

"Sure," I answered.

"Well, you can be a supermodel if you stick with me. Check yourself out, Jane!" Jojo shooed me over to the mirrored medicine cabinet.

A chestnut-haired girl with big blue eyes blinked back at me.

Dead and pretty. Pretty. And dead. Yes. Old me *could* be gone. The girl in the mirror never lived in Mexico. She never found her boyfriend staked to a chair by the pool with a black gunshot hole in his forehead.

This was going to work because I would *make* it work. No more running. My whole life, I never got to stay anywhere. Not with my mom. Or my first foster family. Or the second. It was time for something different. Maybe this was it. That was *my* pipedream: a home.

The girl in the mirror was going to save me.

CADE

The girl I found in the corn had cracked lips and a black eye and smelled sour. She was bloody and scared, and scary, bloody things happened to me because of her. That first version of Jane was not a girl to me; she was someone who needed help. That Jane was a ghost.

This Jane had smooth skin and shiny, dark hair that brushed the tops of her narrow shoulders. It angled around her face and made her bright blue eyes look even brighter.

"Let's get going!" Jojo was excited to go shopping for school clothes before the first day tomorrow. She was running around the house, throwing her things into her purse. Jane and I sat on the bottom bunk, waiting.

The cash my dad gave me for back-to-school supplies was supposed to somehow cover new cleats too, but so far, my patchwork was holding. I figured Jane could get a couple of things, and when she got a job, like she planned, I could get the new shoes then. It would work out. Who knows, maybe we'd find her bag and Jane could pay me back. The thought of using drug money made my stomach turn, though. It was too close to how my mom weaseled her way out when things got hard. I forced the thought out of my mind and looked over at Jane next to me. She was trying to fend off Jojo, who was armed with lip gloss.

"It's pretty on *you*," Jane said with an apologetic smile. "I'm just not really a bright coral sort of girl."

Jojo's makeover had turned Jane back into . . . one of us—someone to call for algebra help or take to the movies, someone I would throw balled-up paper at in chemistry class to get her attention or run faster for if I knew she was in the stands at a game. Someone I shouldn't be thinking about like this. She'd be gone as soon as she had the chance.

"Okay, I'm ready! Come on, people!" Jojo pushed. "What's the holdup? The mall is calling."

But before we could get in gear, Jojo and Mattey's little sisters came barreling in.

"Showtime, everybody!" Nina announced.

"Hiii, Cade." Viviana batted her eyes at me.

"Hiii." I rolled my eyes at her and ruffled her hair.

"Who are *you*?" Nina pointed to Jane.

"Nina and Viviana, meet Cade's cousin Jane," said Jojo. "Jane, meet my roommates. Because sharing space with an eight- and ten-year-old is stupendous."

"We're not stupid, you are." Viviana stuck out her tongue at Jojo in response but quickly spun around to size up Jane. She had the attention span of a puppy. "You're pretty!"

"Thanks," Jane said with a shy laugh.

"We're putting on a show!" Nina announced, grabbing Jane's hand. "You have to be in it."

"Leave her alone, psychos," Jojo said. "Sorry, Jane."

"No. It's okay." Jane seemed pleasantly surprised by the attention.

The girls plugged in a beat-up iPod player and cranked up the volume.

"Is that my iPod?" Jojo lamented. "Did you *ask* if you could take it?"

They just laughed and started a rehearsed little routine for us.

"Now you!" They took Jane by the hands. She hesitated but then gave in to their pleading. She moved slowly, still sore, but even so, it was hard not to just stare at her. Her hips swayed with the beat, and her arms seemed to meld with the music like it was coming out of her body instead of the speakers.

"Wow!" Jojo exclaimed. "Where'd you learn to dance like that?"

Jane abruptly stopped.

"Oh my gosh," Jojo exclaimed. "You are *so* joining dance team with me."

"Oh, no, I . . ." Jane shook her head.

"Oh. Yes. You . . ." Jojo imitated her. ". . . are an amazing dancer. It's happening."

"I . . ."

"Shush! I'm so excited! Okay, *pollitos*, good show!" Jojo planted wet kisses all over her little sisters' cheeks, squishing them against her as they tried to squirm free and wipe off their faces. "More later, okay? We have to get going before the stores all close!"

The four of us squeezed into my truck. Jojo sprawled out in the middle, leaving Mattey so squashed up against the door his elbow and half his face stuck out the window. Jane wound up pressed up against my side, and her arm had nowhere to go except on my leg. Her touch was light at first, but when I didn't shy away she let it rest a little heavier, and that's how we rode into town.

"You guys do your thing. We'll do ours," Jojo ordered.

Mattey and I hesitated. This was Jane's first time out in public.

"It's okay, we can hang with you . . . ," I said to Jojo.

"No, really . . ." She tried to get rid of us again.

"No. Really. It's cool."

"*Fine.* Frickin' pains in my you know what! Better keep up. Let's go, Jane! I know we must have the same taste. I swear I have the exact same outfit you're wearing today."

Jane made a little face behind Jojo's back to Mattey and me. We laughed silently. It *was* her outfit.

"Hey," I pulled Mattey aside to ask quietly, "where are we meeting Sophia?"

"In the food court at three. She's on her break then."

"You sure this is going to work?" I asked.

"Of course," Mattey reassured me under his breath. "Her boyfriend gets fake papers for people all the time. This is easy. Jane Doherty. From California. She'll never be anyone else again."

JANE

I saw him everywhere. Ivan. He twisted the eyes of the clerk in the shoe store, warped the guy serving smoothies. He was the soft-faced dad, the papery old man sitting by the fountain.

And Raff. The mannequins became Raff, haunting me through the glass display windows, their unseeing eyes like his . . . when whatever it was that made Raff *Raff* had already slipped away. I could faint. I shouldn't have come here.

"Mattey." I froze. "Are you sure I look different enough?"

"You look way different. Why . . . hey . . . are you okay?"

Mateo reached out and took my hand. I clenched back hard, trying to make myself breathe.

"What's wrong?" Cade turned back toward us, his eyes instantly locking on our hands.

"Oh, sorry." Mateo let go.

"For what? I was only asking if something was wrong." Cade's cheeks seemed to flush for a split second. "Jane, what's the matter?"

"Nothing. I'll be fine."

"Okay then . . ."

"What's the holdup?" Jojo rounded the corner with a huge soda, somehow already slurping at the ice even though she just bought it.

"Nothing. I'm hungry. Jane, you?" Cade asked.

"I *just* asked if you guys wanted anything!" Jojo said.

"Yeah, sorry. Changed my mind. We'll only be a minute. Mattey, we'll catch up?"

"Sure." Mateo took the hint and steered Jojo back toward the stores.

As soon as they were out of sight, Cade turned to me.

"Hey, look at me, Jane."

I forced my gaze to hold his, focused in on his gray-green eyes, the ocean on a quiet day. His chiseled jaw made me think of Superman— no, Captain America—everything about him from the line of his eyebrows, the angle of his cheeks, the sweep of his shoulders, strong and perfectly symmetric.

"You're going to be okay," Cade said with a firmness that made me believe him. "You can do this."

He pulled his baseball hat off his head, his sandy hair immediately popping up in messy tufts.

"Here. Put this on. It'll make you feel better."

I could have kissed him right then. Honestly. Not like that. I just wanted to be close to him. To somehow tell him he was the only thing keeping me anchored to this planet, that without him I would break into little pieces and swirl around like a dust storm and be gone.

CADE

Jane looked like she wanted to say something, but instead she pulled my hat low over her face and leaned into me a little, our arms touching lightly as we headed over to the food court to meet up with Mattey and Jojo's oldest sister, Sophia.

I could have spotted Sophia from a mile away. As usual, she was a walking makeup experiment. Her passion, she said. A calling. Today her hair was on the top of her head like a plant sprouting some weird branch. Her lipstick was gold.

"The eighties are calling. They want their backup dancer back." I slid into a plastic chair across from her.

"Shut your face, Cade. I changed your diapers. And for your information, *this*"—she gestured to her face—"gets me thousands of views on my YouTube channel. I'm going to get scooped up to do makeup for music videos before you know it. Obviously, *art* is lost on you. Anyway, I only have, like, a minute before I have a client at the counter, so tell me what's going on. Why did you need this . . . favor?"

"My cousin hung with a bad crew and really doesn't want any of them knowing where she moved."

Sophia gave us a squint of scrutiny. I kept my face blank like I knew how to do too well. *No, my dad doesn't hit me. I don't miss my mom. And yeah, this is my cousin.*

"We really appreciate this. A clean slate means more than you know," I said evenly.

Sophia gave us both another long look and then shrugged in acceptance. My shoulders relaxed with relief as she smiled at Jane.

"Hey." Sophia turned to me. "Jojo doesn't know about this, right?"

"No way." I laughed a little.

"Okay, good," she said.

"Why?" Jane asked.

Sophia rolled her eyes and leaned over to Jane. "My little sister is like the paparazzi. Everything she finds out she tells to everyone. And her version of the story is usually only a little bit right. . . . Oh! There he is! Diego! Hi, babeeeey."

As usual, Sophia's boyfriend was decked out like a total sleaze. He had a tacky designer T-shirt covered in roses and skulls, matching trucker hat, and way-too-tight black jeans all skinny at the ankle. His sneakers could probably pay a month of our mortgage. It bothered me that he was wearing dark aviator sunglasses inside the mall.

He leaned down and tilted Sophia's face up toward his, and they French-kissed hello like they couldn't care less we were sitting right there, waiting. I tried to wipe the grossed-out look off my face. Diego finally trailed his fingers off her shoulder, hoisted up his pants, and sat down across from us.

"Cade, nice to see you, bro," Diego said to me before laying out his rules. "I'm not going to ask why you need these papers. And you're not going to ask how I got them. Deal?"

I glanced over at Jane. She gave a little nod.

"Here you go, everything you need to enroll in a new school with a new name. Fake ID. Birth certificate. You're seventeen. *Almost* legal." Diego slid over the papers one by one, cracking himself up with his own commentary. "Immunization records. Good girl, you got your shots. Report card. Mmm, might have to work a little harder in math. And transfer card from your old school. That should cover it."

"Thanks, man." I slid the papers over to Jane fast. Why was he being so showy about it in the middle of the mall?

"You got it," Diego said, and then with a wink toward Sophia, "Bill ya later."

"Wait," Jane interjected. "How much did this cost?"

"Don't worry, sweetheart. Favor for a friend." Diego wrapped an arm around Sophia's waist, resting his hand in her back pocket.

"He's happy to help, right, Diego?" Sophia said.

"Anything for you, gorgeous," Diego said before turning his attention back to Jane. "Where'd you say you were from again?"

"California," we both answered quickly, but he wasn't done.

"Straight from there? Didn't go anywhere in between there and Tanner?"

"Nope," I said. "Right, Jane?"

"Right."

She was clenching and unclenching her hands on the edge of her chair.

I reached under the table and grabbed hold of one of her hands, silently telling her to stop worrying. I didn't blame her, though. It's easy to think anyone who runs a little sideways of the law is linked to the cartels. But Diego was just a car mechanic who knew how to game the system and make money on the side hustling paperwork, especially immigration papers so people could get jobs. I'd known him for years.

He gave Jane an invasive once-over. "You got real pretty blue eyes."

"Thanks," Jane mumbled, looking down.

"Really, Diego?" Sophia fake pouted. "I'm right *here*."

Diego laughed and planted a big, wet kiss on Sophia's neck, biting at her ear until she laughed too and swatted him away. Diego slid his sunglasses down and peered over them at us. He looked from Jane to me and back again.

"Just saying . . . you remember eyes like that."

JANE

My eyes stayed open almost all night.

When I did fall briefly asleep, my dreams twisted everyone into someone else.

In one nightmare I tried to pet Hunter, but then I realized he was a wolf. The wolf snarled, and I started running. But when he caught up with me, instead of attacking, he smiled. And I knew that the wolf was actually Ivan. As its face shifted from animal to human though, I saw that it wasn't Ivan after all. It was Raff.

"You're next," Raff said before he picked up a gun and shot himself in the head. His eyeballs turned black, and he dropped to the ground. I ran over to the body and discovered a lifeless Cade instead.

The sequence snapped me awake. *I won't tell. I won't tell.* I heard my own mid-dream mumble before my eyes even flickered open to stare helplessly at the shadows in the barn, dark and darker.

I lay there thinking about Raff . . . that day he was super messed up on who knows what and got a call directly from the big boss, the one no one ever met and never questioned. Grande. You need to go give people some medicine, Grande told him, and whatever that meant had

Raff scared enough that he told me I had to help. I had to drive him. He could barely stand up and walk straight let alone get behind the wheel. But you don't say no to Grande. There was a kid, Raff told me. They called him the Wolf Cub. He was trying to challenge Grande's turf, take his tunnels. They had to send a message to some of his men.

We drove a long time, at least a few hours from Playa Lavilla, to a little pharmacy outside Montera. Two other cars pulled up. I recognized one of Raff's friends. He looked surprised to see me and pulled Raff aside, speaking angrily and pointing back at me. Raff pushed him away and told him it was fine. Raff took his biggest gun from the trunk. His handgun was on his belt. I'm sure he had his knives. He stroked my cheek. *If I'm not out in one hour, you leave without me. Promise.* He grabbed my face. *I mean it.*

I promised. But I didn't mean it. *Promise* is what you say to people when you're going to do whatever you want regardless.

They pulled three blindfolded men out of the cars and disappeared inside the pharmacy. I stayed with the engine running, lights off, like he told me, watching the numbers on the dashboard clock creep. If you drive the getaway car, that makes you an accomplice, right? Accomplice to exactly what, I didn't let myself answer, even silently in my head.

But I knew.

Forty-seven minutes later, when Raff finally came out, there were tiny sprays of blood across his right arm and the side of his face. Red sea-foam.

This is the tunnel at the end of the light, he said. *Don't you mean the light at the end of the tunnel?* I asked as we sped away. He laughed. *No. I said what I meant. This is the billion-dollar door, babe. You'd never guess, right? Now forget you were ever here.*

Of course that meant I would never forget—the crooked trees and sloppy red medical cross slapped in paint on the side of the building, or that Raff could laugh when he was covered in blood.

If I didn't think about it during the day, I dreamed about it at night.

Like I did tonight, right before I had to get up for school.

Today is the first day of the rest of your life.

I had a social worker who used to say that to me, and it would make me want to squish her cheeks until her words sounded muddled, like a game you play with a baby.

But today it really was.

"Mornin'!"

Cade picked me up at the fork in the road like the school bus and handed me a brown-bag lunch as if we were going on a field trip together.

"I'll pay you back . . . ," I said, my voice trailing off as I climbed in beside him.

"Don't worry. I know. I'll take you by the diner, end of the week, to apply for a job. I told you, they'll be looking because their summer help always leaves this time of year."

"And the school clothes. All of it. I know you can't afford it," I said.

"You calling me poor?" Cade kidded.

"I don't want you to play the hero to the point you're at a disadvantage."

"*Playing* the hero? I thought I *was* a hero."

"You're *my* hero. Swooning." I put the back of my hand to my forehead and fanned myself with the other.

"That's more like it," Cade said. His grin faded as he gave me a concerned double take. "You look *really* tired."

"Thanks."

"Seriously. Did you sleep last night?"

"No. Not at all."

"Sophia's boyfriend?"

"Yes."

"Yeah, I know that was . . . weird," Cade said. "But it's *Diego*. Sophia's dated him on and off since they were in middle school. He's a wannabe high roller who's stuck fixing cars at his daddy's shop."

"The thing about my eyes though."

"It sounded like it was only a warning," Cade said. "Like, don't sell him out because he'd remember you."

"I hope so? Ugh. I hate feeling like this," I said.

"You're overthinking it. We both are." Cade tried to be reassuring.

"Because we're doing something crazy," I said.

"It'll be fine," Cade said. "Look, if we're gonna do this, we have to own it, right? You're my cousin. It's the first day of school. We got this."

He reached over and gave my hand a quick squeeze. I felt the urge to reach out and link my fingers with his, but we were pulling up to Mateo and Jojo's.

Jojo pranced out in the tiny bright orange dress we bought at the mall, ankle-high cowboy boots, and huge hoop earrings. Her mother was two steps behind her, yelling in Spanish.

"It's not too short!" Jojo struck a pose on the front lawn. She ducked away from her mom, using Mattey as a shield, and jumped into the truck beside me. Mateo yanked the heavy door closed, squeezing into the couple of inches left for him.

He handed me a couple of warm tortillas wrapped in foil. "I know you like these."

I scrunched up my face in a little thank-you.

"This must be Jane! So nice to finally meet you." Their mother peeked in. "I'm Mrs. Morales."

"Nice to meet you too," I said, matching her wide smile.

"Good luck on your first day. You kids be good. Now see, Jojo, *that's* how you dress." Mrs. Morales gestured to me.

"*I* picked that out for her, and it's just as short as mine! Jeez, Ma," Jojo protested.

Mrs. Morales threw her hands up, exasperated.

"Buh-byeee. *Besos!*" Jojo blew her kisses while urging Cade to pull out of the driveway.

Mateo gave her an extra wave like the good little only son he was.

"Bye, Mommy, I'll miss you," Cade and Jojo mocked him together.

As we rumbled toward school, the breeze from the open windows tangled my hair. Cade's truck didn't have working air conditioning. I was going to be a mess by the time we got to school, but I didn't care. This was what life was supposed to feel like—crammed in a car with friends, laughing, on the way to school. I hoped Cade was right and that Diego was a nobody.

"We're here!" Jojo announced.

Cade scored a spot right by the front doors of the school. The parking lot was a jumble of junky trucks and beaters, girls hugging and squealing, guys high-fiving. One car stood out, a small red sports car, sparkling in the sun. Leaning on the hood was a curvy blond girl in huge sunglasses, sipping iced tea in a clear travel cup with lemons in it.

"Aaaaah," she screamed happily as we got closer. "Cade! I missed you so much. Hi, Jojo! Hi, Mattey! Oh . . . who are you?"

CADE

Savannah Maddison gave me the kind of hug that lingers. I pulled myself away to introduce Jane.

"This is my cousin Jane from California. How was France?"

"Ah-mazing! I ate all the bread and cheese in the world. And my mom let me drink wine! *So* European. Hi, Jane! I'm Savannah. Welcome to Tanner!"

I could see Jane trying to absorb Savannah's twinkly voice.

Jane smiled back, but her eyes were wary. I watched them flicker over Savannah's long legs, all south-of-France tan, and then take in the shiny new car. She was going to want to hate her. Everyone, even me, thinks they're going to hate Savannah—for her house, her money, her dad and his super successful electric supply company, Maddison Electric. But she's like one of those Disney princesses who makes the flowers bloom, and the birds and animals follow her around. You can't not like Savannah.

"How's sweet baby Hunter?" she asked me, clapping her hands together.

"He's fine," I answered, exchanging a quick look with Mattey.

"Oh, good!"

"Go deep, Cade!" Gunner ran into me hard from behind, ramming me against Savannah's car. Fajardo and the twins, Justin and Taylor, were right behind him, pushing each other around, spilling their sodas, and almost trampling Jane and Jojo in the process.

"What the hell, Farty! Watch it!" Jojo yelled at Fajardo.

Poor guy had had that nickname since first grade, when the cafeteria served refried beans at lunch and he had one serving too many.

"Lookin' good, Jojo." Taylor tried to hit on her.

"Look somewhere else, Taylor." Jojo put a hand up in his face while smacking Justin away as he pretended to dance all up on her.

"Um, *never*. Get away from me, Justin. Jane, meet the football team. Well, some of them anyway. Jocks, this is Jane."

Gunner had quickly removed himself from the tangle. He wiped his hands on his jeans awkwardly. "Hello, Jane. You must be Cade's cousin. It is very nice to have you join us."

His formality sent the guys into hysterics.

"Why, yes, Jane, pleasure to make your acquaintance," said Justin.

"Sincerely yours, fondly, with deepest regards, Gunner," Taylor laughed.

"Oh my gosh, leave him alone!" Savannah swooped in with her magic wand. "Let's go in, so Jane has time to get settled on her first day. Jane, may I take you to meet Principal Jackson?"

I could tell Jane would rather have it be me, but she didn't know how to disagree.

My friends, their laughter, how Gunner looked at Jane, even the way Savannah gently guided Jane off into the building—it felt like when I let go of the football to throw a touchdown and the crowd cheers. As it spirals up and away, even though I'm the one who made it happen, the second it leaves my fingers, it's everyone's.

JANE

Life was full of normal things, which wasn't normal to me at all.

But it's strange how quickly a lie can become routine.

Jane Doherty had a schedule and a locker, teachers and homework, a table to join in the cafeteria. Everyone happily accepted her as the star football player's cousin from super-cool California. The only person who was wary of Jane Doherty's existence was me.

At first I started each day on the library computers, scouring the web for news, anything that might tell me about Raff's old gang and Grande, or Ivan's and the Wolf Cub. But there was never a headline that breathed danger. After about a month it started to feel like I was searching for information for someone else.

Like he'd promised, Cade helped me get a job at the diner in town, Fancy Nancy's. I picked up two shifts a week; it's all they had. *I'll take it*, I'd told Nancy . . . for two dollars and thirteen cents an hour. That was the base salary without tips, and I wasn't wrong to have wondered just how well people in Tanner could tip. Not well.

But it was something. Looking at Cade's farm, you knew that if he lent you even one dollar, he felt it. And he'd been spotting me all summer. So I tied on that smiley face sunflower apron every Friday night and Saturday morning. Each plate of pancakes I served, every bit of bacon grease I wiped up, I thought of the missing bag. Cade and I had crisscrossed all the same places too many times. I'd practically memorized the trees. Each time we rechecked the storm drain it was the same weeds, old shoe, trash. The dead fish rotted and then dried in the summer heat, only bones left behind.

Maybe it was just time to accept I would never see those stacks of hundred-dollar bills again. Maybe that was okay. Jane Doherty from San Diego would figure it out on her own. Two dollars and thirteen cents at a time.

Was it possible that I had found a hiding place that would hold, I wondered as I headed into the school cafeteria.

Jojo screamed my name and gestured wildly for me to sit with her like she hadn't just seen me in history class. I filled my drink and put it on my tray, making it tip, but before I could take a second to balance it, someone swept it out of my hands.

"I got it." Gunner smiled shyly. As usual, his button-down shirt had come untucked on one side, and his hair was sticking up in the front.

As we sat down, Savannah swooped over. She leaned in and whispered in my ear, "I . . . know . . . your . . . secret."

I froze.

Savannah cocked her head and wagged a finger at me. "Jojo tells me you dance."

I almost started laughing with relief. I could breathe again.

"No, that's not true," I said.

"No, it is," Jojo interrupted. "The girl can move. We *need* her."

"I can't believe you've been holdin' out on us, Jane! We can schedule a tryout for you." Savannah slid onto the bench beside me. "Don't worry, totally a formality. I'm the captain. If I say you're in, you're in."

"Thank you, but I'm all set."

"Don't be scared! It'll be fun." Savannah was persistent. "If you start now you'll be ready for the big homecoming game."

"What else are you going to do after school?" Jojo added, putting her hands out like a scale weighing the options. "Hang out with your crabby uncle on the farm and do homework. Hang out with your amazing new friends and dance."

"My job . . ."

"Totally won't get in the way." Jojo wasn't having it.

Gunner touched my arm. "You'd get to perform at all the football games. You're basically our cheerleaders."

I couldn't help it. I broke out laughing. Me? A cheerleader? Poor Gunner looked so confused by my outburst though, I choked it back.

"Will I have to use *pom-poms*?" I asked, mildly horrified.

"It's dance team, not cheering!" Jojo said. "Don't listen to Gunner."

"I was just meant it would be fun to have you at the games," Gunner tried to explain. Jojo turned to him with raised eyebrows and a knowing smile, which made him quickly backtrack. "I mean, because the whole group, you know, like, all of us, we would all get to hang out and stuff."

"We'll see. How's that?" I said.

"Perfect." Savannah clapped. "We so need fresh talent. Are you comfortable getting thrown?"

I ran my fingers along my stomach. "No. I, uh, have an old injury. I shouldn't."

"No problem, we'll put you in the regular lineup. No tumbling."

No tumbling.

Somehow I had not only tumbled into life as a regular high school girl but was the shiny new thing. Savannah made sure I knew where to go, which teachers were cool, which ones weren't, and was pretty much booking my social calendar full of football games and rallies and dances. Her birthday party was coming up and I *had* to be there.

"What are we talking about?" Cade came in for a landing at our table, munching on some candy. "Want some?"

I peeked at the packet. "I only like the pink ones. No thanks."

"I'll have some." Savannah cupped her hands out to him with a little pout. "All I've been getting is veggies with a side of . . . veggies. My mom says I ate too much in France."

"Jane is joining dance team!" Jojo announced.

"No . . . ," I protested.

"She's going to be fantastic," Savannah said. "I already know it."

Cade shot me an amused look.

Somehow, when Savannah decided something, people wound up doing it.

That night, I asked if I could borrow Cade's iPod to practice in the barn. When he brought it out to me he plopped down on the mattress and folded his arms behind his head like he was settling in.

"Um, what are you doing?"

"You're gonna be performing on a dance team. Did you not catch the part about people watching?" Cade teased.

"It's awkward if you're just, like, sitting there."

"Fine, fine!" He surrendered, then grinned mischievously and, in a dramatic whisper, said, "Dance . . . like no one is watching . . ."

"Shut up!"

"Okay, okay. Do your thing. Seriously . . . have fun. You deserve it. See you in the morning." Cade did a lousy pirouette and saluted me goodnight at the door.

I put the earbuds in and dimmed the hurricane lamp, shuffling through his music. There was a lot of country. I smiled. Of course there was. I found a couple of upbeat songs that matched some of the go-to dance team moves Jojo had shown me and launched into the practice routine.

My muscles were wound tightly. What was I thinking? Everyone would be wondering who I thought I was showing up to join last-minute. The beat picked up. Did they really want me on the team? Did I even want to be involved in something so . . . conventional?

The music surged through me, skin to heartbeat.

And I stopped worrying about it.

I stopped worrying about anything.

Every twist and dip, each time I went up on my toes or spun, the weight on my shoulders lifted. I had missed this. Ever since my mom first taught me how to waltz, dance had been my getaway car peeling out, the wind in my hair. *One two three*, *one two three*, she used to chant as we bobbed across the room, until we were moving too fast to keep count and the three turned into *wheeee*, and we would fall down dizzy, laughing.

I didn't learn how to dance alone until I was alone.

An afterschool program for "at risk" kids had a modern dance class. That's where I found out that thoughts can become movements, that you can convert the darkest parts of your mind into the fuel that lightens your limbs. Anger can shoot your feet off the floor. Tears can be spun back inside.

I danced alone in the barn until I was sweating and out of breath, ignoring the dull ache in my stomach as the motions pulled at my scar, a new part of my body unfamiliar with movement like this.

When I finally sat down on the floor to stretch, I absently thumbed through Cade's music lists. "Most Played" caught my eye. A country song was at the top. I hit play. Very soft, minimal chords strummed, and then a deep voice mused:

Has it been that long? No, it's been much longer. Wanted to see if it's true, that if I'm not dead, I'm stronger. Yes, is a guess, when you say it too soon. You'd know that, if you knew me . . . anymore.

My mind abruptly flashed to my mother, the last time I saw her, getting small and smaller in the rearview mirror. She wouldn't know me. I wouldn't know her.

She disappeared the morning she sent me away with my aunt. *Wave bye-bye*, Aunt Nikki cheerfully said, like we were just running some quick errands, not driving across the country to Houston and leaving New Hampshire—and my mother—behind forever.

I wondered how strong the things that killed me made me.

Four foster families who don't want you anymore. Metal beds lined up in a group home, a place for children to dream the lie that they will be loved.

Raff, by the swimming pool, in a blood pool.

I found myself swaying to the dark melody. I stretched my arms over my head.

The pharmacy. The blood. The threat of Grande and the Wolf Cub.

I stood and let the words fill me up, moving with the pensive progression.

My shadow from the lamp was dancing with me, a melancholy waltz.

Yes is a guess if you say it too soon . . .

I realized I knew this song. A heavy metal band sang it first. They'd scream the chorus, "you'd know that if you knew me *anymooore*." Raff used to play it in the car. Crazy how different this version sounded. The same words, same melody, but completely different. I was like that, wasn't I? The girl in Playa Lavilla, Mexico. The girl in Tanner, Texas.

I raised my arms like a ballerina. My shadow answered.

I arched my back, grabbed my stomach, and then let my body flop over at the waist. My shadow showed me what it looked like to be stabbed.

I will lie to you. No, I'll just turn away. Wanted to see if you were true . . . but the world I want can't stay. A guess is a yes when you need it to be. You're counting on nothing if you're counting on me.

I started spinning up on one foot, pushing with the other and snapping my head to a focal point to keep my balance.

Even if the world changes around you, how do you know if you're changing with it or simply spinning out of control? This broken, slow version of the song was Cade's favorite. Maybe it was mine now too. My throat clenched for him. I stopped and held out my hands. My shadow reached back, and for a moment I felt like it was Cade.

CADE

The first two months back at school felt like a total blur. It was October already, and we were still undefeated. First time in the history of Tanner High. If we kept it up we'd be in the playoffs for homecoming on Thanksgiving weekend.

"Hi, it's me." I creaked open the door of the barn.

Jane was lying down, doing homework by the light of the hurricane lamp. The glow made her look like someone had drawn a fuzzy yellow line around her.

The barn felt more like my house than my house these days.

Jane had spread my sleeping bag over the top of the old mattress to make it softer, and I found some extra pillows in my mom's old sewing room, along with a quilt with blue rabbits on it from when I was little. Mattey brought a faded sheet with sun designs on it from his house to use as a tablecloth for the old card table. He or Jane, I wasn't sure which, had picked some black-eyed Susans and stuck them in a Coke bottle.

"I hate numbers," Jane complained.

"What did numbers ever do to you?"

"There are too many rules," she said. "And if you make one mistake at the very beginning of the equation, even if you get everything right after that, you're still wrong."

I lowered myself down on the mattress with a groan.

Jane put down her pencil. "What hurts?"

"What doesn't?"

"Your coach is diabolical."

"Pain is weakness leaving the body."

"If you say so," she said doubtfully.

"He says so."

I reached over to grab some candy from beside her notebook. "Wait. Why are there only pinks in here?"

"Gunner saved them all for me."

I let out a little snort of laughter. "Of course he did."

"What's that supposed to mean?"

"What do you think it means? He wants to jump your bones."

"Stop," Jane protested.

"Y'all gonna be bumpin' uglies."

"What?!"

"You never heard that phrase? Bumpin' uglies. You know . . ."

"Yeah, I mean, I get it. But come on, really? *Uglies?*" Jane sounded appalled.

"You really think a guy is pretty down there?"

"Uh . . ."

"Well, I mean, *I* am."

"Oh my God. *Cade!*"

I busted out laughing and rolled out of arm's reach so she couldn't smack me. We lay there for a while, eating Gunner's candy offering.

"Hey, guess what?" Jane said.

"What?"

"I went to Savannah's today to practice our routines."

"I'm surprised you came back," I said with a laugh. "Waterfront views. That crazy big kitchen. Flat-screen TV in her room. And did she show you how her bathroom floor is heated? Because who wants cold feet after a shower?"

Jane's voice got tight. "Oh, you've been there?"

"Of course."

"Of course."

"She's my friend."

"That's it?"

"Yeah, why?" I asked.

"She's gorgeous."

"That's true." Couldn't argue with that.

"So why just friends?" Jane asked.

Wait, was she jealous? Really? That was so very . . . regular high school girl of her.

"Why do you care?" I teased.

"Who said I cared?" she fired back with a smirk.

"I think you do."

"I think you want me to."

I laughed and shook my head.

Back in the day, my father found a stone when we went camping with Gunner and his pops all the way up in Montana. *Crack it open*, he'd told me. *It might be a geode.* Sure enough, there was a line of blue on the inside and all these little crystal ridges.

Jane was layers and layers.

"So?" She looked at me expectantly, waiting for an answer.

"So . . . Savannah used to be just one of us, before Maddison Electric started making millions. Lived in a little place up the road from here. Didn't have that car and the fancy clothes. It's different now."

"She asks about you a lot," Jane said.

I brushed it off. "I mean, don't get me wrong. I like her and all. But some people don't . . . match. Can you imagine her . . . here?"

"In the barn? Um, no."

"Of course not in the *barn*; I mean on the farm at all. Savannah should be away at some private school, but her father's too overprotective, wants her where he can see her."

"I didn't meet him. No one was home except Savannah and the housekeepers."

"Yeah, none of us really hang out over there. It's awkward being someplace so fancy. I always feel like I'm going to break something."

I rolled over, trying to hide the wince, but Jane was onto me.

"Rough practice?" she asked, suspicious.

"I'm fine. This is nothing. I mean, I've played with a broken wrist before."

"Are you serious?"

"Yeah, my dad said not to tell anyone or they'd make me sit out. So we waited to make it through the playoffs to go to the ER."

"That must have hurt like hell."

"Coach says blood makes the grass grow."

"Right," she said, narrowing her eyes at me.

My silence told the truth. Jane tossed me my old quilt, fluffed up the second pillow, and patted it, motioning for me to lie down under the threadbare bunnies.

"So how often does your dad hit you?" Jane asked.

"What are you talking about?"

"I'm not dumb. Come on. I want to know."

I sighed. "It's not like . . . an everyday thing. He just gets himself all worked up over nothing sometimes, and if he's drunk too much . . . then . . . yeah."

"Why don't you tell someone?" Jane asked.

"Why don't you tell someone about everything that's happened to *you*?" I countered. "Other people will start making decisions for you about your life. I don't want that. If I get put in the system, who knows if I even stay in this county? I have to protect my football position. It's my only way out."

"So it's about survival more than loyalty."

I thought about that. "Mostly, yes. But I also feel like he deserves the benefit of the doubt from me. My mom never even gave him a chance, you know? She didn't come to him and say, *Oh hey, I kinda hate my life on the farm. Let's talk about alternatives.* She traded up and never looked back."

"I just don't get how your mom could have ever left you behind to get beaten up." Jane shook her head.

"It only started after she left."

"What if you told *her*?"

"She doesn't answer my calls."

"Oh." Jane was quiet for a few minutes. "I don't talk to my mom either."

"When did you last see her?"

"When I was four."

"Where did she go?"

"Last I knew, jail. For stealing credit cards. I'm sure she's out now. My best guess is she went back to where we lived in New Hampshire. Manchester." Jane shrugged.

"What about your dad?" I asked.

"I don't know anything about him," she said.

"Maybe that's better than thinking you know who someone is . . . and then they're . . . not."

We lay there side by side, our stories so different and so similar.

"You can stay out here too, you know," Jane whispered. "This used to be your spot. To get away from your father. It still can be."

That was the first night I slept in the barn next to her.

JANE

Daylight hides the shadows. For every echo that haunted night-time, life at school was the opposite. The smile I pasted on during dance practice didn't feel so foreign on my face anymore, and that was foreign. The bounce in my step was no longer forced. At first, I would catch myself, like I wasn't allowed. But wasn't this the whole point? When I was with everyone at Tanner High, I really did have hours, even entire days, when I didn't think of running, or blood, or Raff. Those thoughts were thoughts to lose.

"Ah! So exciting. Your uniform came in!" Savannah ran across the school gym, waving a bright blue leotard with a puffy silver skirt. "Just in time for homecoming!"

Jojo swooped in, holding it against her and posing with it, one hip out. "It has your name on it and everything! Look! *JANE!*"

She handed it to me, and I ran my fingers along the sequins. Who ever thought a fake name in sparkly cursive would make me feel more real than I had in years?

"I love it," I said. And I wasn't lying.

The music kicked up. We moved in unison, in tight leggings and

128

tiny tank tops, ponytails that flopped back and forth. But instead of feeling ridiculous, I felt . . . safe. One of them.

After dance practice each day, I would walk over from the gym to the football field to meet up with Cade and ride home. He was always the last one left, jogging a few extra laps or lifting for a little longer than everyone else.

That afternoon, with the big Thanksgiving homecoming game around the corner, Cade stayed especially late. I could see him at the far end of the field doing push-ups. When he spotted me though, he hopped to his feet.

"Goooo, team!" Cade teased.

"Don't knock it till you've tried it," I challenged. "Show me what you got."

Cade cocked his head and opened his arms wide as if to say, *Watch me*. But then when he tried to do a cartwheel he couldn't get his legs up over his head. He landed in a heap on the grass.

"That's what you get for making fun of me." I plopped down on the empty field next to him and grabbed his water bottle to steal a sip.

"Wait, what's this?" He grabbed the uniform from me. "Look at you! Official."

"Shut up."

"You'll look so cuuute," he teased.

"Whatever!"

"Next step: homecoming queen," Cade said, cracking up at my appalled expression.

"Never that."

"Don't try and tell me you don't dig all this." Cade grinned. "I've seen you practicing in the barn."

"Ah! Spy!" I squirted some of the water on his face.

"You look like you're ready for game day," he said, wiping it off.

"So do you."

"Thanks, but I, uh, question your expert opinion." Cade grinned. "You're not exactly a fan of football."

"Sure I am."

"Okay, go for it. Tell me what you know."

"See those lines at the end of the field? Those are called end lines. And the ones on the side? Sidelines." I nodded like I was very smart.

"Oh. Impressive," Cade said. "And what line are we sitting on?"

"The starting line."

Cade cracked up at me. "You're hopeless."

"And you're relentless. This is a record workout even for you," I pointed out. "The sun's already setting."

Peach light cut over the bleachers. Cade's grin faded when he looked over at the stands.

"Did she used to come to your games?" I asked.

"Who?"

"Your mom? I thought maybe you were thinking about her."

"What, you read minds now?"

"Only yours. Side effect of living in your barn."

Cade pointed. "Right there, ten up, in the center. That's where she sat. She held court in those bleachers. Farty's momma always parked it right next to her because she ain't scared of loud."

"Your mom's loud?"

Cade nodded. "Hell yeah. And everything my mom yelled, Farty's mom would yell louder. She'd get so fired up at the referees she'd hurl every insult she had, English, Spanish, whatever popped out. That's how I learned to swear in Spanish." He smiled at the memory. "The two of them were as much a part of the game as the game. All the other mothers, they'd set up shop around them, even if they didn't know them, because that was where the party was at."

"Sounds like she was fun," I said.

Cade sighed. "All that yelling and cheering is what got the attention of one of the cops working detail. I laughed the first time my mom told me he was making fun of her for being so passionate. Then one day, when my dad started getting real moody over the farm sucking so bad, he just up and left in the middle of the game. No explanation. Just took off. So we were gonna hitch a ride with Farty's family in their pickup. But the officer said it wasn't safe to be in the open back like that. So he gave us a ride instead."

"So that's how it started."

"That's how it started."

Cade's expression was a practiced blank slate, but his eyes looked so sad I reached out and slipped my hand into his. He looked surprised but then squeezed back. We rested our hands on the white line painted on the grass between us..

"By the way, your 'starting line,'" he said, "is actually the fifty-yard line. It divides the field."

"So we're right in the middle?"

"Yep. Same distance in either direction." Cade let go of my hand and placed his football in it, shaping my fingers around it. "Hey, I wanna show you something. Get up."

I stood up.

"The way football works is that you have a line you're trying to reach. See that ten-yard line? Get there."

"What do you mean?"

"Take the ball and try to get there."

"You mean, like, run with it?"

"Run, dance. Whatever you want to do, just get there."

"Okay . . ." I started to jog toward the line.

Cade got in front of me and grabbed my shoulders and firmly pushed me back a good distance past where we started. "See, now you're more than fifteen yards away. But you still have to get to that same spot. Try again."

I tried to dart around him, but Cade easily blocked me and guided me gently to the ground.

"You got a little closer, but you're still farther away than where you started, and you're running out of chances. You've got two more. Try again?"

I tried again. The last time Cade let me get closer before he expertly took me down. He pulled me against him so he hit the ground first and I landed softly on top.

"You almost made it, right? But not quite. And now you're out of chances to try."

"So that's it?"

"This would be when the other team gets the ball. Or you have the option for a field goal. But we're not close enough for that. When you keep getting pushed back, over and over again, you have to be realistic about what you can reach. Or you're just going to be disappointed."

THE WOLF CUB

Tip the scale to even the field.

Gaining ground, underground.

There was a new tunnel on which our future hinged, owned by my rival, Grande, and hidden well. I would find the people who could find that tunnel. It was a giant hand reaching into the United States, so we could take what we deserved.

One day I will go to school in los Estados Unidos. I will live in the USA.

That's what I used to say to my friends as we kicked a soggy ball between us in an empty lot, the tattered leather flapping. Stale bread. Rotting garbage. Dirty engine oil. In the summer, with the rain, our barrio smelled.

Me too, me too, they would say. We would talk about what cars to buy when we were rich, in which city we would have a fancy house with motorcycles, purebred dogs, and swimming pools, maybe even a girlfriend who was a model or a movie star. One day, someday, we would live like royalty.

Some kings are born. Others, made.

My father made the border run when I was thirteen.

He said he would send for us as soon as he had the money and a safe way to get us there. But there was no call. No knock on the door. No letter with a stamp from the USA.

I told myself there were several possibilities.

He made it there and it was not good enough for us.

He made it there and it was so good he did not need us.

He never made it there.

Who really knows how far he did or didn't get? But we still owed the money for his crossing. Even with no proof that he was dead or alive, the men who promised to get him there came for the payment. They were men we knew by name. We knew their kids. And we knew what they did to people who did not pay their debts.

Manada de Lobos. The Wolf Pack. The Lobos always collected.

My mother's factory job at the maquiladora would never bring in the cash they demanded. And when she got sick and died, the debt fell to me. They offered me a job delivering packages for them.

First I delivered their drugs. Then I started collecting money for the drugs. I was good at . . . convincing . . . people to pay their bills. When the Lobos dug their first tunnel, they trusted me to oversee construction. I took notes. And then, I took over.

The cub rose to rule the pack. Now it was time to rule the rest.

Across the border, loyalties still lay with Grande, and those small towns were the other half of the equation. A tunnel needs a beginning and an end.

It was time to send a message, I told my three best friends.

First Alamo, like the fortress. He had that nickname from back when we played ball in the street. You could never get around him when he guarded the goal.

Then Asesino, the Assassin, a skinny kid who had his first kill even younger than me. He was wire slinking along walls, my shadow.

And Pozolero. We called him the Soup Maker. He learned how to get rid of bodies from the internet. He didn't say much. He didn't have to.

Wolves have territories they will aggressively defend. They howl. And if their howls are not heeded, their next step is to crouch, fangs bared, and clash their teeth. They don't usually bite at that point. It's just a loud snap to remind everyone who is dominant.

That was the sort of warning I would send.

CADE

Something was wrong. The second we pulled up at school I knew it. No one was in the parking lot.

"Are we late?" Mattey asked, glancing at his watch in confusion.

Jojo scrolled fast through her phone.

"Oh . . . damn," she breathed.

Jane didn't say a thing, but her body had gone rigid beside me in the truck.

"What is it?" Mattey asked.

"Bunch of guys got killed on the bridge!" Jojo read.

"What bridge? The one right behind the practice field?" I craned my neck to try and see down the ravine.

"Hey, there's Gunner's mom," Mattey pointed.

Two cruisers blocked the back entrance of the lot, lights flashing. The sheriff jumped out and jogged across the field.

"Everyone in the building immediately." Principal Jackson had taken Coach Hollis's bullhorn and was waving the last of us inside. Two sheriff's deputies flanked him, hurrying us through the doors.

"Come on." I put a hand on the small of Jane's back as teachers waved us into the auditorium.

We filled up the seats fast, everyone falling in line quickly out of nerves and curiosity. Even my teammates, the twins included, shut up and sat down.

Principal Jackson looked very serious at the podium.

"Overnight a violent crime took place close to school grounds. It was only discovered a short time ago. Police are currently on the scene, so the school is officially on lockdown in accordance with our policies, even though they have everything under control. We've sent reverse 9-1-1 calls to notify your parents and guardians so that they don't worry."

A murmur buzzed through the room as everyone grabbed their phones and started pulling up information.

"We're told it's an isolated incident. And it was not random. The victims were specifically targeted. But out of an abundance of caution, no one comes, no one goes until we get the all clear. In the meantime, the school day will proceed as normal."

Yeah. Good luck with that.

Even the teachers were scared. They didn't try to stick to their lessons, instead letting us look up stuff and talk. Until lunchtime. That's when all the details started coming out. They told us to put away our phones. We should discuss it at home, with our families. But it was out there by then.

I didn't have any classes with Jane, and my lunch schedule didn't line up with hers today either. I couldn't get the look in her eyes out of my head as we went our separate ways from the assembly. She kept glancing back at me even after I'd grabbed her arm and told her this sort of thing isn't new. It's Tanner. But that was before I read everything. This was worse—way worse—than anything that had happened here before.

I saw Mattey real quick in the hall. "It's cartels."

"I know," he said.

"Have you seen Jane? Is she okay?" I asked.

"Hard to tell. This couldn't have to do with her, right?" Mattey looked as worried as I felt.

"You heard Principal Jackson. He said the victims were specifically targeted," I reassured him . . . and myself.

"True. But don't you think we should maybe tell someone?"

"*Now?* No way. We'd be in so much trouble."

"But—"

"We can't do that to Jane. Let's wait and see once we find out more, okay?" I said.

"Okay," Mattey tentatively agreed.

"Hey!" Jojo came blowing around the corner. "Did you hear? Some of the guys who were killed worked for *Savannah's* dad!"

"That's awful."

"I know, right?"

"Did she read *how* they died?"

"Yeah."

We got quiet. The bell rang in the emptying hallway, shrill metal.

Four men. One was missing his hands. One had no eyes. Another's tongue had been hacked off. The last was burned to charred-black nothing. They were left hanging from the bridge behind the school, on the road that leads to the border crossing, hanging with a sign that said, in Spanish: *Defect or die.*

JANE

Defect or die. The warning on the bridge was a claw around my neck.

I was trapped. Killing time. We were stranded on lockdown for hours after the school day would normally be over, waiting for the all clear. Our teacher pretended to read a book, like we couldn't tell she was constantly checking her phone.

I stared at the leftover algebra equations on the board, but all I could see was the number four. Four people tortured to death. I closed my eyes for a moment and watched the inside of my eyelids—my own gray and black, fuzzy dots like white noise blotting out the past.

The static scramble of emotions collected. The pool. The blood in the water and on the deck. Their faces . . . *No.* I wouldn't think about Raff. If I thought of him I would stop being . . . this. There'd be no way to do things like brush my teeth or tie my shoes. Lunch. Lockers. Laughing. I wouldn't be able to sit in this classroom. I would have to run screaming out the doors.

Bury it. Bury him. He gets no grave in the ground. He's frozen somewhere in the coldest parts of me, the Ice Age in my head.

"Remember what happened to Lola Javier?" Jojo was whispering with a group of girls in the back, all of them straining to lean over their desks and listen.

"Her boyfriend was one of them. When she broke up with him, he took her to one of their hideouts and they sliced her tongue so she could never tell their secrets."

My head shot up.

"What about the old postmaster?" another girl, Lucia, added. "The one who stopped delivering the cartel's packages because he thought the feds were onto him?"

The girls nodded. I didn't ask what happened to him. I could imagine all too well the body parts that got mailed to his family.

"And whatever happened to Hector?" Lucia continued. "Remember how his mother witnessed that huge shooting at the nightclub where she worked back in Mexico, and the cartel came and found her here? They kidnapped her husband, and the whole rest of the family had to go into witness protection."

"Oh, and our neighbor's cousin," Jojo added. "She was a doctor who treated a little boy who got hit by a car. He couldn't be saved. It was too late. But he was a cartel leader's kid, so they ran over the doctor."

"I still think the post office fire was the worst," said Lucia.

Jojo argued. "That was years ago! I think the doctor is worse."

"That's just because you knew her."

"*That* much has happened here? In Tanner?" I asked, heart pounding. "Because of cartels?"

"My dad calls them the devil puppet masters," Jojo said. "But they come and go, you know? Like every couple of years some bad stuff will happen. Then the police crack down and it goes away."

"Which cartels?" I tried to sound casual but my voice was high, and I'm sure my eyes were flashing panic.

Jojo gave me a funny look. "Haven't you been checking your phone? Some new cartel trying to make a statement."

She hadn't noticed I didn't own a phone. "They didn't *name* them?"

"I mean, no. Aren't they all, like, the same?"

Jojo's voice started sounding far away and muffled to me, as if she were talking into her hand. I held on to each side of my desk like it was a boat about to capsize.

The intercom cracked. Thank God. I couldn't listen to any more. We were finally cleared to leave school, the murder scene deemed secure. We'd been on lockdown for almost ten hours. It was already five thirty. I walked out of the classroom in a daze.

"There you are! I've been worried about you. Come here," Cade's voice cut through.

I almost broke into a run as I hurried toward him. He held out his arms . . . and a blond head collapsed against his chest. I stopped in my tracks. He hadn't been talking to me.

Savannah's shoulders shook as she cried into his shirt. I immediately slowed down to act natural as I approached, like I never thought his arms were open for me. I melted in with the rest of the group of friends, trying to disappear. An arm slipped over my shoulders. Gunner.

"Hey, don't be freaked out," he said. "My mom says we shouldn't worry. None of us have anything to do with people like that."

I blinked at him. No idea. I mean, how could he? The girl he thought he knew, Jane from San Diego, gave his hand a little pat to say, *Thank you for the effort.* Gunner responded with a sweet half smile of reassurance.

"Did you know them?" Cade was asking Savannah.

"I mean, I knew two of them by sight. Not well." She sniffed. "But still . . . they worked for my *dad*."

"Jane!" Savannah reached out as soon as she spotted me, pulling me in so I was right there next to her, pressed against Cade. I quickly untangled myself from the awkward group hug.

"You okay?" Cade asked.

"I'm fine."

Cade frowned at me. "Sure?"

"Yes."

"Do you all want to come to our house?" Mattey asked. "For dinner? I don't know. I feel like none of us should be alone tonight."

"Oh, Mattey, that's so sweet." Savannah wiped her eyes. "I would love to, but I'm supposed to go straight home."

"Call your parents and ask?"

"Yeah, actually, I think . . . I think I will." Savannah pulled out her phone and dialed. "Voicemail. Let me try my mom . . . annnd . . . voicemail."

She bit her lower lip, thinking. "You know what . . . forget it. I'm coming. If they're worried about where I am, they should pick up their phones, am I right?"

She looked proud of her tiny rebellion.

"Gunner? You coming?" Jojo asked.

"That'd be real nice, actually. My mom will be busy all night, and my dad's on the road."

As soon as Gunner and Savannah left the lot, Jojo spun around to us, her eyes wide and challenging. My whole body constricted at what she said next.

"Let's go to the bridge."

CADE

If Jane had said no, I never would have driven by. But she didn't say a thing. She hadn't even really looked me in the eye since the school hallway. And I was curious.

"I don't know," Mattey hemmed and hawed. "Why would we want to see something like that?"

"Don't be that guy!" Jojo interrupted. "Everyone is going!"

Almost every car that left the student parking lot banged a right, like us, slow-rolling past the bridge, as close as we could get to the police tape.

The bodies were long gone. News trucks lined up along the street, reporters picking their way down the muddy embankment in fancy suits to do their live shots.

"Wow, even the national news is here." Mattey pointed.

"Of course *national* news is here," Jojo exclaimed. "So are the FBI, the CIA, and Homeland Security. I mean, please, it's, like, a *mass murder*. They gouged out the one guy's eyes and—"

"Please, don't."

Jane's voice was the smallest I'd heard since those first few days I found her. I glanced over at her. She was pale, and her mouth was a thin line.

"You okay?" I asked her.

"I need to get out of here."

I sped up and got us out of there.

"Sorry." Jojo patted Jane's shoulder. "I forget you're not used to this stuff. I mean, first that guy who tried to rob Cade's house, now this. Tanner's going crazy."

Jane stared straight ahead, giving Jojo only the tiniest nod that she'd heard her.

"You sure it's okay we all come over?" I double-checked as we neared the Moraleses' house.

"Are you kidding? You know my mom cooks enough to feed the whole school," Mattey answered.

As we piled out, Jane's fingers dug into my arm. She eyed Jojo and Mattey, waiting until they were out of earshot.

"I have to leave," she whispered.

"You don't want to go to dinner?"

"No. I need to *leave* leave. Like, leave Tanner."

I froze.

"The bridge. It has to do with *you*?"

"It might."

I swore under my breath. "Are you serious? Are you sure?"

My throat had a weird tightness to it when I thought about Jane leaving. Jane tried to read my face. I tried to read hers. We stared at each other for a second too long.

"What the heck are you two talking about back there?" Jojo called back to us from the porch. "Come on! Savannah and Gunner are already inside."

"I guess let's go in for now," I said. "And then we'll figure it out?"

I nudged Jane forward, and we stepped in to find Savannah already smooshed into one of Mrs. Morales's bear hugs.

"Savannah! I haven't seen you here since you moved to the big house!"

"I know," Savannah said, squished against her. "I miss you! And your cooking. What can I do to help?"

"Here, honey, you set the table. Days like today, you hug your children extra, you know?"

Mrs. Morales grabbed each of our faces and planted big, wet smacks on our foreheads before a loud sizzle on the stove forced her back into the kitchen. She spilled some dry rice on the cluttered counter as she went to dump a scoop into a boiling pot of water. She shook a finger at the rice like it was at fault, not her, making a joke of it. But I could tell the events of the day had her stressed.

"Everyone, come and help yourselves. It's all ready."

She put Jojo and Gunner to work plopping enchiladas onto a row of colorful plates. Gunner managed to spatter sauce on his shirt almost immediately.

"Here, sweetie." Mrs. Morales took her apron off and draped it over Gunner. "Okay. Better."

"Mrs. Morales, come on," he protested. Everyone cracked up at him in the ruffled apron except Jane and me. She barely seemed to notice what was going on around her, and I couldn't ease the sick worry sitting in my core.

"How much?" Jojo asked.

"The usual," I said. Jojo heaped a giant serving onto my plate.

"Jane, what about you?" she asked. "Jane . . . Jane?"

When she didn't answer, Gunner reached out and touched Jane's arm. "You okay?"

Jane nodded. "Yeah . . . sorry, just a little distracted."

"It's scary, what happened," Gunner said. "But remember, they're not after people like us."

"Right," Jane murmured.

"If you want, we could maybe go to a movie this weekend. Get your mind off everything?" Gunner said.

Smooth, Gunner, I thought, trying not to roll my eyes.

"We have a lot of work to do on the farm," I interjected and sat down next to Jane before Gunner could. He gave me a funny look and slid in next to Mattey, who was also giving me a double take.

"Why don't we *all* go see a movie?" Savannah sat down across from me with a big smile. "It's so nice to be together, isn't it?"

No matter what was going on, it had always been easy to find comfort in the chaos of the Morales house, the food, the noise. I searched for it now.

The little girls, Nina and Viviana, burst into the kitchen and claimed their spots at the table. They immediately started arguing and teasing each other as they passed the bowls of food around.

"Ow, it's hot—take it, take it, take it."

"Put it down, *boba*, what's wrong with you?"

"Hiiii, Cade. How's foooootball?" Viviana flirted.

"It's good. How's school?"

"Well, *today* school was scary because of the people who died," Nina announced matter-of-factly.

"Let's not talk about this at the table," Mrs. Morales said.

"Where else are we going to talk about it?" Dr. Morales walked in and flipped on the television before even taking off his shoes or washing his hands. "Savannah! How nice to see you. Hello, Gunner. How's your mom?"

"She'll be living at the cop shop for a while with all this going on," Gunner said.

"No doubt. Well, you're always welcome here. And you must be Cade's cousin," Mr. Morales said, extending his hand to Jane.

"Yes, sir. I'm Jane. Thank you for having us over," Jane responded softly.

"Anytime. Where's Sophia?"

Mrs. Morales looked down. "Late."

"Is she with . . . *him*?"

"She's with Diego, yes."

"I'll call her. I want my family home." Dr. Morales pulled out his chair noisily. "It's dinnertime. We eat together."

"Do you really eat together every night?" Savannah asked, folding her napkin neatly in her lap.

"Of course," Viviana piped up. "Don't you?"

Savannah gave her a little smile. "My parents are very busy."

"That's sad," said Nina.

"Nina!" Mrs. Morales scolded.

"No, it's okay," Savannah said softly, and got very busy cutting her dinner up into small and then smaller pieces.

The door slammed. Sophia came storming in, all riled up.

"*Three* missed calls. Are you serious right now, Papa?"

"You still live under my roof. So please, have a seat. I *said* . . . sit with your *family*." Dr. Morales was having none of it. "Jojo, please pass the corn."

Sophia plopped loudly down in a chair, scraping it closer to the table and resting both elbows on the edge, refusing to eat, like a little kid. She glanced up at Jane, clearly recognizing her from the mall. I stiffened, but she didn't say anything.

We should caution you that the images you're about to see are very disturbing, the television anchor warned us in the background. We all turned to see.

"*Dios mío*." Mrs. Morales was the first to look away from the distant images of four silhouetted bodies dangling from the bridge. Jane choked back her food.

Dr. Morales cleared his throat loudly.

"So, about what happened today . . ." He put down his fork. "I want you to think about it. Sophia, pay attention. This is the kind of violence we see when one cartel moves to take over another's territory. This is the time when you can get caught up in it if you're not careful."

Sophia slammed down her glass. Water sloshed onto the embroidered tablecloth. "Why do you say *Sophia*, pay attention?"

"You know what Diego is."

"Yeah . . . my *boyfriend*."

"He's a *halcón*."

"Nice, Dad. Really? You've decided Diego spies for the cartels based on what?"

"I know who does what in this town."

"Oh, really? *You* have informants too now? Your own *halcones*? Who are they? The sick cats and dogs at your office?" Sophia countered.

"Enough," her father ordered.

"No, *I've* had enough. He's not like that."

I thought about Diego's getup in the mall. The clothes, the attitude. Jane shot me a nervous look. What if he was something more than a con artist who could get documents for people? *Halcón*. I knew what that meant. It was slang for street-level informant. A falcon. Circling the skies with laser-sharp vision and talons that could scoop up even the smallest things to carry back.

Dr. Morales spoke softly but with conviction.

"These four bodies. This is only the latest example. You think back over the years. You think about Lola. The post office that burned down. Our neighbor's cousin. How many crime scenes will Thomas Mack and his workers clean up? He thought his company was going to handle cleanup for floods or fire damage. The cartel is no natural disaster. It is avoidable. No one chooses a tornado. But the devil is a different story."

An uncomfortable and long silence filled the room. Even Nina and Viviana went quiet.

A loud, official-sounding knock snapped us out of it. The rap on the door repeated, louder. Dr. Morales frowned and walked over to check the peephole.

"Aha!" he exclaimed, and opened it. "Garrett Maddison, long time no see, come on in."

"Hey, Doc, nice to see you too. Is, uh, Savannah here?"

"Right here. Would you like to join us?"

"Oh, that's kind, but not this time. We have to get home."

Mr. Maddison tapped a fancy watch, peeking out from where his cuffs lined up with his light gray blazer. The suit, the shoes—all of it breathed success. An image of my dad flashed to mind, unshaven, stained jeans, undershirt.

Savannah got up quickly from the table and walked to the door.

"What are you *doing* here, Daddy? I texted you where I was," Savannah said quietly, but I could still hear.

"You didn't answer your phone. I was concerned," he said.

"You didn't answer *yours*," Savannah mumbled.

"Tone," her father warned.

She blushed. "Sorry, Daddy."

"Let's go. Your mother's been worried."

Savannah circled back and hugged us all goodbye. I could tell she was stalling.

"Thanks for taking care of Savannah on such a nerve-racking day," Mr. Maddison said politely, holding the door open for his daughter and ushering her out. She gave a little wave and hurried down the steps.

Another awkward silence fell.

"It's getting late. I should, uh, probably go too," Gunner said. "Mrs. Morales, thank you. You know I love your enchiladas."

"Same," I added, picking up my plate to take to the kitchen.

Dr. Morales held up a finger, motioning us back to the table to listen.

"I wouldn't be a good father if I didn't remind each of you: Helping the cartel is no better than being in it. *Anyone* who has *anything* to with them could wind up dead."

JANE

"All right. Talk to me," Cade said the second we got in the truck and were alone.

The truck smelled like the Mexican food that lingered on our hair and clothes. The Moraleses' house disappeared in the rearview mirror, kitchen-glow windows getting smaller, eyes closing against the night. Being in their home was like being placed into a bright mosaic. Even when they argued, even when the news told them the world was broken, they took those broken pieces and glued them into a picture. That's what a family was.

"What's going on?" Cade pushed.

"It's bad," I whispered.

Cade was waiting for more. I didn't help.

"*It's bad* doesn't really explain anything, Jane." He ran his hands through his messy hair, fed up with my silence.

"It's time for me to leave Tanner."

"You already said that. But I want to know *why right now*?" Cade demanded.

"You never told me everything that happened here: the post office, the girl whose tongue they cut out."

"That stuff all happened a long time ago," Cade said. "And I thought *this* would be over once Ivan was gone."

"I never would have stayed if I had known all those things," I said.

"That's not fair." Cade got huffy. "Why would I ever do something to put you in danger? Any of us? Don't get mad at *me* when you're the one with all the secrets."

He was driving faster than usual. "I only know what you tell me, which isn't much."

"I don't tell you things to protect you," I said.

"You *need* to tell me some things so *I* can protect me," Cade responded. "And *you*."

The candor in his voice put a lump in my throat. I opened my mouth, closed it again. Anything I told him put him at risk. But he was right. Keeping him in the dark did the same.

"I don't know where to start," I mumbled.

"Start with who killed Raff."

I struggled to find the words. "Raff was killed by his boss . . . to keep him from selling their secrets to a new cartel. . . . That new cartel sent Ivan after me."

Cade stayed quiet as he let that sink in.

"And you think that new cartel is who's behind the bridge murders?" he asked.

"Defect or die. That was the message on the bridge," I choked out. "That's the same thing the new cartel offered Raff: Join them or die. So he joined. And then he was killed by his old one for the betrayal."

Tears welled and then overflowed. Cade took one look at me and threw the truck into park. "Come here. I'm sorry. I'm sorry for yelling at you."

I slid across the seat, and he wrapped one arm around me. A light rain spattered droplets across the windshield.

"You're right," Cade said, letting out a long hiss of a held breath. "This is bad."

We sat for a couple more minutes, the only sound the nervous taps of rain.

"Why don't we go back to the barn?" Cade asked. "And come up with a plan."

"Okay," I whispered.

I knew the twists and turns of the road back to the barn in my body, the rumble of the seat up my back, the slight yank left at the fork, then back around right, the last few bumps before we came to a stop. Cade tried to hold his sweatshirt over my head to keep me dry as we darted through the rain to the barn.

"Gotta check in on my dad and get something."

"All right," I said.

"I'll be right back. You gonna be okay alone for a few?"

"Yes."

But I couldn't stop shaking, even after I changed out of my wet clothes into a threadbare T-shirt of Cade's and a pair of his sweatpants and curled up under the faded baby blanket on my mattress. The drizzle outside had picked up, and the rain on the weathered wood drummed in impatient fingers, counting down.

Cade knocked lightly.

"Come on in."

Once inside, Cade moved the table and chairs and then even the old wheelbarrow against the door as barricades. He leaned something carefully against the wall.

"Wait . . . is that a gun?" I asked.

"It's one of my dad's. He's passed out for the night. I don't like what you told me. Just being extra careful."

He double-checked that the doors were jammed closed.

"And this is exactly why I have to leave," I said. "It's not right to do this to you."

Cade shrugged. "You don't get to decide that for me."

He took off his rain-soaked T-shirt and climbed in next to me, pulling the blanket over his bare chest. Hunter happily plopped down in his favorite spot between us, and I breathed in the popcorn smell of his paws. As Cade and I both absently stroked Hunter's fuzzy back, our hands crossed over each other's. Outside, rain dragged diagonal. The hurricane lamp swung in the slightest of breezes, illuminating the gun and then dropping it back to the shadows.

"Why would you ever put yourself through this?" I asked.

Cade's face was closer to mine than I was used to. I could see a thin scar between his lip and the edge of his nose, just a thread of a line, and another over his eye. Cade noticed me looking and took my hand. He traced my fingers along the scar, down his jaw to a bigger one that went all the way around the back of his neck. Then he pushed the blanket down and ran my hand to his rib cage to a scar new enough that it still had shiny patches of skin. I flattened my palm against his chest, feeling his heartbeat. It seemed to quicken under my touch, and my breath audibly caught as my own heartbeat sped up too.

"Because you get it," Cade whispered, placing his hand over mine.

I took his other hand and placed it over his old T-shirt, along the raised edges of my long, thick knife scar. I couldn't bring myself to let him touch the ragged ridges directly.

"I win," I joked.

Cade let air out his nose in a little laugh. "Like I said, you get it. Life can suck."

"Sure can."

"Hasn't felt that way though . . . as much . . . lately," Cade said. "Since you got here."

"Oh yeah? Because I think I've brought you nothing but problems."

"There's been some crazy stuff that went down . . . but for some reason I feel more normal than I have in a long time," Cade said. "I like having you here."

"I find that hard to believe."

"Why? It's nice having someone to talk to . . . make breakfast for . . . meet up with after football."

"That's pretty much 'insert girl here.' That's just . . . company," I said. "That's nothing specific to me."

"Fine," Cade said. "I like your ponytail."

"What?" I had to laugh.

"I like how it bops around when you dance. It looks silly. And I like how you start to smile before you say something sarcastic."

I gave him a wary look.

"Um, what else *specific*? I like how you smell," he said.

"Well, you bought me the soap."

"Fine, how's this? All the trouble is what kind of makes you amazing. You're tough as all hell. I don't know anyone like you."

Cade placed my hand back beside me and let go. "And that's about as mushy as I'm going to get, Jane Doe."

"That's pretty mushy."

"You gonna leave me hanging?"

"If I didn't feel the same way, I would already be gone. How's that?" I said.

"It would be better if you said you would stay," Cade answered.

"It's not that I don't want to."

"You'll need money. For a bus ticket. And to cover you till you get a job wherever you go."

Cade was being realistic. Without that bag of money from Raff, it was dollar in, dollar out from the diner. I had nothing. And after all this time, I had to assume that bag was just . . . gone.

"A bus ticket to Portland, Maine, from here only costs about a hundred and sixty dollars," I said. I'd searched that day one, on the school computers.

"Right. The puffins," Cade snorted. His voice went flat. "I don't even have enough for new cleats right now, Jane."

"I'm not asking for your money," I said. "I can probably make enough at the diner for the ticket and enough extra to live off of for a little while in about two or three weekends, if we don't spend it on anything else."

Cade shook his head. "I hate this."

"Me too."

He shrugged in defeat. "So . . . two more weeks then."

"Two more weeks," I echoed. "At least we're committing to something, right?"

"Right."

"I mean, go or stay . . . stay or go. Hide or run. This back-and-forth dance, it's been killing me."

Dancing, back when I was little girl, was simply to twirl as fast as I could, then abruptly stop, arms over my head for balance, barely able to catch my breath while the walls blurred around me.

First you spin.

Then the room does.

Even when you hold still, if you've been moving too fast, the world around you keeps going. Even when you want to see clearly, you can't. At least not right away. You have to wait for everything to come back into focus. And as the dizziness fades, sometimes there's that little pulse of nausea. The sick reality.

I kicked the blanket off of us and stood up on the mattress.

"Will you dance with me?" I asked.

"Here?"

"No, in chemistry class next Monday. Yes, here."

"That crazy dance team stuff you do? Hell no."

"Just . . . normal."

Cade shook his head at me like I was nuts but stood up beside me. He took my hands and placed them on his shoulders and held his rigid at my waist.

"How 'bout like a middle school slow dance?" he asked, keeping a ridiculous amount of space between us. It had the intended effect. I started laughing.

"You've got skills," I nodded and widened my eyes wide in mock sincerity.

"Girl, don't judge." He swayed awkwardly and pretended to step on my feet.

We cracked up laughing some more but didn't let go. Instead Cade eased out of his stilted joke dance and pulled me against him. I relaxed my arms around his neck and rested against his chest.

The amazing thing about music is that it stays. Our brains can somehow recall and play back the melodies without any instruments or singers there. I don't know what music Cade was hearing, but we swayed to the same slow rhythm in the silence of the barn, and even though I wasn't spinning in a little tornado like I used to, all the sharp edges and straight lines still smudged around us. The world is softer when you're dancing.

Dancing is a lie.

We lay back down on the mattress, staring at the ceiling for a while. Cade settled against me, the weird platonic-not-platonic way we slept, shoulder to shoulder, on our backs, like that kept it from becoming something we had to talk about. But I was always aware of each point of our bodies that touched: shoulder, elbow, wrist, hip, ankle, outside edge of my left foot. My eyes got heavier.

Cade's face flashed across my mind, the first time I ever saw it, going in and out of focus against the sky as I lay bleeding in the dirt. And then there was blood on his face and chest instead of mine, a big red *X* painted on his body like Raff. . . . The wolf was back, and it was laughing and . . .

"Hey, wake up! Wake up!"

Cade was shaking me awake. How long had we been asleep?

"You were dreaming. Crying."

"Sorry."

"You wanna talk about it?" Cade asked.

"It was a just bad dream." I tried to brush it off.

Cade propped himself up on an elbow. "Not the first time."

"What do you mean?"

"You talk a lot . . . in your sleep."

"Really? What do I say?"

Cade looked uncomfortable. "You, um, you say *Raff* a lot. You call his name."

I sighed. Of course the whisper of the only person who ever cared about me until now still lingered. The memory might always bleed.

"You kept saying, *I won't tell.* And mumbling something about . . . a pharmacy?"

"Don't worry about it," I said, but Cade wouldn't leave it alone.

"It's always the same though. Blood. The pharmacy. Is that where . . . your boyfriend was killed?"

"No. It's where he killed people."

I knew that would shock him. Maybe I wanted it to.

"Oh" was all Cade said.

Oh. Oh yeah, that's right, Cade, I used to be a murderer's girlfriend. I'm not just some girl with a cute ponytail. Still like having someone to make breakfast for? He needed to remember who I was before I could believe any of what he said. Cade might think it was worth it to keep me around, but he was wrong. And just because he was allowing me to pull him into my mess didn't make it okay.

I would leave, and he would go back to his life. Date someone like Savannah. Get scooped up by a college to play football. Forget the weird months a fugitive lived in his barn.

I would work on the docks in Portland and make friends with the fishermen. They would smuggle me across the bay to Nova Scotia, and I would disappear into Canada. I could work at a coffee shop on one of the islands, frothing designs into lattes and telling the tourists I'd lived on there all my life. The lighthouses would blink back the darkness.

As Cade fell back asleep, I listened to the sheets of rain. The perfect storm is to leave before people don't want you anymore.

CADE

The heavy rain overnight must have blown in from the tropics, bringing in an Indian summer heat wave. Jane was still asleep, her hair falling in damp strands across her forehead. I brushed them lightly aside, and her eyes flickered open. I pulled my hand quickly away.

"It's hot," she mumbled sleepily. "Feels like when I first got here."

"Sure does."

But it didn't. Not beyond the weather. Everything else had shifted. The empty barn was full of Jane. It would feel like she was here long after she left. I knew that.

Jane had to be one day at a time. That was it. No more angst bullshit. I don't dance. I run. I fight for the wins. I had to stop worrying about the long term and only think as far ahead as the big game on Sunday. My chem test on Wednesday. Savannah's birthday party. Simple as that. And today.

"Let's go swimming," I said.

"Now?" Jane asked.

"What, you got plans?"

"Um, school?"

"Screw school. You're leaving anyway."

"Not for a couple of weeks."

"Exactly. Soon. So let's go swimming."

"Cade, I'm serious."

"*Jane*, so am I."

"The cartels are no joke. I need to be lying low. Not doing things that will attract attention, like skipping class."

"Ivan's dead. Who's gonna tell anyone about some teenage girl who maybe knows something about something?"

"You make it sound so simple."

"Christ, Jane, we're *kids*. It should be that simple. We're going swimming, okay?" I was amped up. "Fuck it."

"Yeah, *okay*."

"No, say it," I told her.

"Say what?"

"Fuck it."

"Why?"

"Just do it."

"Fuck it."

"No, say it like you mean it. Yell it. FUCK the cartels!"

"FUCK the cartels."

When she shouted it with me, in that small moment, we said the cartels didn't matter, so they didn't. We could make them sound like nothing, and they would be.

"Let's go," I said and pulled her out of bed and the barn before she could change her mind.

Hunter ran ahead of us and jumped into the back of my truck. Mud flew out behind us as we tore down the road. A sagging fruit stand caught my eye, and on a whim I stopped and pulled out the few crumpled bills I had to buy a little green carton piled high with strawberries. It had been a long time since I threw down money on something to eat just because I wanted it.

I kept my eyes peeled for the turnoff. I hadn't been this way in years. We bounced deeper and deeper into the woods.

"Where are we going?" Jane asked.

"Spot my dad showed me. Long time ago. He used to take me swimming there after we harvested the corn. We'd celebrate. Splurge on empanadas, lemonade, and"—I pointed to the carton—"strawberries."

I threw the truck into park and rummaged around my football duffle bag for a towel.

"Time to walk. Let's go."

I led the way down a narrow path that eventually opened up to the quarry and its crystal-clear water.

"Careful—it's slippery from all the rain last night," I said.

But Jane was already peeling off her clothes, running ahead of me in lacy pink underwear with little flowers. I stripped down to my boxers and jumped in behind her.

The ice-cold water kicked my breath out but felt so good at the same time. I came up for air with a big grin. Hunter picked his way down the rocks to explore the shallow water, happily lapping up mouthfuls.

Jane treaded beside me, her dark hair slicked back so her whole face was just those big, bright blue eyes. She gave me this sweet little smile, all innocent, and then wound up to send a big splash in my direction before trying dunk me. We wrestled around a little before she swam out deep toward a big, flat rock. I caught up and climbed beside her. We lay flat, letting the hot sun bake us dry.

Jane Doe. Jane Doherty. If anyone ever told me back when I found her I was gonna be talking to her every night all night and laughing my ass off with her, I wouldn't have believed it. When she was all matted and sweaty and bloody, if someone said I'd be sneaking looks at her like I was right now, I would have been like, *Sure, okay*.

But I couldn't stop myself from glancing over to where she lay with her eyes shut. Her bra was soaked and stuck to her. I rolled over onto my stomach to keep everything under control, but I peeked out from under my arm at her. Her skin was so tawny smooth that the puckered purple cut on her stomach seemed like some stick-on Halloween scar.

"Don't look at it," she said. How did she know? Her eyes were still closed.

"Maybe that's not what I'm looking at," I couldn't help saying.

She sat up and folded her arms over her chest. "What's that supposed to mean!"

"It means your bra is see-through," I teased, bursting out laughing as she yelled at me to shut up and dove off the rock.

JANE

I pulled on Cade's T-shirt back at the shore as fast as I could and grabbed the strawberries. Up the path a little ways there was a big old wooden swing. Once I got it going good, it swung right out over the water. This place was perfect. It was secret and pretty, and there was a stillness that went from my fingertips to my heartbeat.

If anyone had told me when I was lying in that cornfield watching the clouds move inch by inch overhead that I would smile again, let alone laugh, I would have said, *You're crazy*.

But the sun was warm. The strawberries were sweet. And then I felt Cade's hands against my back as he gave me a push, sending me soaring even higher.

"You gonna share any of those berries?" Cade walked around the swing to face me and tried to grab at them.

I laughed and took a bite of one right near his face before the swing arched up again. He kept trying to steal them, and I kept holding them away, popping them in my mouth, until he grabbed the ropes on the swing and yanked me back in.

Laughing, Cade started twisting the swing in a circle, trapping me, the rope braiding up on itself until there was no more give at all. Just when it seemed like the ropes were so tight they would snap and I would fall, he let go.

I spun with the rapid unwind. Fast, faster, the quarry a blur. Through the whirl of the swing I caught flashes of Cade's face, his hair wet and tousled like a little kid's. In the frantic wash of my spinning surroundings, Cade was the only focal point. I could get lost in the safety of his steady gray eyes. Who leaves Captain America? How could I leave when I was finally home?

The swing slowed, leaving me dizzy. Cade swooped in for a strawberry. I gave him a look like *nice try*, raising one to my mouth to eat dramatically, when he leaned in and bit it out of my fingers, his lips right next to mine. My feet slipped from where they were anchored on the ground, and I swung even closer to him. Our lips pressed against each other for a split second before he gave the swing a huge push, sending me up and away. I'm sure my eyes must have looked as surprised as his, my face flushing so hot. I let go of the swing and let myself fall down into the water.

I swam underwater as far as I could before surfacing to take a breath.

It was an accident. He was playing, trying to get the strawberry. But I felt like I was still on that swing. The backward us and forward we, pendulum perfect, changing minds and circumstances . . . I forced myself not to look back at where Cade was standing. *What are you doing to me?* I wanted to ask him. *You catch me, kiss me, or at least I think you do. Maybe I kissed you. And now Tuesday will never be ordinary.*

CADE

It shouldn't have happened. We were running a play that worked, and it had to work now more than ever. For just a couple more weeks, people had to believe Jane was my cousin. Last I checked, cousins don't kiss. But was it even a kiss? Maybe I was feeling something she wasn't: flight risk. From the get-go, Jane was perpetually one headline, one wrong glance away from running. My house was already haunted by my mother. I didn't need the ghost of Jane to steal my barn.

"You went swimming without us *and* I had to take the bus!" Jojo yelled at us all the way to school the next day.

"It would have been nice if we could have all gone to the quarry," Mattey said. "On the weekend, though, so we wouldn't get in trouble for skipping."

"It wasn't like it was a plan," I tried to smooth things over.

Jojo still stomped off as soon as we pulled into the school parking lot, only to come to a screeching halt the second she rounded the corner. "What the . . ."

Graffiti covered the wall.

WETBACKS GO HOME.

"Nice way to start the day." Fajardo came up beside Jane and me. His grim expression was one I'd never seen on his happy-go-lucky face.

Gunner was right behind him. He put a hand on the small of Jane's back. I stifled the urge to push it off.

"You know my mom will get her guys on this," Gunner said.

"This is real nasty, man. I'm sorry," I said to Farty.

Farty shrugged. "You didn't do it. Who cares?"

But he cared. His mouth was in a weird upside-down smirk, trying to hide how upset he was. "Our lockers have pig's blood on them."

"What?" I couldn't have heard him right.

"Yeah. Whoever did this knows where our lockers are. They sloshed it on all the Mexican kids' lockers."

Jojo and Mattey looked at each other. Their lockers would be drenched too.

"You've gotta be kidding me." Gunner's face twisted in disgust. His hand had stayed on Jane's back. Why was he still touching her? Why was she letting him?

Jojo stood there taking the graffiti in, her eyes dimming angrier and angrier.

Savannah's voice suddenly sprinkled above the murmur. She was shaking her head dramatically, talking to a group of other kids. "It's awful. I mean, I realize that the drug problem is because of the Mexicans, but to write hate speech at school . . ."

"Wait, the drug problem is *because* of the Mexicans?" Jojo turned on her, blazing. "I'm sorry, what?"

"Well, you know what I mean," Savannah stammered.

"No. I don't. Maybe you should explain. Who are 'the Mexicans'?"

"Jojo . . ." Mattey tried to step in, but she threw her hand up in her little brother's face in a way that made him step right down.

"I'm just saying"—Savannah regained her composure—"we know who brings the drugs in."

Jojo was fired up. "And who's that? *The Mexicans?* Or rich white men like your daddy? Because last I heard, some of the guys that got killed work for *him*. What's up with that?"

"Don't bring my dad into this."

"Don't bring *mine* into it then."

"I didn't say anything about your father!" Savannah's eyes were getting all teary.

"You talk about Mexicans, you're talking about my father and mother. You're talking about Mattey. You're talking about *me*."

"Jojo Morales, you're being ridiculous," Savannah mock-scolded her with her hands on her hips, trying to pretend she wasn't thrown by the attack.

"Savannah Maddison, you're being a bigot," Jojo fired back, copying her pose.

"Hey now," Gunner tried to defuse things. "Everyone's upset by this. Let's not blame each other."

"Yeah, well, someone's to blame. Someone we go to school with thinks this stuff. Someone I sit next to in class," Jojo said, noticing the crowd that'd backed away from her and gone quiet.

"Show's over," Jojo sighed. Gunner and I exchanged a helpless look. Mattey shook his head. He wasn't gonna go there. We knew to let Jojo walk away alone.

Savannah sidled up next to me.

"I didn't mean anything by it." Her glossy lip was quivering.

"Well, then why were you talking trash?" I asked.

"I wasn't. It's true. The drugs come in from Mexico."

"Doesn't mean it's Mexicans' *fault*."

"I know that!"

"Well, you don't have explain yourself to me. Save it for Jojo."

"I can't believe how mad she is at me."

"You'll patch things up," I said.

Savannah slipped her hand into mine. "Thanks, Cade. You always make me feel better."

She rested her head against my arm.

"I'm going to go, uh, check on Jojo," Jane mumbled.

"Do you think Jojo and Mattey hate me?" Savannah asked.

"Mattey doesn't hate anyone," I answered, distracted by Jane's awkward retreat down the hall.

Savannah took a deep breath and blinked back her tears, pasting on a big, bright smile. "I hope they'll still come to my birthday party."

CADE

Football practice couldn't end soon enough. I just wanted to get out of there—away from the graffiti and the gossip, the rumors and the drama—and scoop up Jane at the diner to hang in the barn. I was worried about her.

I decided to shower at home to save time, even though my feet were soaked, especially my right one. The tape on my cleat had peeled up, and mud was squishing in, the practice field totally waterlogged from all the rain.

All summer, this was all we'd needed. And nothing. Now it'd been raining on and off all week when all we wanted was for it to clear up by the homecoming game. College scouts.

Everything was on the line.

And none of it seemed to matter if Jane wasn't going to be around to see it unfold.

The creek runoff was overflowing into the edges of the field and parking lot. A fish flopped in the shallow street flooding. I reached down and tossed it back into the stream by the fence and then sloshed through the parking lot to my truck.

I rested my head against the window. I was frickin' wiped.

Worrying was more of a workout than football. It made me feel like an old, old man. And I suddenly missed being a little kid. Tree forts. Treasure maps. Pretending to be a tiger or frog. Catching lightning bugs. Racing our little boats until they were sucked under the interstate and out the other side—the other side we never dared cross to see. Funny to think there was a time when the only danger was a busy road.

I called out a couple of goodbyes to my friends and peeled out, loud, through the puddles to make them spray up around me.

It hadn't rained this hard since right after I found Jane in the corn.

Wait.

Wait.

The fish on the practice field just now.

There'd been a dead fish in the drainpipe where Jane hid.

The fish would only get in there if the creek crested, which it could have during that early summer storm.

All the times Jane and I had crisscrossed the ditch and the drain looking for her bag, I never thought to cross to the other side of the interstate and look there.

What if Jane *had* lost the bag in the storm drain and it got swept under and out like our paper boats did back in the day?

I pulled off right before the woods near the farm and got out by the factories. This was a total shot in the dark. I was being stupid. Wasting more time. But still . . . I had to see.

I started jogging and then broke into an all-out run, trying to still the adrenaline of my crazy theory and prepare myself for the same letdown of every trip to the storm drain.

I slid down the embankment and peeked in.

Muddy water coursed through the normally dry concrete. I ducked in and waded through to where it streamed out, followed the flow down, down, to where the road passed overhead. The water was almost waist-deep, but I kept going, through the darkness underneath the interstate, toward the light of the grate on the other side. It butted up against the drainage ditch from one of the factories—Savannah's dad's place, Maddison Electric.

I felt along the grate, under the water. Sticks and leaves. More nasty dead fish. Rusty toy truck. Cooler. Beer cans. Fast-food wrappers.

And . . . a soggy, sludge-coated backpack.

My heart pounded. My hands shook.

I unzipped the top of the bag to find it stuffed with girl's clothes. I pulled a couple of balled-up shirts off the top.

"No way," I breathed.

Tucked in each folded piece of clothing were stacks of hundred-dollar bills. I was legit dizzy, like I could pass out, as I counted one of the packets. Twenty hundred-dollar bills with a rubber band around them. Two thousand dollars. Right there. And there were how many of these packets? Damn. There had to be more than two hundred thousand dollars.

Did Jane realize *how* much was in the bag?

I took one of the bricks of money and riffled my thumb along the soggy edges. What could someone do with this much cash? Even if I shoved just one stack of twenties in my pocket, I could buy the shoes I needed for the homecoming game. And pay the water bill before they cut it off.

This could change everything.

But it wasn't mine.

The bag felt heavier and heavier in my hands.

Forget two weeks.

Jane could leave right now. The second she had this money, she was gone.

JANE

Maybe I could leave even sooner. This lunch shift plus one more might actually do it for the bus ticket, if I could wrangle enough tips.

"Well, hey there," a vaguely familiar voice called out. "Ding, ding. Do I gotta ring a bell for service or what?"

I realized I'd been wiping the same spot on the counter over and over, so deep in thought.

"Sorry, zoned out." I grabbed a menu and pushed it over to the customer, looked up, and froze. "Oh. Hi."

It was Sophia's boyfriend, Diego. He slid onto one of the sea-green vinyl stools, its metal legs screeching as he dragged it across the checkered tiles.

"Heard you were working here. Like it?"

"Sure," I said. "How about you? Everything good in the, uh . . . where do you work again? Something with cars?"

"Everything at the shop is fantastic. Had some guys stop by this morning though, made me think of you . . . What's the pie of the day?"

My back stiffened. "What?"

"Pie of the day? I hope it's pecan. I sure do like pecan pie."

"It's apple. What guys?" I nervously looked around. Nancy was busy in the back. The only other people here were Mr. and Mrs. Hillcrest in the corner booth. They weren't listening, peering over their matching bifocals at the newspaper they shared, waiting for their meatloaf special.

"I guess I'll have a slice of the apple then," Diego said. "And a coffee—extra cream, extra sugar. I got a sweet tooth."

I cut him a slice of pie and placed the plate in front of him with a louder clatter than I intended.

"Will you tell me what you're talking about?" I leaned in close.

"Why don't *you* tell me what I'm talking about?" Diego said and took a big bite of pie. "Mmm. Can I get some whipped cream?"

Frustrated, I accidentally sprayed out a huge blob.

He laughed and scooped up a fingerful and licked it off. "Why you stressin', girl? I'm looking out for you. Sophia asked me to help. I'm helping."

I turned and grabbed the coffeepot, trying to act as normal as I could. But I couldn't hide the sharp edge in my voice. "Tell me what you're getting at, Diego. *Please.*"

He leaned both elbows on the counter and gestured for me to come in close.

"Some guys have been asking if there are any new girls around . . . with big blue eyes . . . Know of any?"

The steaming coffee I was pouring him overflowed and splashed out onto my arm. I jumped back with a wince.

"Nope," I said, looking him straight in the eye. "Do you?"

"Sure don't," Diego said. "I told you: any friend of Sophia's . . ."

He slid an envelope across the counter to me, hidden under a couple of dollars for the pie.

"I'm on your side, *Jane*," he said, pointing at my lopsided name tag. "And if I were you, I would take this and run."

CADE

I shoved the money under the driver's seat of my truck. My hands gripped the wheel white-knuckled.

Maybe the police would figure out who was responsible for the bridge murders. Maybe they'd arrest someone. Maybe all this cartel stuff would die down. And then Jane could stay and finish out the school year, and we could ditch Tanner together. Start over.

I would tell Jane after the game. Say I had a surprise. Take her out to dinner somewhere or something. A nice place. The new one, by the river.

I drove like frickin' NASCAR to the diner, lost in my thoughts, not noticing the sports car with cheesy flames painted on it until I pulled right up behind it to park. I glanced in the big front window of the diner and recognized Diego in his sunglasses.

He was talking to Jane. I leaned over my steering wheel to get a better look.

He handed her something. She tucked it into her waistband under her shirt. Diego sauntered out, hopped in his car, and drove off. Jane hung up her apron and cashed out.

"Hey," she said casually as she climbed in with me.

"Hey," I said. I waited for her to say something about Diego. "How was work?"

"Fine."

"Anything interesting?"

"At Fancy Nancy's? Oh, you know it," Jane said.

My jaw clenched. She wasn't going to tell me?

I found myself pushing the bag deeper beneath the seat with my heel as we drove.

At the next stoplight, my phone buzzed with a text from Savannah: *Can't wait to see you all tonight! Please make Jojo come*, it read.

"Who's that?" Jane asked.

"Savannah. You sticking around to go to her party?"

"Um, I mean, yes, right?" Jane said. "Everything status quo . . ."

"Till it's not."

"I wouldn't leave without telling you." Jane frowned.

"You sure about that?" I asked. Because that's exactly what it looked like she was going to do.

"Trying to get rid of me?" she hesitantly joked. "You know I don't have enough money yet. What's going on? Why are you being weird?"

I took a deep breath in. I was overreacting. I should give her the benefit of the doubt. Jane only kept secrets when she thought it would keep us safe. Still, the sight of her with Diego made my stomach drop to my ripped-up shoes. It killed me that she would trust someone like him over me.

"Nothing. Been a long day."

"As long as that's it," she said, trying to read my face. "I was, uh, going to get ready over at the Moraleses'. Jojo is letting me borrow a dress."

"I'll drop you. I didn't shower after practice," I said. "I need to go home."

"Yeah, you're *really* soaked and muddy," Jane said. She reached over and pulled a twig off my shorts. "What did you do? Run into a tree?"

"Putting in the work. Sunday's everything." I pulled up in front of Mattey and Jojo's. "Anyway, see you in a bit."

"See you in a bit," Jane repeated.

As Jane walked away she glanced back, and it was like we both had X-ray vision. I could see through to the envelope under her shirt, and she could see right into my head and know I found the one thing she needed the most and hadn't said a word.

When I got home I hid the bag of money under the loose floorboard under my bed.

Jane would say something to me about Diego and whatever it was he had given her. She had to. Probably tonight, in the barn, after the party. And then I would tell her about the money, and we could figure out what to do next. I paced the slanted, creaky floor of my room. The walls felt like they were closing in. We'd never lied to each other before.

JANE

We shouldn't be punished for dreaming. But until something is real, it's just a cruel game of make-believe. My time in Tanner, Texas, was pretend. Here I was, back in Jojo's room, trying to blend in and stay hidden, but everywhere I turned, it seemed the searchlight was getting closer to illuminating everything.

Jojo was on a tirade as she pinned her dress to fit me, still so angry with Savannah that she was boycotting her birthday.

When Cade walked in, all cleaned up, I tried to catch his eye, but he didn't look my way. Something was going on with him. I felt a knot form in my chest. I should have told him right away about what Diego had given me. But I didn't want him to know that I had accepted more help from a . . . *halcón* or whatever it was Mr. Morales had called Diego. I could still feel the bite of Cade's sharp words from when we first met: *Y'all can rot with the cartel together.*

And now I wasn't sure how to even back into it. It was like when you hesitate crossing a busy street. You probably could have made it, but the second-guessing cost you the chance, and then the traffic is coming too fast. The moment felt gone. If I tried to say something now I was going to get run over by the big speeding Mack truck that carried all my secrets.

Cade interrupted Jojo's rant. "Gunner says his mom found who did the graffiti. School surveillance camera caught some guys getting the spray paint out of their cars. And she checked with Joe's Hardware, and sure enough, they sold paint to some kids from our school the day before."

"Oh my God, *who*?" Jojo asked, eyes wide.

"Couple of freshmen who think they're tough. Won't be seeing them for a while, that's for sure."

"Good. I hope they're kicked out."

"Me too," I said, "but maybe we can try to put this behind us now. You and Savannah have been friends since diaper days. And she did apologize."

"She said she was sorry she hurt my feelings," Jojo argued. "She didn't apologize for what she *actually* said."

"Why don't you explain it to her then?" Cade asked.

"I shouldn't have to! Why do you always defend her, anyway?" Jojo demanded.

"I'm just sayin', all it would take is a conversation and you two would be back to normal."

"So you're going to her party."

"Look, I get why you're mad. I told her it was messed up too," Cade said. "But I think if you're still upset you should call her and say how you feel. Otherwise all this ranting is just going to make you crazy."

He helped himself to a soda from the Moraleses' fridge.

"Jane?" Jojo turned to me as her next possible ally.

"Um?" I looked to Cade to get me out of Jojo's line of fire. He passed me a plate of snacks without making eye contact.

"Yes, Jane is going. Everyone's going. You're the only one," he said.

"Ugh," Jojo groaned. "Fine. Jane, we have work to do."

"What do you mean?" I asked through a mouthful of chips and Mrs. Morales's pico de gallo.

Jojo let out a dramatic sigh. "If you're going to compromise your integrity by going to Savannah's stupid birthday party, you think I'm going to let Jane go there looking anything but perfect? *One* of you needs to look decent." Jojo unleashed a huge cloud of hairspray right in my face like a weapon.

"What's wrong with how I look?" Cade protested, coughing and backing up.

"You're wearing *jeans*!" Jojo was apparently appalled.

"They're dark jeans. They're my *fancy* pants." He did a little two-step to bug her.

The second Cade joked around, I felt myself relax a little bit. I didn't want to be walking on eggshells with him. I wanted to soak this in, all of it, the laughter, the normalcy. I wanted to believe in this story for a few more days.

"I think he looks nice," I said.

"Sure, defend your cousin." Jojo brandished the curling iron. "Do you really want to mess with me right now? I mean, your hair is in my hands. I could make you look like a disaster."

"Okay, okay. Do your thing," I surrendered.

"Oh, and then there's this situation," Jojo pointed to Mattey as he strutted into the room. "He thinks it counts as a silent protest against what Savannah said."

Mateo was wearing a suit embroidered with intricate gold designs, with a matching giant bow tie and wide-brimmed hat. He gave us a cheesy double thumbs-up.

"I'm embracing my heritage."

"More like playing to the stereotype." Jojo snorted.

"That's the whole point. La cucaracha, la cucaracha . . ." he sang right next to Jojo's face.

"Like Savannah will even get it. Please. She'll just think you came as her own personal mariachi singer," Jojo said. But Mattey's attention was suddenly fixed on me.

"Wow, Jane, you look so pretty," Mattey said earnestly.

"Told ya." Jojo took a little bow.

"You are red-carpet ready, girl. Now go be hotter than Savannah for me, okay?" Jojo said, motioning for me to go look in the mirror.

My face was framed in soft waves, and the makeup Jojo put on my eyes made me look like an old-time movie star, one of those actresses you see in flickery black and white, so beautiful they don't seem real.

CADE

A long line of cars went from the front gates of Savannah's house down the side of the street. How many people were invited to this thing?

"The whole school, of course. And then a bunch of my dad's friends. We invited three hundred," Savannah announced when I asked on the way in. "And then I *un*invited two guests. Did you hear Sheriff Healey solved the graffiti?"

"Yeah. Gunner said."

Savannah grabbed my hand. "Does Jojo know?"

"Yeah, she does."

Savannah stood up on her tiptoes, looking for her.

"She's sitting this one out," I said, then quickly changed the subject. "So, three hundred people. I didn't even know there were that many people in Tanner," I joked.

"Actually, no," Savannah said. "Not that many important people, anyway. They're all, like, state people. Senators and stuff. A lot of businessmen my dad says *had* to come. I think he thinks it's his birthday."

She looked tired. But only for a second.

"Jane! You're, like, stunning. Doesn't she look drop-dead? Cade? Mattey?"

I had been trying *not* to look at Jane. The way her dress swung, how her hair fell, her smooth, suntanned skin—everything about the way she looked tonight contradicted my doubts and made me want to grab that money, grab her hand, and never look back. Just me and her and whatever came next. But . . . Diego. Raff. Mexico. Her past was catching up to her . . . to us. The future seemed impossible.

"She looks good," Mattey agreed. "Like *my* outfit?"

"You look very . . . festive," Savannah answered. "You remind me of the guys who worked at the resort where we stayed in Cabo last year."

Jojo was right: clueless. Mattey laughed and rolled his eyes behind her back.

"But seriously, Jane! Not fair! No one's allowed to be prettier than the birthday girl." Savannah tried to pretend she was kidding.

She smoothed the skirt of her short pink dress and looked back and forth between Jane and me for a split second before clapping her hands together and leading us around. A murmur, the proper level of loud, filled the mansion as guests made their small talk. Glasses and silverware were all clink-clink fancy, and servers wearing black and white handed us things to eat on toothpicks with napkins in way-too-small bites.

Mrs. Maddison kissed us on both cheeks and cupped our hands in her cool dry ones.

"It's a pleasure. Welcome," she said over and over to each guest.

"Psst." Savannah leaned in as soon as her mother was out of range. "I paid off a couple of the servers to sneak us champagne."

She grabbed Jane's arm and motioned for Mattey and me to follow her.

"Have some." Savannah shoved a glass into my hand. "Here's to us!"

I hesitated.

"All of us," she added, making sure Mattey and Jane had some too.

"Come on, *Cade*, cheers!" Savannah pouted.

We tapped our glasses together. I touched the sour bubbles to my mouth and tried to make myself take a sip. The second Savannah looked away to point us in the direction of the door, Jane quickly switched glasses with me so it looked like I drank mine. *Thank you*, I mouthed. She gave me a knowing look and shrugged one shoulder. I felt my stomach flip. That smile. *Tell me what's going on. What did Diego give you?* I wanted to say, but I held it in.

Savannah was about to steer us all outside when I heard someone call my name.

Gunner's mom. She looked out of place in a dress instead of her sheriff's uniform and hat, and she'd put some lipstick on for the party.

"Hey, Cade, how are you doing?"

"Look at you all fancy, Mrs. H," I teased.

"This is as good as it gets, kid," she answered. "Everything okay at the farm? Tommy Mack clean everything up good?"

"Yes, ma'am."

"And your father?"

"He's all right."

"You know you can come to me if anything's ever . . . a problem."

"Sure, Mrs. Healey. I know that. Thanks."

There was an awkward pause.

Gunner looked dumbstruck beside her, staring at Jane.

"Hi, Jane. You look really beautiful."

"Thanks." Jane shot him a shy smile.

"Sheriff, nice to see you." Savannah's dad swooped in to shake her hand. "Wasn't sure I could get you to take a night off."

"Only once in a blue moon, Garrett. How's business?"

"Electric," he said, chuckling at his own joke. Savannah made a face.

"Any progress looking into the bridge murders?" he asked the sheriff.

"Come on now, that's not party talk," Mrs. Healey said. She glanced over at us. "Why don't you kids go have fun?"

"Yeah, let's go dance!" Savannah said, tugging at my hand. "The band is out back."

"Hang on a sec, I wanna know," I said, glancing over at Jane and motioning for her to come closer too. "Did you figure out who did it?"

"We've got Homeland Security helping," Gunner's mom reassured us. "It's a temporary flare-up while the cartels have their little power struggle. But don't worry, we'll snuff 'em both out. Grande and this new one . . . the one they're calling Lobenzo . . . the Wolf Cub."

As soon as she said their names, a glass came crashing to the floor beside me. Jane stood, stricken, champagne spilled at her feet, her hand outstretched and empty.

THE WOLF CUB

Guisado. **The stew.**

People get dumped into giant kettles and boiled alive. Kerosene. Gasoline. Whatever's available. We had each of the four men in Tanner killed in a different way, but when asked my all-time favorite method, that is what I say.

"When people don't understand things, they like to blame the devil and God. I don't blame anyone for anything, and certainly not some higher power. I think when you die, you simply stop and slip into a silent nothing, as vast as the beginning of the universe. When I slit a throat I think about that, how everything started."

I crossed my legs on the table and admired my new sneakers as I addressed Alamo, Asesino, and Pozolero. I motioned for Alamo to light my cigar with his. The room was already full of smoke, making it look like their faces were swirling, modern art paintings.

"I want a Picasso."

Someday I would be someone who could make that happen.

"Grande thinks he can keep his tunnel a secret, look what happens," I extolled. Once we had Grande's super tunnel, the entire Gulf Cartel would answer to me. We had been so close to getting the location from a gang loyal to him. But when Grande heard they were considering our ultimatum—come be a wolf, or be slaughtered like a lamb—he slaughtered them first. I admired Grande, I did. He was unflinching. Cutting off the arm to save the body.

But the whispers reached me. They always reached me.

There was one other person who might know the tunnel's location. One of the gang had a girlfriend who escaped the massacre. I sent my favorite bounty hunter after her months ago.

"Any news from Ivan?"

"Not yet."

"Track him down. We need to find that girl."

JANE

Grande. Lobenzo.

The sheriff took a surprised step back as my glass shattered.

My brain felt like it was moving backward. Counterclockwise. Candle snuffed, relit.

When Lobenzo wants something, you give it to him, I remember Raff telling me. *Some people aren't really even people anymore. He's possessed by demons or something. The Wolf Cub.*

Sorry, I said. Or thought I said. No sound came out. I tried again.

"Sorry. The glass slipped."

"Oh!" Savannah said. "It happens! Don't worry, we'll get you more . . . uh, *soda*."

She waved over some of the servers to clean up my mess.

"Y'all wanna go out and find that band?" Cade tried to get the attention off me.

"Finally!" Savannah said and then whispered to us behind her hand: "And more champagne. Let's find some more of that too!"

She grabbed Cade's hand and pulled him along behind her, grabbing new flutes of champagne for us off a tray. I followed like I was in slow motion.

"What's wrong?" Mattey whispered.

"Don't worry about it."

"Come on. I'm in this too, you know," Mattey said. "You can tell me what's going on."

"I . . . I don't know." I shook his hand off my arm. It was bad enough Cade knew so much. No way was I getting Mattey more involved. It wasn't safe.

Mattey let out a frustrated sigh and sped up ahead of me as we walked outside. As soon as we reached the back patio, the music hit us, some happy country band that people had to shout over to be heard.

"Want to go dance?" Gunner asked. I could see the twins and Farty dancing with some of the girls from school on the other side of the lawn.

I somehow made myself answer him. "Maybe after I finish my drink. Don't want to spill again."

Cade leaned in so close I could feel his breath on my neck, mouth near my ear.

"Is it them?" He hooked his fingers protectively through the back strap of my dress, standing close enough that no one could see. "The cartels the sheriff named? Are those the ones after you?"

A sudden boom tore through the sky, practically stopping my heart right there.

The crowd made *oohs* and *aahs* of surprise as fireworks lit up the night. The band started playing "Happy Birthday."

"Oh, it's for *me*." Savannah jumped up and down. "This is the best day of my life!"

She turned around and flung her arms around Cade's neck, pulling his face down to meet hers, and on tiptoe, one leg back for balance, gave him a long Hollywood kiss. Cade's fingers dropped from my back. His eyes stayed open, confused. They locked with mine in what felt like some strange apology. But he didn't break away.

My face tingled, and everything inside me shrank. I had to *do* something. I swallowed the lump in my throat, and in what felt like a total blur, spun around to Gunner, took his smooth face in my hands, and kissed him hard. So I didn't fall apart.

CADE

My eyes were so glued to Jane's that for a second I felt like it was her kissing me, not Savannah. The fireworks were going off in the sky, but it might as well have been my brain flashing all bright and dark and bright again. My whole body heated up, and I wanted to pull Savannah, or Jane—no, Savannah—closer against me. She smelled like vanilla, and her mouth melted into mine like frosting.

Then Jane kissed Gunner. It hit me like a tackle midair.

Gunner pulled her onto the lawn to dance. I watched them together over Savannah's soft, blond hair. Gunner kept stepping awkwardly closer to Jane as they moved with the music, hands placed on her waist and back like he was following instructions—ten and two, driving a car for the first time.

We danced like that for a while: Jane and Gunner, Savannah and me. I tracked their movements across the lawn. But Savannah pulled me away to get closer to the band, and I lost sight of them as the night wound on. I scanned the crowd. Gunner was with Mattey, but I didn't see Jane anywhere. I gently unhooked Savannah's hands from behind my neck and motioned them over to us.

"Where's Jane?"

Gunner shrugged. "She said she was going to find y'all."

"When did you last see her?" I asked.

Mattey looked worried. "Not for an hour, at least."

"What's wrong?" Savannah asked.

I tried to make it sound like no big deal. "Sometimes Jane just gets overwhelmed by stuff."

"Stuff like my party? Was she not having fun?" Savannah looked devastated.

"No. This is an amazing party. She's probably at the truck just taking a break. I'll go check. Come on, Mattey."

"You'll be back, right?" Savannah asked.

"Sure. If not, though, I'll see you at the game."

"So . . . tomorrow," Savannah said, like she knew we were probably leaving for the night.

"Yeah . . . thanks for having us." I took a minute to give her a hug and a kiss on the cheek. "Happy birthday, Savannah."

"Thanks, Cade."

Savannah looked like a beauty pageant contestant who didn't get the tiara but still had to smile and wave as Mattey and I hurried away to the truck.

No sign of Jane.

"Uh-oh," Mattey said.

"Will you go tell Savannah we found her but she doesn't feel good, so I'm taking her home?"

"But . . . we didn't."

"Yeah, but I don't want anyone to worry," I said. "I have a pretty good idea where Jane went."

"Where?"

"Cartel stuff has her freaked out. I think she might be trying to take off. I'm gonna go check the bus station. Can you hitch a ride home with Gunner?"

"I want to come."

"Please, Mattey, I need you to handle this. Can you make them think everything's normal?"

"Fine," he said. "Text me you found her though, okay?"

"Of course."

Mattey jogged back up the hill and steep steps to Savannah's mansion, and I took off for the bus station. The factories churned their smoke in the distance like fat businessmen puffing cigars. I passed the old post office. The burnt scaffolding looked like I could blow it over. The charred walls still smelled of gasoline, just another mile marker of violence telling Jane to go.

When I got to the bus station, the lobby doors were unlocked, but the ticket counter was hooded shut for the night. Sticking out against the tile and plastic chairs was a girl in a bright red dress.

Jane sat alone, the bull's-eye of an easy target.

I looked up at the departure board.

"The next bus isn't for six hours." My voice cut through the empty room. She didn't turn around. "Come on. Let's get out of here."

Jane shook her head no.

I sighed and walked over to her, sliding into the stiff plastic chair beside her.

Jane stared straight ahead. "Sheriff Healey said Grande and Lobenzo. You asked if those are the ones. The answer is yes."

I pressed my lips together. "So . . . worst-case scenario."

"Right."

"Damn it." It wasn't fair.

"I *can't* stay here any longer," Jane said.

"What are you gonna do, wait all night and then take off in a little dress and heels with no plan?"

"I have a plan."

"You gonna share it with me? Clearly not . . ."

"Please don't be mad at me."

But I was. "This is messed up, Jane. I've helped you every step of the way since I found you."

I slumped in the chair and raked my hands through my hair.

My mom never told me she was leaving either.

I just woke up one morning to a note with the same doodle of a daisy she would put on my lunch bags, like she hadn't just blown up our lives. *I need something different. I have for a long time. Please try to understand. Take care of your father. Love you always.* And the fucking flower.

"You'd rather have *Diego* help you than me?" I said.

"What?" Jane acted confused.

"You heard me."

"I don't understand."

"Yes you do."

Jane's face twisted as she realized. "Oh. You saw."

"Yeah. I *saw*. Why did you lie?"

"I didn't. I just didn't mention it."

"Same thing." I stood up.

Same thing. Same thing as me not telling her about the money. I hated this. We had to undo what was happening, get back on the same side.

"What if I hadn't thought to come here or if there had been a midnight bus?" I asked her. "You'd be gone. Without ever knowing if maybe there's a different path out of this mess."

"Different path like what?" Jane scoffed.

"Maybe you should come home and we can talk about it. . . . Come on, Jane, please. We can get you on a bus tomorrow," I said. "Right now, you're a sitting duck. We both are."

Jane didn't move.

"Do you *wanna* get found?"

Jane looked around. She knew I was right. "Fine. Let's go."

When we got in the truck, she reached out and took my hand, placing an envelope in it.

"*That's* what Diego gave me," Jane said.

I opened it. Inside was a passport. It had a picture of a girl who looked just enough like her that it could work. Lilly Ford. Age twenty-one. From Wisconsin. She'd been to Ireland and Costa Rica, according to the stamps on the pages.

"He said to get out of town; people are looking for a girl with blue eyes. He was trying to help."

I handed back the passport. I didn't feel better.

"Why wouldn't you just tell me?"

"The less you know, the better."

"I think we're past that point now, don't you?"

"You still have no idea." She shook her head at me like I was too dumb to understand.

"I kinda think I do," I snapped.

"Do you? Do you really? The cartels destroy *everyone* who gets in their way." Jane's voice shook. "Grande left Raff and his friends in nice poolside chairs at our condo complex with warnings written on pieces of paper . . . pinned to their chests . . . with ice picks. *That's* what I came home to. That's what I was trying to run from. I had no idea Lobenzo, the Wolf Cub, was after me too until Ivan caught me. Ivan said he would slice me into little pieces unless I told them where Grande's tunnel is. They are *both* after me." Jane's eyes filled up. "And I don't need them to come after Mattey and Jojo . . . and *you*."

The weight of the violence she described closed in.

"But what if they come after *you* once you leave here?" I asked.

She didn't have an answer. There were no answers. We drove in silence.

After a few minutes, Jane asked, "Cade, what did you *think* was going on with Diego?"

"I didn't know."

"You don't trust me," she said. "At all."

"Yes I do," I said. But it was a lie. If I trusted her I would have already told her about finding the money, the biggest lie of all.

Seeing her whispering with Diego had knocked me sideways. I hated that it had made me question Jane. But it did. It made me wonder if at the core she was someone who would take her cartel money and wrap herself back up in their mess.

We had reached the fork in the road.

"I want to be alone tonight," she said.

"That's not a good idea."

"I'm serious. Don't come. I need to think about what to do on my own."

"I'm coming."

"I said no."

Jane stalked away down the path to the barn, completely out of place in her dress and high heels walking through the corn. She had to know I wasn't going to listen, that the second I pulled up to my house to check in with my father, I would hurry back out there. I pulled in front of my house and hopped out of my truck, debating whether I should get the money.

Jane was mad at me. Or hurt. Same difference.

If I told her about the money now, what would she do? Say, *Thanks, bye*.

I would never see her again.

I will tell her. Just not yet, I thought as I trudged up the walkway. I heard the screen door slam and looked up.

"You're late." My dad lurched down the porch steps.

"Am I? Sorry. It was Savannah's birthday. I told you."

"I don't care if it's the pope's birthday. You got a curfew."

Lord, he'd been drinking. Like, all day, maybe all the way since last night drinking. He was swaying and squinting and twitching his neck around. I backed up toward the truck.

"Where do you think you're going?" he demanded.

"Dad, you're being crazy."

"Get in the house, Cade."

"I'm not gonna stay here when you're acting like this."

"What, you're like your mother now? Just do what you want when you want and don't pay anyone else no mind. Well, who do you think puts food in your mouth? Who breaks their back to keep a roof over your head?"

He approached me in two quick strides. We were face to face. Alcohol on his breath.

"I won't let you turn into her."

When I tried to push past, he shoved me back. Hard. My foot tripped over a rock, and I went flying toward the trailer hitch of the truck. There was white. And then black.

JANE

I paced the barn.

Even if I left on a bus tomorrow, would everyone I cared about actually be safe, or the next targets?

The cartels are the food chain. They are rats that whisper disease across your face while you're sleeping, always in the walls, even if you think you are alone, the bites you wake up to, red rings on your skin. They are the strange wail of a street cat in heat, a wanting that sounds like pain. Nighttime outside Montera. The cross on the pharmacy.

I waited for Cade's knock on the barn door. I thought for sure he wouldn't listen when I told him not to come. I didn't really mean it. Obviously.

Hunter came. He licked my face and then collapsed into his little curl and was asleep in seconds. I carefully took off Jojo's beautiful red dress and put on Cade's old shorts and T-shirt and crawled onto the sleeping bag to wait. The minutes collected. No Cade.

I guessed I would have to say goodbye tomorrow before his big football game. Playoffs. Savannah was supposed to be picking us up at Jojo and Mattey's.

Savannah. Why did she get her life and I get mine? I tried in my mind to jab at some ugly spot exposed and obvious but could find no blemishes. Her lips were like a rose—there, I said it. It took an infinity to make them. Eyes, nose, skin, strawberries. The left ventricle of hope, somewhere. The phoenix falls to its ashes. Again. The world will collapse to Tanner, Texas. She wins everything. Roses, warmth, a scream.

I'm sorry for kissing her, Cade whispered. Or so I thought. Then I realized I had drifted off to sleep and dreamed it. I should have known it was a dream, because Cade's footprints were red. My dreams since Raff died were always filled with blood. Even if I dreamed of something simple, something nice, I found it streaked on a table, or window, or pooling on the ground. When I caught my own reflection I realized blood was smeared across my face like war paint. It was a parade of violence in my head every night. Gunfire drumbeats. Gritty trombone heartbeats. Bone confetti.

When I woke up, it was morning and I was still completely alone, thinking and rethinking where Lobenzo's men might be, hungry wolves who would eat each other's ragged bodies to survive. The cartel, the food chain, survival of the fittest. The heads of cartels are male lions lounging under a tree, hiding from the orange sun, waiting for the pride to bring them the kill, eating the hunt without having to move.

And at the top, the ones like Grande and the Wolf Cub think they are gods. Maybe they are—deciding who lives and who dies, deciding what happens to me.

I went through the motions: Showering from the whiskey barrel. Picking an outfit from the few items of clothing hung on nails on the old stall walls. Checking my reflection in the warped mirror the boys got me from somewhere.

I couldn't show up at Cade's and risk running into his dad. Instead I headed down the dusty shortcut over to Mattey and Jojo's . . . to see them one last time.

And then? Canada. Use my brand-new passport to get to Montreal, maybe, where I could begin to forget them . . . Cade and Tanner, Texas.

Snow outside could remind me to be ice inside.

CADE

Five minutes. Damn it. That's all I needed. Five more minutes and I would have been out of there and back to the barn and Jane with no one seeing, none the wiser. Instead what happened? She and Jojo walked in while I was still sitting at the dining table with Mattey stitching up my head and blotting the blood with a paper towel.

"Oh my God, Cade, what happened?" Jojo exclaimed.

I stared straight ahead. Does it get any more mortifying than this? I was pathetic. I let out a long exhale through a tiny opening in my lips to try and calm down. It came out in a weird hiss. Seriously, who gets beat up by their old man over and over again and takes it?

"I've got this," Mattey said without breaking his concentration.

"What about the game tonight?" Jojo insisted.

What about it? I would be on that field no matter what. Everyone would cheer and depend on me. And I'd put my arms in the air like I was in control, a hero, like I was the king of everything. Like I was proud of who I was. What a joke. I was a joke.

"He's shouldn't play," Mattey answered Jojo. "He's lucky not to be hurt worse."

"Lucky?" Jojo stewed. "That's not how I'd describe it. Cade, what can I do? You want food or soda or something?"

"Something to drink maybe would be good. And I'm definitely playing. Don't listen to Mattey."

"You could have a concussion. You get hit again on the field, you're in big trouble," Mattey warned.

"You said *mild* concussion."

"You want to make it major, go play tonight." Mattey sounded like his dad.

"It's not an option. I have to play. College scouts . . ."

"Scouts won't want a brain-dead vegetable."

"Oh, come on. I got a whack to the head."

Jojo scowled. "Cade, I *hate* him. I hate your dad. I want to tell some-body. It's getting worse."

Jane interjected. "What do you think will happen if police or the state get involved? He'd get put into foster care."

"I don't wanna go to the police on my own dad," I shut the discussion down. And it was true. I didn't.

"What happened this time, Soldado?"

Oh no. Dr. Morales was home. Dr. Morales always said our names the Spanish way. But there was no name equivalent for Cade, so instead he called me Soldado. Old soldier.

"Hood of the truck came down on me while I was working on the engine."

"For all your moves on the field, you're one clumsy kid off it." Dr. Morales stepped in to take over the stitches from Mattey. I quickly turned my arm over so he couldn't see the finger marks on the inside of my wrist.

Jojo let a burst of air out her nose like an agitated horse and spun around dramatically to go into the kitchen. Jane sat down at the table with me, her eyes going from my messed-up face, to the cut, to Dr. Morales's hands at work.

"Let's numb you up. You knocked yourself good this time," he said.

It felt weird with half my head numbed. It went up the side of my face, even into my nose. No feeling—in my skin, in my mind. My brain had a dull, flat buzz. Turning off emotion. I tried to grin, like everything was normal.

"Am I even smiling?" I turned to Jane.

"Sort of."

"Do I look like shit?"

"Sort of," Mattey answered for her.

That made me laugh a little, at least.

"Jauna, you make sure Soldado here rests, okay?"

Jane nodded as Jojo came blowing around the corner with root beer. I reached for it without thinking, and Dr. Morales grabbed my wrist and turned it. He looked from the bruises to the cut on my head.

"Cade." He used my real name. His eyes were serious. "You know you can always be honest with me, right?"

"Sure."

"Everything okay at the farm? Your father . . . isn't drinking too much, is he?"

"He's fine."

"Jane?"

"Yes, sir?"

"Our doors are always open."

Dr. Morales cleaned off my skin around the stitches with a sting of alcohol and started reciting a verse.

"Break up your fallow ground, for it is time to seek the Lord, till he come and rain righteousness upon you."

Jane's eyes connected with mine before flickering back to Dr. Morales.

"What does that mean?" she asked.

"It means ground that's been tilled and farmed before but that now lies waste," Dr. Morales explained. "It need to be broken up and mellowed before it is ready to receive grain."

"It means you have to be open to goodness," Mattey offered.

Break up your fallow ground.

It's not that simple, I wanted to tell him.

My farm will never be anything but dry and dead. Jane will always want to run. I will always be sitting here, keeping other people's ugly secrets, because deep down, no matter what, I love them. My father. Jane . . .

I lowered my gaze from hers, face flashing hot.

I mumbled thank you to Dr. Morales and bolted outside. Jane caught up to me. I gave her a little nod but didn't say anything. We headed back down the path toward the barn, sipping the cold bottles in silence for a while, until Jane asked me a question.

"You really would never turn in your dad?"

I sighed.

"It's child abuse," she persisted.

"I'm not a child," I mumbled

"You're *his* child. He's abusing you."

"Look, I'm really not in the mood for some sort of heart-to-heart here. We've talked about this. We all know he's not winning father of the year. But it's the booze. It's not who he really is."

"When does a person become what they *do* though? When do their actions take over what you think you know about them? How can you trust that someone doesn't mean to hurt you?"

"Maybe you can answer those questions better than me," I shot back. She looked down at the ground. I tried to soften it. "Sorry. I don't want to talk about it."

"So, this is why you never came last night?" she asked quietly.

"Yeah. Got knocked out. It was a bad one. Did you really think I wouldn't show? Come on, now."

"I don't know. You were pretty mad about the passport."

Jane's hair was messy. The back was sticking up a little bit. Her big blue eyes looked tired. She must have been up all night deciding what to do.

"Are you really leaving today?" I asked.

"It's too dangerous to stay." Jane bit her bottom lip lightly as she thought about her answer. "You need to go back to your lives, like nothing ever happened."

It's not nothing, I wanted to say. *It's everything. You're the only thing that is going to get me through senior year. Let's keep hiding you. Don't leave Tanner until I can leave Tanner. Stay, stay, stay.*

Instead I said, "You're part of the group now. Me, Jojo, Mattey, Gunner, Savannah."

"Yeah . . . Savannah," Jane said.

"Look, about her party—" I started.

"What about it?"

I stopped walking and leaned up against a fence post. "Come on, Jane."

"What?" She leaned next to me and crossed her arms.

"Don't act like it wasn't awkward."

Jane turned to face the other way, staring out at the endless flat fields. She climbed up onto the bottom rung of the fence. We stood shoulder to shoulder, but looking in opposite directions. Old barbed wire sat rolled in the grass—metal tumbleweeds.

"You should be with someone like Savannah. She's like sunshine," Jane said softly. "I want to feel like sunshine."

I found myself reaching out and pulling her in front of me, so our legs and hips were up against each other, her feet staggered with mine. She arched her back away from me and placed her hands against my chest, keeping distance between us.

"I'm scared that even if I leave, someone will come looking for *me* here and find *you*. I'm so terrified of what they could do."

"Well then, that defeats the purpose of running off, doesn't it?" I wrapped my hands around her wrists and pulled them up against my shoulders, so her elbows fell against my chest and she was that much closer.

A flash of lightning zipped across the sky behind her. Jane jerked around to see what was going on and finally gave into the lean, letting her body fit against mine. I rested my chin on top of her head. The pounding in my skull where I got slammed into the truck got that much quieter. My father's sweaty face faded. When I wrapped my arms around Jane, it felt like how coming home is supposed to. And as we watched the dry lightning come down in skeleton fingers, then break into smaller and smaller veins dying into the horizon, I knew I would do anything to protect that home.

"Stay until after the game," I said. "It's important. I promise."

THE WOLF CUB

"Party's over."

I didn't shout it. I simply turned off the music. Waited. So then when I banged my fist on the pool table, it made everybody jump. "Take off your shoes . . . and pants. Watches, all of it."

"Lobenzo, man, what are you trying to prove?" Alamo asked. My compadres looked at me, confused.

"Shut up and go outside."

Alamo, Asesino, and Pozolero stood, in their underwear, on my balcony.

"Now toss it all over the edge."

Their clothes and shoes, sunglasses and jewelry landed in the gutter below.

"Who puts the clothes on your back?" I asked. "Buys your cars? Diamonds?"

"You do," they mumbled.

"You have nothing without me. So when I say I *need* something, I don't expect you to be partying. We're not little kids playing games anymore."

"Can you just tell us what we did wrong?" Pozolero pleaded.

"Ivan is dead."

The hiss of their collective inhale told me they were as surprised as me.

"I'm told he broke into somebody's house and the man who lived there killed him," I said. "In *Tanner*."

Alamo rubbed his temples. "Ivan was our best tracker."

"Exactly. So if Tanner, Texas, is where Ivan died, the girl he was tracking for us is somewhere close," I said. "Clearly loyalties still lie with Grande there if we are only hearing of this *now*. We must make the birds sing. It's time to send another message."

"*Plata o plomo?*" asked Asesino.

Silver or lead. Those who cannot be bought with money get eliminated with bullets.

"Whatever it takes."

JANE

The tiny apartment outside Manchester, New Hampshire, with my mom, snow collecting on the windowsill, flakes falling so softly it was like the world had slowed down.

My aunt's house in the Third Ward in Houston, police sirens warping the early morning hours.

Tanner High . . . It was just my latest foster home. Another temporary resting place on my way to . . . *what*?

Somewhere in Mexico, Lobenzo was whispering to his wolves to find me.

But instead of racing north, I was standing in a silver-and-blue dress on a football field. Because Cade asked me to.

My world is full of worlds, ceilinged with stars that don't align, constellations jagged as this afternoon's lightning. It made the sky look cracked enough to fall down around us, but then rain never came. How long can a person live like a terrible storm is about to hit? That isn't really even living. It's waiting.

I was tired of waiting. But I would, because Cade said he had something to tell me before I took off. After the game, he said, we needed to talk. What was one more night, he asked. It was important, what he had to say. Please wait. And I couldn't say no.

"Are you so excited?" Jojo bounced up and down next to me. "First big performance!"

Gunner's mom paced nearby.

"Hi, kids," she said to us as she passed. "Jane, nice to see you here."

Jojo dug her elbow into my side and whispered, "Yeah, Jane, nice to *see* you."

"What's that for?" I elbowed her back.

"Gunner so has a thing for you if the sheriff is going out of her way to say hello."

"Oh, please."

"Oh, please yourself. *I* heard y'all made out at Savannah's party. You have a *boyyy*friend."

"Gunner's not my boyfriend."

"But he wants to be."

"Whatever. It was just a kiss," I tried to brush her off.

"I've never seen Gunner like anyone like he likes you. It's for real, Jane!"

That made me sadder instead of flattered. Gunner liked the version of me that Cade and Mattey and I had made up. Jojo too. My only friends had no clue who I even was. It was anything but real.

"Ready?" Jojo squeezed my fingers.

The band marched onto the field, and we fell into our routine. Savannah led the moves, front and center. We plastered smiles on our faces. It wasn't her fault she was who she was. Or rather, it wasn't her fault I was me. That was more like it. We spun around and then dropped into splits, hopped up, swished hips. We were born into our fates. Mansions and barns. Fathers who protect us, fathers who hit us, fathers who never even meet us. The formation shifted, and I fell in line next to her.

As Savannah and I danced, arms and legs and bodies moving the same, I noticed her eyes looked as determined as mine to see something beyond what was right in front of us. Maybe I was wrong and we weren't that different. I had nothing. She had everything. But we both danced like it was the only way to pump color back into the world.

The band cleared the field, and the football team came running through the paper mouth of a roaring cloth lion to line up in the foggy green light. We fell back to the sidelines as the crowd cheered and the game launched into action.

"Go, go, go!" Jojo hollered.

Cade had rolled out for a pass, but at the last second he decided to run it. He dodged guys left and right and kept running and running. His legs moved in a blur. His body angled as he darted by everyone and flew across that field for a touchdown. Everyone started cheering. I did too. The smile that crept across my face stuck there and wouldn't go away. Cade was good. He was so good. Even someone like me, who didn't know the first thing about football, could see that.

"That's my boy!" A gravelly voice rang out from behind us. "Did all y'all see that? That's my boy!"

"Oh jeez, it's your *uncle*," Jojo hissed in my ear.

"Who?" It popped out before I realized what she meant. "You mean Cade's dad. Really? Here?"

"I know, right? He hasn't been to a game in forever. Must have felt bad for beating on his own son," Jojo mumbled, shooting a pointed glare over her shoulder.

Cade's dad teetered on the bench above us, where Mattey was sitting. "Oh hey, Mattey, how you doin', boy?"

"Fine, Mr. Evans." Mattey looked nervously over at me.

"That was a hell of a run, wasn't it?" he slurred. I tried to turn away so that he wouldn't notice me. He was drunk again. Or still drunk. Either way, it wasn't pretty.

"Hey, Danny." Gunner's mom had homed in on him. "How you feelin', my friend?"

"Feelin' fine, Connie. I mean *Sheriff*. And how are you?"

"Oh, I'm just dandy. Why don't you go ahead and sit down with your niece? Take a break . . ."

"Niece? I ain't got a niece."

"Wow, he must be really drunk," Mateo quickly interjected as Jojo and the sheriff looked on in confusion.

"Boy, who you callin' drunk?" Cade's dad lurched his way closer, looming over Mattey.

"All right then, Danny," Sheriff Healey stepped in. "Let's take a walk."

Mr. Evans swayed back and forth. She put an arm lightly on his back and guided him off the bleachers. He and the sheriff headed out to the parking lot, toward her cruiser.

"That's so weird," Jojo said with a frown. "He acted like he'd never seen you before in his life."

Just then, a giant boom ripped through the stadium.

All consuming.

The sound had a sharpness to it that put ice in my veins, the kind of noise that leaves a sick vibration in your heart and throat.

The players froze on the field. Everyone went completely still.

Then we heard screaming from the parking lot. Smoke spiraled up.

People around us were starting to panic, racing to get off the bleachers. The metal clanged with hurried footsteps, and the whole structure rattled like it was about to fall down.

My legs felt fused in place, but Jojo grabbed my arm and Mattey's and forced us through the crowd to the field.

"What the hell happened?" she yelled.

A paramedic running by answered. "Car bomb."

CADE

I figured that if a leg got blown off, it was gone, like a clean sweep. Sure, it would be bloody. But I didn't think about the fact that the skin and muscle would be shredded and a long piece of the bone would still be left sticking out, jagged where the foot flew off.

Gunner's mom's pants were in shreds. There were little pink pieces of flesh all over the pavement. I didn't know how she was even conscious. "*Get back, get back.*" The police tried to push us away, but Gunner and I were too fast and got in right next to her. His voice was raw as he yelled, "*Mom, Mom, oh my God, oh my God.*" Gunner took her head in his hands, and his dad dropped to his knees, breathing in a panic, stroking her face, telling her in a whisper that she was going to make it. She was the color of ash. Her eyes didn't understand.

Police taped off the lot, pushing us back, and I allowed myself to disappear into the crowd and away from Sheriff Healey, Gunner, and Gunner's dad. They were huddled together like they were physically connected. I could feel the prayers coming off of them, and I added my own. *Please let her be all right. Don't let Gunner lose his mother. Don't let Tanner lose our sheriff. Let this be the worst it gets.*

Bomb-sniffing dogs funneled their way through the lot. Every cop's car, every elected official's, was getting searched first, but you could tell nobody here was going near their own cars until they got cleared too.

And then I saw him. My *father*? What in the world would he be doing here?

"She was going into the cruiser to get me some water," he was mumbling to the police officers. "And then, out of nowhere, kaboom."

My dad was covered in blood—the sheriff's blood though. Other than some shards of glass that had sliced his face and forehead, he seemed to be fine. And, God dammit, drunk.

I was up in his face before I even realized what I was doing.

"Did she come out here for *you*? She was trying to help you, and this happened?"

He wrapped his hand around my wrists, forcing me back. Two cops stepped in fast to separate us.

"That bomb woulda gone off either way, now or later. Cartel thugs blow shit up and you're gonna yell at me?" My dad was getting louder. Everyone who wasn't still staring at the emergency workers loading up Gunner's mom and rushing her off in the ambulance turned their attention to us.

"Why don't you yell at your *mother*?" he hissed. "She's married to one."

"You know what? Stumble around into a frickin' IED, for all I care."

I turned around and walked away. Then I broke into a jog. Everyone, it seemed, was going in a different direction, crisscrossing like cattle gone crazy from a coyote. Except for Jane. I spotted her, standing still, on the edge of the football field, frozen in horror.

Jane was the eye of this storm, but I ran toward her, the only place to run.

THE WOLF CUB

I turned on the television while lounging in bed. The sheets were tangled. That bothered me. I liked them pulled tight and smooth. But the whisky was smooth. When I finished my glass, I placed it on the back of my leather-bound copy of *Crime and Punishment* and flipped to the news.

The reporter said officials were investigating a brazen attack during the classic American institution of high school football. I wondered whether if I offered her an interview, she would dare meet me somewhere alone.

"How did you become so powerful?" she'd ask.

"Let me tell you a story," I would say, and the pretty reporter would hang on my every word, impressed by how much knowledge I held. I would tell her about Paricutín, a volcano I read about, uncovered by a farmer here in Mexico. He was tending to his crop of corn when a huge crack appeared in the dirt. A rotten smell seeped out. It was sulfur. There was a massive rumble, and the earth gave way into a giant fissure that started spewing fire and rock. No one had any idea a volcano could come from nowhere like that. It is called a scoria cone. It can appear suddenly, and the eruption . . . it can build a mountain.

The reporter would understand I was also talking about myself. I had been here all along, a volcano sucking down the countryside to rise. *I* was the mountain.

A sharp rap on the door interrupted my daydream. "Come in."

It was Alamo. He smirked. "We brought you a present."

I turned off the television and grabbed my gun, following Alamo downstairs. He called for Asesino and Pozolero. They forced a man with a bag over his head through the door and to his knees, hands tied behind his back.

"We found Grande's accountant. He doesn't know where the tunnel is, but he has some interesting information about who might."

The man was shaking. Whimpering.

"Answer all of our questions, or I'll kill you in a way your *family* will remember," I ordered.

The man's voice trembled. "Grande is working with someone in the United States. We call him the Mad Son."

"And where is this Mad Son?"

"I don't know," he swore. "I've never met him. I only coordinate the payments. He's overseeing construction on that side of the border."

"The *Mad Son*," I pondered. I pointed to Asesino. "Peel back the layers. I want his real name. His address. His home. His business. Find out *exactly* who he is. And then . . . find out who he loves the most."

They had done well again—my Fortress, Soup Maker, and Assassin.

I stepped around Grande's accountant to my liquor cabinet and got out a bottle of imported vodka I'd been saving.

"My friends," I said. "This is triple distilled through birch charcoal, then filtered again through a tube of precious stones inside the bottle as you pour."

"What stones?" asked Alamo.

"They let you choose when you order. Enjoy. This is as close as we can get to drinking *diamonds*. *Salud,* amigos."

I turned to Pozolero and gave a slight wave back toward the accountant quivering beneath the bag on his head.

"Go make some soup."

JANE

Boiling water wheezed into the Styrofoam cup of soup from the vending machine in the hospital lobby. I stirred the flecks of noodles around until they got soft and handed it to Cade. He walked it over to Gunner.

"Please eat something, buddy," he said.

Gunner sat with his head resting on his father's shoulder like a little kid. He shook his head no and slumped lower into the hard chair. Plastic chairs should not be used in hospital waiting rooms. It makes it that much colder. And the colors are always wrong for whatever it is you're feeling. Tan is not enough. Orange is too much. Both of those colors dominated the room.

"How about something from the cafeteria instead?" Cade offered. "I'll go see what they have."

"How much longer before you think we hear something?" Jojo thought she was whispering, but with her there was really no such thing.

We'd been waiting outside the ER for almost four and a half hours. Two buses out of Tanner had come and gone since last night, but there was no way I was leaving right now.

Gunner reached out for my hand. I looked down at Gunner's fingers grazing mine, dark brown against pale, so pale it was almost blue, as if there was no blood flowing through me. I was empty, a black hole that would swallow his goodness. I should let go. But I didn't. I couldn't, or I would cave in on myself, like black holes tend to do.

"Thank you for sitting with me," Gunner said. His eyes were dewy and wide like a puppy's, and his bottom lip was wet from where he nervously bit it.

"Henry Healey?" a doctor called out.

Mr. Healey and Gunner jumped to their feet. I gave Gunner's hand an extra squeeze before they disappeared down a hall for an update.

"This is the craziest, worst thing that has ever happened to anyone I know." Jojo leaned in. "Do you think Sheriff Healey's going to live?"

"Don't even say things like that," Mattey said.

"What? It's a legit question."

"Be quiet, Jojo." Mattey stood up. "I'm going outside."

Jojo looked surprised. Mattey rarely snapped at anyone, let alone her.

"I think I need some air too." I followed him out.

"Hey . . ." I jogged to catch up.

"I can't do this anymore." Mattey shook his head. "I feel like . . . like . . . It's what my father said: Anyone who has anything to do with the cartel winds up dead. That guy who was chasing you, he was cartel. Don't you think that after what just happened, we should tell the police the truth about him? I know Cade thinks . . ."

"Cade thinks what?"

Cade had come out of the hospital looking for us.

"We need to come clean." Mattey was getting riled up. "Cade, I'm *really* freaked out. I know you think police are bad, but there was a *bomb*."

"Calm down. No one's fighting you on this, Mattey," Cade said. "You're right. The bomb changes everything. We need advice."

I remember somebody saying to me once that advice is what you ask for when you already know what to do but don't like the answer.

"I guess it was stupid to think this could last forever," I said.

"It was stupid to start it in the first place," Cade answered. "But we did."

"We're going to be in so much trouble for lying. We need to tell someone *now*," Mattey pleaded. "A grown-up. If not the police, my dad. Someone!"

"It's the middle of the night," Cade said. "Let's wait and see how Gunner's mom is doing. She's the only one we can trust."

"What if she's not okay?"

"I don't want to think about that."

Cade hopped up to sit on top of a big electrical box. Huge air conditioning units buzzed and hissed around us. Massive pipes climbed the cinder blocks of the hospital walls. A row of dumpsters blocked us from view. I pretended for a moment we were on a spaceship full of machines and engines rumbling us far away from here. The night was cloudy, cool, the heat that lingers deep into late Texas fall coming to a close. It was trying to hold on. I was trying to hold on.

"No stars," Mattey noticed.

"They're there," Cade said. "Even if we can't see them. They're out there."

"We're *kids*," Mattey mumbled.

"It's going to be all right," Cade said.

"How? How is it *possibly* going to be all right?" Mattey asked.

Silence fell between us. No one knew.

CADE

Sheriff Healy was going to make it. Gunner's mom would live.

First thought: *Thank God.*

Next thought: *Now what?*

We promised Mattey we would go talk to her first thing in the morning, the second the doctors let us, and take it from there.

Jane and I trekked back to the barn, exhausted from being up all night. We fell asleep as usual, side by side on our backs, then back to back facing away from each other. But when I woke up, I was curled around Jane, holding on like someone was going to take her away. My knees pressed against the backs of hers, my arms around her waist. Even our fingers were laced together. She was still breathing steady and soft. I didn't want to move. We were all wrapped up against that first chilly morning.

The sun peeked through the slats in the barn. I took a minute to soak Jane in, her hair that Hawaii-smelling shampoo I bought her. This was the girl I knew. When we were in the barn, alone, all the doubt dimmed.

I couldn't help it. I pressed my lips against the curve where her neck and shoulder met and let my face rest there in the warmth a minute. Jane's breathing changed. I froze, my lips still on her skin. Her breath caught and went a little deeper, and she pressed closer. She was definitely awake. I wrapped my arms tighter around her. She gently stroked the back of my hand with her fingers, then traced them up my arm. I let my lips trail along her neck, over her cheek, stopping by her ear. I should tell her right now: *I have your money. We can run away.*

I pushed at her shoulder a little bit, trying to get her to face me. What would her lips feel like? Her body? I pictured Jane lying in the sunshine on that rock in the quarry in her see-through underwear. I wanted to run my hands . . . everywhere. Both of our breathing was the same now, too fast, too hot. *Turn over. Kiss me.* But then what? What would that make us? *Don't do it. But do it. But don't. It will ruin everything. It will fix everything.*

We moved away from each other quickly, kicked off the blankets, and stood up. I pulled a sweatshirt over my head. Jane did the same. Our eyes connected for only the briefest second in a way that hurt. Everything that we would never say. Or do. Or be.

Today was reality—the cold air that seeped in, everything that happened last night.

Summer was over.

The barn was over.

Game over.

"Gunner's mom has surgery today," I said.

We were both quiet.

"I'll go wash my clothes at the Moraleses' and pack up my things," Jane broke the silence.

"I should go check on my dad," I said. "I'll let you know when we can talk to the sheriff?"

"Okay."

"Okay."

There was nothing else to say.

I wanted to punch someone. I wanted to kick something.

As I rounded the corner to my house, a black car pulled up. The driver's-side window rolled down, and a man in a suit leaned out.

"Can I help you?" I asked.

"Do you live here?"

"Why?"

"We have some paperwork for Mr. Daniel Evans."

"That's my father."

"We didn't want to leave it in the mailbox, and no one came to the door. It's important," he said.

"I can take it."

"Can you show me some ID?"

"Can *you*?"

The man handed me a business card.

I dug around in my pocket and fished out my wallet and handed him my license to look over. He nodded and handed me a big fat envelope.

I stared at the business card he gave me. His name blurred as my eyes focused on the title underneath. Bankruptcy attorney.

It's not so easy to break up fallow ground.

JANE

"It was all over the ground! I can't believe how much blood there was from her leg. I mean, I know it got completely blown off, but still, it was like *three* people exploded."

Jojo sat on the dryer in the Moraleses' basement while I did my laundry, zippers and snaps clanging and clinking against the metal as they circled beneath her. Cade hadn't had a working washing machine at his house in two years, so she was used to the routine. She chattered a mile a minute about the bombing. She was horrified, sure, but in the excited way that people who have nothing to do with terrible things are.

"If I were Gunner, I would want to kill whoever did that. I kind of want to kill them *for* Gunner. I am definitely capable of murder," Jojo said. "Like, if someone hurt any of my family or friends."

"You don't know that," I answered.

"Sure I do. I would straight-up shoot them. I'm not scared of the cartel."

"I am." Mattey appeared in the doorway.

He was beyond edgy waiting for us to talk to the sheriff, but too used to going along with Cade to make a move on his own.

"I'll bet the feds come sweep Tanner. I wonder who they'll find out is connected." Jojo took a bite of her sandwich. "Want a pickle or some chips?"

"No thanks, I should head back." I pulled the last of my laundry out of the dryer.

The sound the bomb made yesterday was caught in my brain, like an alarm on a ship warning that the whole thing is going down.

"Keep us in the loop," Mattey said. "You know, if you hear anything about Gunner's mom."

"I will."

The walk back to the barn was slow and sad.

Being in the barn was even sadder. I watched the sunlight shift across the floor, noting the last place the afternoon brushed, staring at the spaces where the roof was uneven with the walls. I needed to pack my bag for when they made me leave here.

D-day. I would tell law enforcement everything I knew. I would tell them about Ivan and the money I lost. I would tell them about Raff and how he died, all of them left with their blood X'ed on their faces like the cross on the pharmacy wall. What they knew killed them— that was the message. *They call it the tunnel at the end of the light*, I would tell the police. And they could go to the pharmacy near the boney-looking forest full of starving coyotes and shallow graves and see if there was gold.

What would it be like to really say goodbye, I wondered. I could only think of how it felt waking up to Cade wrapped around me, turning me into the sunlight I wanted to be. Stop. I needed to stop. In the middle of this huge and horrifying mess, being with Cade felt perfect. Perfect is terrifying. Perfect breaks.

I glanced down at the barn floor and noticed that Mattey had left one of his sketch pads behind from our long, hot days here. I thumbed through the pages. He didn't share many of his drawings, brushing them off as doodles, so I was surprised to find a perfect rendition of my own face looking back at me. Mattey was beyond talented. Here was my life in the barn, in this book. At some point he must have drawn me sleeping right after they found me. Hunter was against my legs. The lines of my body were jagged, and the shadows on my face, deep.

He had also sketched Cade and me talking at the table. We appeared so relaxed, not a care in the world. But then I looked closer. I was laughing in the picture, but he'd captured something in my eyes that scared me. I looked like I didn't believe in anything.

I put the sketchbook down and wandered out to the back of the barn, where the three of us had watched so many sunsets, talking as the sky turned colors over the faded fence. There was something about the edge of white sky meeting wind-spindled trees, charcoal limbs cutting and cut by their own offshoots, lines inside lines, the bleached horizon crosshatched to gray, that made me wonder if I could still hope for a version of what we built. This view used to catch fire in the summer, raspberry, lilac, goldenrod, the vanishing colors of hummingbirds darting to take the smallest sips of nectar and quickly gone. How can a pinpoint of honey be enough to keep them flying? We can't even see their wings. They blur white like those lines on the side of the road we are told to stay inside, but don't. A thousand nerve endings ending.

The day scraped to a close, as frayed as the flakes of white paint on the shingles behind me. My home, cracking to settle. I squinted up at the barn's weather vane as it pointed to me and then away. I wished I would dissolve in a whisper, passing like Texas dust in the sky.

Fallow ground is hard to break.

CADE

It seemed like God never let me catch a break.

In all of the papers in that envelope, there was one word that stuck out clear as day. It might as well have been painted in the sky.

Foreclosure.

I couldn't find my father. I looked for him passed out in his bedroom, checked the backyard, even the basement. Since when did he go anywhere?

I sat waiting, numb, on the couch in the living room. He stumbled home around noon.

"Why didn't you say something about this before?"

The question exploded out of me. I didn't mean to be loud. I didn't want him to know I was mad. That meant letting him have control over my emotions. And he didn't deserve that.

It took my father a minute to focus on what I was holding. I shoved the papers against his chest.

"Got nuthin' to do with you," he said after a heavy silence. "Choice already been made."

"Yeah, you chose to give up."

"Cade, there's nothing here." My father spoke like his tongue was too big for his mouth. The whiskey on his breath was so strong it was like I was smelling it straight from the bottle.

"This farm's dead. Been dead for a long time now. You know that."

"Well, what do we do then?" I demanded.

"We let things take their course with the legal stuff, and when we gotta move, we move into an apartment in town or something."

"You don't know how to do anything but be a farmer."

"I'll work on someone else's farm." My father shrugged like he didn't hate what he was saying with every fiber of his being.

"That'll last," I mumbled.

"What the hell's that supposed to mean?"

"Nothing."

"No, say it."

"You know you can't drink on the job when someone else is paying you, right?"

My father let out a snort of disgust. "I don't need my *son* lecturing me. First your mother, now you . . . Christ, this week."

"Wait, what? You saw Mom?"

"Well, shit, son, we had to sign the damn papers at the courthouse. Course she was here."

Sometimes words can hit you. I mean physically slap you in the face. My *mother* was here. And I didn't know. She didn't tell me. My dad didn't tell me. No one thought I needed to know anything about anything.

"Why the hell didn't you say so?"

My father stood up and placed his hands hard on the table. "She didn't want to see you."

"That's not true."

My dad gave me a nasty smirk. "Guess you don't really know your mother."

"You're the one who made her leave. Not me."

"Think what you want, son. She left us *both* . . . for a good-for-nothing cartel rat."

Disgust filled my throat. "Like you're any better? You're a good-for-nothing alcoholic. You're lucky I don't leave too—"

Before I could even finish the sentence, his fist slammed into the side of my face. I wasn't ready for it. I mean, I should have been, but I wasn't. I was too caught up in all the stuff I was saying, so the force made me lose my balance, and I stumbled backward.

"You want to leave me?" He was huffing. "You wanna be like her?"

I managed to scramble up. I snaked my foot out against his ankles and kicked like I was punting a football. My dad went down like a bear hit with a tranquilizer dart. He let out a grunt but rolled right over and tackled me hard, pinning me down. He started slapping me lightly on the face, over and over.

"Oh, you wanna fight? Come on, show me what you got."

I wound up and swung my fist against the side of his head. My father crumpled. He looked small. Drunk and sloppy.

Shaking, I felt for a pulse. There it was. There I was. I bolted out the door before he could get up.

For the first time ever, I'd hit him back hard. And now I couldn't even bear to see what I'd done. Who beats up their own dad? Who leaves their own kid? How could my mother have come back to Tanner and not have seen me? How are we all so messed up?

Jane. I wanted to be with Jane.

JANE

I still couldn't make myself pack up what little I had. I'd finally gotten around to at least dumping some clothes onto my sleeping bag. I kneeled down to start folding when I heard the tap-tap at the barn door that let me know not to worry—it was only Cade.

"Hi," I said without turning around as I smoothed out one of my shirts.

"Hi." His hello was cracked and raw. I looked over my shoulder with a start to see what was wrong.

"Oh my God. Cade, what happened to you?"

"I hit him. This time . . . I . . ."

The side of Cade's head was smeared in blood. He was holding his ribs. He didn't finish his sentence, just walked over and dropped to his knees in front of me so that we were the same level, half our height, kneeling there, staring at each other. I reached out and tentatively took his hands, and he melted right into me.

"What did he do? What did he do to you?" I repeated softly. I cradled my arms around him, and he let his head sink onto my shoulder, his face hidden in my neck.

"She was here," he whispered.

"What . . . who?"

"My mother."

"At the house? Now?"

"No. In Tanner. My dad . . . needed her to sign some papers about the farm. He's foreclosing on the place. Bankrupt."

"Oh no. Cade . . ."

"I couldn't give two shits about the farm."

"Then why—"

"She was *here*! Don't you get it? I haven't heard so much as a *happy birthday* from her. I don't even know if I still have a working phone number for her, because she never answers. She left me. And she comes back, signs some papers, and leaves *again*."

I shifted off of my knees to sit back on the ground. Of *course* I understood.

"I hate that when I look at myself, I can see my mom . . . more and more the older I get," I started slowly and softly. "She had hair the same as mine. Well, mine the color it normally is. And my eyes when I see them in the mirror remind me of hers every day. I remember she met this guy, and they started going out and leaving me home alone, leaving me for so long it would be night and day and then night again, and I would get so hungry but there'd be nothing in the fridge. One day I ate toothpaste just to have something in my stomach."

Cade's ragged breathing evened up a bit as he listened to me.

"And then . . . one weekend," I continued, "I was so excited because she said I was going on a trip. I remember her putting me in the car, and off I went with my aunt Nikki. And . . . she never came for me. So, yeah, I *get it*."

"How old were you?" Cade asked.

"Almost five, maybe? I wasn't in school yet," I answered.

"So, that's how it ended . . ."

"Are you kidding? That's how it *started*. Aunt Nikki never left me at *home*. She brought me everywhere with her, and then . . . left me in the *car*. In the cold. In the heat. And then one night when she left me outside a bar, someone called the police, and then it was foster care."

Cade's eyes were fixed on mine.

"Every family I thought would be my 'forever family' . . . my aunt, every foster parent I dreamed was 'the one' . . . I was wrong," I continued. "Something would happen. It always fell apart. My mother was only the *first* person to leave. Everybody leaves me."

"I didn't," Cade interrupted.

"No." I looked back into Cade's eyes and couldn't break away. "No, you didn't."

I reached up with one of the towels from my laundry and went to dab off his head, but he caught my hand and wrapped it around the back of his neck instead.

Cade climbed toward me, still on his knees, leaning me gently back onto the pile of clean clothes. They smelled fresh, like the color green, like curtains blowing in an open window. I got lost in the piles, the clothes a cushion against my back, as Cade lowered himself gently down over me, brushing my hair away from my face.

"What are you doing?" I whispered.

"Nothing," he whispered back.

"No, really."

"Really."

"Really?"

"Stop talking," Cade murmured against my mouth.

Nothing, he'd said.

Nothing in the way of our lips, the warm air we breathed, heavier and faster. Nothing but this kiss, the way his mouth felt, hungry on mine. Nothing but each other. Or we were nothing.

CADE

"Let's get out of here," I said against Jane's mouth. I couldn't stop kissing her, not even to talk. If I didn't stand up right now, we would never leave the barn. And I didn't want it to be like that *here*. On the farm. In Tanner. She was better than that. *We* were better than that.

"Where do you want to go?" Jane asked, the words more breath than voice, and the heat against my mouth made me grab her that much harder. I raked my hands through her hair and kissed down her neck like I was never going to get the chance to again. I picked her right up with me and moved us against the wall, kissing her all the way to the door. The night air was so different than it had been all these months. It was thin and crisp. It was new. *Get in the truck*, it said. *Roll down the windows. Drive away, fast.*

"Grab your bathing suit and some clothes. Meet me at the fork in the road."

It was so hard to let go of her even for a second. I sprinted back to my house, but when I got to the front yard I dropped low. I went in through the bulkhead, down to the basement, and up the back staircase. I went up to my room like I was special ops in my own house. I heard the hiss of the shower. My dad had come to. I had to get in and out quickly. I crawled under the bed and grabbed the stacks of money and shoved them into my backpack and bolted.

I jumped in my truck, heart pounding, and waited till I got around the bend to turn on the headlights. They lit up Jane standing there with her bag, hair all tangled around her flushed face, and she smiled the biggest, most real smile I'd ever seen on her. She threw open the door and jumped in before I'd even come to a complete stop.

"Before we hit the road, I gotta call Mattey."

I hadn't really even thought about what time it was. He answered all sleepy and fuddled-sounding.

"What's wrong?"

"Listen, buddy, my dad flipped out on me."

"Again?"

"Yeah, again. But bad. Real bad."

"What do you need?"

"Can you feed Hunter for a couple of days? And have your pops call school and tell 'em Jane and I got the flu?"

"Where are you going?"

"I have no idea."

"What do you mean? Did you talk to Sheriff Healey? What happened with the police?"

"We haven't gone yet."

"What? Cade . . . what the *hell*? You promised!"

"We'll talk to Gunner's mom when she's recovered from surgery. Right now, I have to get away from this. Just for a bit."

JANE

We drove in the dark. I fell asleep for a while and woke up and couldn't remember where I was, and then when I did, I scrambled up and kissed Cade to make sure I hadn't dreamed the whole thing. The sun was rising, and we were going over a long bridge so narrow and low it looked like we were driving right on the water.

"Where are we going?"

"South Padre Island."

"Really?"

"I think so?"

"You're not sure?"

"Not entirely. But almost." He grabbed my hand. "Hi."

"Hi."

"You okay?"

"Yes. You?"

"Yes."

"You look like you killed someone," I informed him. It was the truth.

"Thanks."

242

"You need to wash the blood off."

"I will."

"Also, I need to pee."

"Okay, let's stop."

Cade pulled over at a fast-food restaurant. When he came out of the restroom, his hair was wet and the crusted blood was gone. He still had a pale purple ring under his eye from the other day, along with the stitches on his forehead. And now there was a weird scrape down the other side of his face, and I noticed in the harsh light of the rest stop that his lip was kind of puffy. He was a total mess. And he still looked hot. His T-shirt clung right. His wet hair stuck up in this perfect way. Even though he'd driven all night, his gray eyes had a little spark in them I'd never seen before. I grabbed his belt buckle and pulled him toward me. He looked around kind of self-consciously for a second but then gave in. I wrapped my arms around him, and he kissed my forehead, my nose, then my mouth. And then we couldn't stop. Again.

"Get a room," someone said.

"Oh, we will," Cade fired back.

"We will?" I asked.

"Of course we will," he joked. Or wait—was he serious? My palms got tingly, and so did my face.

"Want some breakfast?"

"Um. Yeah." I stepped back to breathe a second.

Back in the truck we chugged our coffees and wolfed down the food. How long had it been since we last ate? I could actually feel the food translate to energy. I rolled down the window and stuck my face out into the salty air.

"God, I needed this," Cade said.

"The egg sandwich?"

"No, dummy. *This.*"

He reached over for my hand. We had crossed the last bridge to South Padre. The sky was shifting from pink to orange to real daytime.

"Me too."

CADE

I drove the truck right up to the seawall. The ocean was the color of a tornado sky, corroded-penny green.

"Wanna jump in?"

"Obviously."

Jane grabbed her bathing suit out of her bag and started shimmying out of her underwear under her dress and putting on her bikini.

"Wait . . ."

I grabbed her face in my hands and kissed her, probably too hard, probably too messy, but she answered it the same way. We were all over the place, all over each other, and I ran my hands all the way down her body, with only that sundress between me and her skin. Jane moved closer to me, leaning against her door as I pressed back.

"I think," Jane said breathlessly, "I think we should go swimming."

"Okay."

"Like, right now."

"Yeah, yeah. You're probably right. There are, uh, people around."

Jane fumbled with the handle behind her and practically fell out of my truck.

"Race you to the water," Jane said and took off.

I caught up easily and grabbed her. She screamed as I picked her up over my shoulder, and we tumbled into the water.

"Let's never go back," she said. "Let's live in your truck and swim in the ocean every day."

"We—"

"I know, I know. Don't say it. Let's pretend for as long as we're here . . . that this is the only place we will ever be."

Jane wrapped her legs around me in the water, and I cupped my hands under her like a seat as we bobbed up and down together with the waves.

"I can do that," I said. "I can definitely do that."

We swam. We lay in the sun. We swam some more.

"What do you want to do next?" Jane asked as we sat on the sand drying off.

"Anything you want," I answered.

"Let's find somewhere to dance," she said.

"That's anywhere on South Padre," I said. "Let's go find a party."

Jane threw on her dress, I grabbed my shirt, and we trekked toward the sound of music down at the far end of the beach. It was only noon, but the music was already bumping from a big stage on the sand. We worked our way up close, Jane expertly guiding us past guys showing off their six-packs and girls in tiny string bikinis. She seemed in her element—the sand, the music—nothing like the quiet, uncertain girl in the halls of Tanner High. Was this her scene? This is what made her happy?

"You like it here."

"I do," Jane said.

"Is this the kind of stuff you liked to do in Mexico?"

Jane gave me a suspicious look.

"I like it *here*. With *you*. What are you getting at, Cade?"

"Nothing. It's nothing."

Jane grabbed the back of my neck and pulled me down to kiss her.

"Everything stops this weekend. No thinking about anything except right now."

Her warm tongue flicked over mine, and I wanted to feel it everywhere. I hooked my fingers with hers, and even our palms pressing together made me all crazy, like it was somehow our bodies up against each other, not just our hands.

The beach got more packed as the afternoon went on. Everyone around us was watching Jane dance, but she had no idea. When Jane got to dancing, she was in her own world, so when the DJ pointed at her and a couple other girls to go up on the stage, she looked surprised.

She looked at me. I shrugged. "Go for it."

But when the other girls started stripping down to their bikinis, Jane abruptly bowed out, sliding off the edge of the stage. I knew immediately what was wrong.

"It's not that bad," I lied.

She knew. "You're lying."

"I don't even notice it."

"Everyone else would."

"You're still beautiful." I ran my fingers along the ridges of her awful scar.

"Lying again."

"No, I'm not. Honestly. Be proud of this thing. *We* stitched you up. No doctors, no nothing. You, me, and Mattey. And now we're *here*, dancing. Exactly what you said you wanted to do."

I caught her and spun her around, and she gave in with a reluctant smile.

The music picked up. And she started to really dance all up on me. Her hips ground into mine. It was like she was lighting me on fire. Where did she learn to dance like this? My head flashed real quick to frickin' Raff. Again. The guy who almost got her killed. I thought about when she lived with him, hitting the clubs, dancing with him, doing everything . . . with him. Her life I still knew so little about. No, I didn't want to go there. Knock it off. I grabbed Jane's face and kissed her hard, kissed her until that was the only thing.

JANE

Breakfast was the sun coming up over the bridge. Lunch, searing blue skies on an outdoor deck, stealing fries off each other's plates, sitting on the same side of the table with my legs draped over his. And after we got too tired to dance anymore, the late afternoon became bodysurfing, and Cade's wide smile, his hair sticking straight up from the salt and me running my hands through it.

"It's like we're kids who ran around so much we have to suddenly lie down and sleep right where we are," Cade said as we collapsed onto our backs in the sun-warmed sand.

"Do you ever miss being little?" he wondered.

"Never."

"You didn't even think about it for a second. Really?"

"Really."

"There's nothing?"

"There's nothing about being a kid that was like being a kid for me. I'm more of a kid right now than then. When I think of things like ice cream and sandcastles, I'll think of today."

"It was really that bad?" Cade asked.

"It was that *empty*."

"What's something you remember liking to do?"

"I don't know. Sitting on the carpets in whatever crappy housing project we were living in, fake painting."

"Fake painting? What's that?"

"I would trace stains on the rug or walls with my fingers, pretending it was paper and I was a painter."

"That's kind of sad."

"That's kind of what I mean."

As we rested there, with our eyes closed and fingers woven together, I could feel the wind picking up off the water.

"It's going to rain," I said.

"No it's not."

"Look. See that line of gray out there? That's the rain. I give us five minutes, max."

"I'm too tired to move," Cade mumbled contentedly. "What else? Tell me something else you liked."

"Sleeping on my mom's folded-up winter coat."

"Why would you sleep on a coat?"

"Because she was on the only bed."

"What's to like about sleeping on a coat?"

"I liked the way the fuzzy hood felt on my face and how it blocked out the sound if I wrapped it around my head so I wouldn't have to listen to her fight with whatever guy she was with at the time."

"Jeez. What's your happiest memory?"

"Leaving with Raff." The answer popped out. Cade looked away, and I instantly wanted to swallow the words back up, but it was too late.

"I meant as a *little* kid," he said flatly.

"I know. Sorry. It's just . . . that the happiest part of my life *then* was when it ended."

He nodded with an upside-down sort of smile that I didn't believe.

"I have happier memories than that now," I tried to turn the corner.

"Yeah? Like what?"

"Like every day with you. I don't need . . . all this. The beach is great, but the best times I've ever had—*ever*—are sitting there talking to you back home, in the barn."

"You don't have to say that."

"I'm not saying it because I have to."

I matched Cade's glare, mirroring his ridiculous furrowed expression up close, until he couldn't help but let it go and laugh.

"Fine," he said.

"Good," I said. "You really shouldn't be jealous of someone's *dead* boyfriend."

"Aw, come on, Jane, that's not fair."

"*I* know."

Cade scratched the side of his nose. "I have nothin' to say to that."

"I *know*."

"You play dirty," he said.

"I'm not playing." But I was, a little. "The only way for me to talk about something like this is to be a little irreverent about death in general."

A rumble of thunder made us both sit up, and then the rain reached us, icy drops pummeling us.

"Told you!" I yelled as we raced back to the truck.

"You're *so* sunburned," Cade pointed out once we climbed in. "We should go get you some aloe. And find a place to stay."

"We can sleep on the beach once the rain passes."

"I was thinking somewhere nice," Cade said.

"Oh, you mean like your truck," I joked.

But Cade was pulling into a big resort called Pearl. It looked like it was out of a magazine. He had to be using it to make a U-turn. But no, he threw the truck in park.

"Cade . . ."

"Wait here one sec." He left me in the running truck and dashed into the front lobby. A couple of minutes later a valet came out. He gave the rusty, banged-up truck and the two of us a scathing once-over. I didn't blame him. There was no way we looked like we could afford this place. And we couldn't. Unless . . .

"Cade, are you out of your mind? We don't have the money for this."

"Sure we do."

Cade leaned against a pillar by the big double doors and pulled me against him. Rain streamed down his face and off his chin. It beaded on his lips. His eyes were serious.

"Let's go up to our room. There's something I need to tell you."

CADE

I told her because she deserved to know. I told her because I finally dared to. I told her because I was crazy about her and never wanted to have a secret from her ever again. But I'd be lying if I didn't admit that a little part of saying it right there, when I did, was because I wanted to show her I was better than him, than Raff. It probably doesn't make sense to anyone else. I mean, Jane said it best: You shouldn't be jealous of someone's dead boyfriend. But I needed her to see me as the good guy. I didn't want to be another person who lied to her, stole from her. *I* wanted to be her favorite memory.

"I found the money."

"Ah! I knew it!" Jane screamed and jumped up and down, clapping her hands. "That's amazing! Where was it?"

"The storm drain—"

"But we looked there so many times."

"I know. All the rain got me to thinking, though. After big storms Mattey and I used to race boats there when we were kids. We'd follow the boats all the way to the drain and watch them get sucked under the road. That's when I realized we never thought to look on the other side of the highway, right? So after practice . . ."

The smile fell off her face. She cut me off.

"Wait . . . after *practice*?" Her eyes looked so hurt I wished I could kick the shit out of myself. "Why . . . why didn't you tell me right away? Cade . . . I was *leaving*. Were you going to let me leave without it?"

"No! Of course I wasn't. But then *you* almost left without telling me."

"And that's on me," Jane said. "But this . . . I mean, Cade, you were mad at me about the passport . . . and all the while you . . . you didn't tell me about *this*?"

I sank down to sit on the bed facing the wall. "I'd never seen that much money before in my life."

I could hear Jane breathing behind me, waiting for what I had to say.

"I *was* going to tell you right away. But then I saw you with Diego. I worried that maybe you were still mixed up with the cartels somehow . . ."

"So *you* would keep the money?"

"I thought . . . when you told me about him, I would tell you about the money."

Jane let out an angry huff. "But you didn't."

"I was going to! So many times. After Savannah's party. Then after the game. But first my dad went ballistic, and then Gunner's mom got hurt." My voice dropped to a whisper as I tried to keep it steady. "I'm telling you *now*, Jane. I'm sorry I didn't before. But for God's sake, who cares? You have two hundred thousand dollars to do what you want with. You wanna leave, fine, take it and go."

Jane didn't say a thing for what felt like a really long time.

"Do you mean that? You'd want me to just take all the money and leave?"

"Do you really have to ask?" I said, staring at the wall. And that's when I realized what this was really all about. I hadn't even been honest with myself.

"It's less about not trusting you . . . than being selfish," I tried to explain.

"You wanted the money."

"No. I wanted you," I blurted out.

"I don't understand."

It was time to lay it all on the line.

"The truth is, I held off telling you about it because the money meant you could leave sooner. And . . . you're . . . pretty much the only person I have."

I felt the mattress sink down as Jane climbed onto the bed behind me. She hesitated but then crawled over and wrapped her arms around me and then her legs. She rested her head against my back.

"Same," she softly said.

I relaxed into the coil of her body. I could feel the stress of the lies dissolving. *This* was us. This was the version we wanted. But it wasn't the only version. And we both knew it.

"What if we never go back?" Jane asked. "What if we just . . . leave . . . from here?"

"What about football? Hunter? My life . . ." I trailed off.

"Right . . . your life."

"I mean, trust me, I'd love to never see Tanner again . . . but I also . . ."

"Need to see the football thing through. Everything you've worked for. I know," she said.

Jane had to leave. I had to stay. This weekend was all we had. We would go back and spill everything to the sheriff for their investigation. They'd send Jane somewhere far away. They'd have to. At least she'd be safe. There was no running off together. And there was no going home, the home we felt or made or knew . . . because every secret was catching up to us and making our world smaller and smaller. We could barely fit.

JANE

"No more secrets," Cade said.

"No more lying," I answered.

We lay side by side, looking up at the fan flicking moonlight across the ceiling.

"Promise," he said.

"Are *you* promising or asking *me* to?"

"Both."

"Promise you'll let me know you're okay," Cade said, "from wherever they hide you."

"Promise you'll come find me when you graduate?"

"What, are we negotiating here? A promise for a promise?"

"Is that so bad?" I asked.

I could see a flicker of a smile cross Cade's face. The bed was so soft, the sheets so smooth. If I looked at him for too long I would get lost in his eyes and then his lips, his arms, chest, warm skin, and that would be it. I would forget that this was temporary.

"I don't want to go to sleep," I said.

"Me neither."

"Being awake here with you right now is like the dream. And when I go to sleep, the nightmares . . . that's reality."

"What are they about?" Cade asked. "The dreams you always wake up from crying?"

I stopped myself from answering.

"No more secrets," Cade reminded me. "Why do you always say *I won't tell*?"

"Because I saw stuff I never should have." I could still see it all so clearly. "I dream about that small-town pharmacy where Raff killed God knows who . . . and the pool back at our condo where I found him dead . . . every. Single. Night."

Cade sucked a big breath of air in and out. "Everything you've been through . . . you're stronger than anyone."

"Even when it looks like I'm being strong, inside I'm falling apart. Strong can break too," I said into my pillow. "Like concrete. It's supposed to be so strong, right? But you drill into it wrong and fissures go out every which way . . . and even the sturdiest-looking branches snap under too much weight. . . . There are so many different ways to break."

"Glass shatters," Cade said.

"Ceramic cracks," I answered.

"A door is kicked down."

"Bones fracture."

"Legs get blown off."

We both got quiet, thinking of everything that had happened.

I felt like all of those things: shattered and cracked, beaten and empty. And somehow Cade gluing me back together made me all the more aware of the seams and scars. I was so used to being made of sad, disconnected parts that to be whole felt wrong somehow. Happy was for other people. People who deserved it. Not someone who ran away and left her boyfriend staked to a deck chair. Not someone who sucked innocent people into her mess. The blood was chasing me. It was a wildfire consuming a forest, a city, all of America.

"I wonder if the college recruiters will come back," Cade said. "After the bomb . . ."

"They will," I said. And I believed it. I had to. I had to believe that good things would still come to good people. I had to believe that Cade would get everything he ever wanted.

I sat up and looked down at him, tangled in the white sheets . . . this boy who picked me up from the mud, hid me in a barn, ran with me from a hitman, put a roof over my head. This superhero who literally had saved my life was still only human. Cade hadn't told me about the money right away because he was just like me, trying to find his way to a better version of life. He was stumbling into his own holes, as he pushed away from Tanner, a railway town with no locomotion, no engine to make anything turn, move.

I felt what I said next in my heartbeat.

"You're taking half, you know."

"What do you mean?"

"Half the money. You're keeping it."

"Jane . . ."

"Just in case you somehow don't get a scholarship."

"It's not my money."

"It's not mine either. It was Raff's."

I tucked my head under Cade's chin, letting my lips brush his collarbone. I didn't want to think about Raff. Life was Cade now, this perfect body curled against me. I traced my fingers along his arm, the muscles along the front and back of it from football. I needed to memorize this moment: half a year's events—or a lifetime's—rolled inside a two-day trip, separately beating hearts compressed too suddenly in a gasp of honesty. I thought about paper burning, so pretty as the edges glow orange and then fold in on each other, like a flower blooming in reverse . . . so pretty that you forget it's disappearing.

Raff's name hung between us.

When Cade finally rolled over, he took my face in his hands. "It's strange for me to think . . . you were in love with someone. I never felt like that before."

"Before what?"

"Nothing."

"Come on," I sighed. It was hard for me to explain Raff to Cade. "I told you, we weren't *in* love."

"You moved to a different *country* with him."

"Why wouldn't I? We were each other's best chance. But . . ." I wasn't sure I should continue out loud. "I feel terrible saying it."

"You can say anything to me."

"Of course I wish he were still alive. I will never, *ever* forget what happened to him. But . . . I'm glad I'm not with him anymore. We . . . we were like prisoners who escaped jail together. We ran away, and that kind of bonded us together."

"Why did you stay with him then?"

"He was the only thing I knew. But we would never be better than the lives we left. It's not like you and me."

"You and me how?" Cade asked.

"You know . . . *you and me.*"

"I don't know." Cade had to be playing dumb on purpose.

"You want me to say it?" I challenged.

"Say what?" Cade faked innocence.

"What you wouldn't say a minute ago. You *know* what."

"No, what?" Even in the dark I knew that Cade was all-out grinning his big teasing grin now.

"I don't care, I'll say it," I announced. "I'm not scared."

Cade abruptly pulled me against him and kissed me. "Neither am I."

"I love you," we said at the exact same time.

CADE

I woke up to Jane outlined by sunlight, her hair sweeping down over my face, her hands planted on my chest, a leg on either side of me.

"Today, we get whatever we want," she announced.

"Oh yeah?"

I put my hands on her hips.

"We have, oh, a couple hundred thousand dollars at our disposal. We can talk about what we want to do for real later. But today, let's be stupid."

"I think I like stupid."

I moved against her a little, letting our bodies settle into each other. Jeez, she felt good first thing in the morning like this, in this fancy room with the nice sheets and the bed that swallowed us up. Jane let out a little murmur and melted down on my chest, draped on top of me. I raked my fingers up her sides, under her shirt, starting to pull it up and off, when there was a polite knock on the door.

"Oh," she said. "I forgot I ordered room service!"

"Now?" I groaned.

She gave me a devilish look and slid off me. "Why? What *else* did you have in mind?"

Breakfast came served under a big silver cover, like in the movies. Jane had ordered Belgian waffles with strawberries and whipped cream.

"Want a bite?" she asked.

"How about later?" I wanted to get back to *her*.

"Now, or I'm going to eat it by myself," Jane warned.

"Seriously? You care about breakfast right now?"

"You don't?"

She held an overloaded forkful to my mouth, and I wasn't really sitting up far enough, so it spilled down my chin. Jane laughed and leaned over to grab it with her mouth, her lips lingering. She kissed down my chest then back up again and abruptly crawled away. I reached out for her, and she rolled even further.

"Are you torturing me on purpose?" I groaned.

Her eyes glinted with mischief.

"Oh," I realized. "You totally are."

"You deserve it," Jane said.

"No I don't."

"You lied to me," Jane said.

"You lied to *me*."

"You have to make up for it."

"What about you?"

"I said it first."

"What do you want me to do?"

"You're a smart boy. Take me on a date. Somewhere amazing. I'm going to go take a shower."

I rolled out of bed. "Game on, girl."

While she was showering, I thumbed through a binder from the bedside table, full of things to do. I felt a smile creep onto my face. I had an idea.

JANE

They said the boat could carry twenty-eight people. Cade said he wanted it for only the two of us and offered to pay in cash.

"Are you serious right now?" the guy asked.

"I'm sorry?" Cade gave him a discerning look. He pulled off the role well.

"No, no. *I'm* sorry." the man backpedaled. "You look like a couple of high school kids."

"We robbed a cartel out of Mexico," Cade deadpanned.

The guy let out a guffaw. "No, really . . ."

"Really? We're very lucky to have the parents we do." Cade smiled charmingly.

"All right then, what excursion you want?"

"All of them."

"Wait, what?"

"You heard me," Cade said. "Everything."

The guy shook his head. "You for real? Okay. Everything it is. Welcome aboard, trust-fund babies. I'm Bob. You can call me Captain."

"Um, what's everything?" I asked Cade under my breath.

"Snorkeling, sunset cruise, dolphin watch, and tubing."

"Hold on . . ."

"And parasailing."

"Did you book us for every activity this company offers? In one afternoon?"

Cade grinned at me. "Is it a date?"

"You're crazy."

"Well, is it?"

"Uh, *yeah*." I squinted up at Cade in disbelief.

He kissed me on the forehead and walked off ahead of me, proud of himself.

"First up, parasailing!"

We got strapped into a little two-seated harness that hooked to a colorful parachute. We crouched into a seated position as the guys pulled us back as far as they could. The wind filled the chute, our feet left the ground . . . and we suddenly lifted. The motorboat ahead of us shot forward, and I screamed as we flew higher and higher over Port Isabel. I kicked my bare feet against the cool rush of air. Suddenly the wind let up and we dipped abruptly down, only to catch again and stretch back tight. Cade was laughing beside me as we snapped into the sky.

The resort skyscrapers of South Padre Island turned to tiny blocks below us, and I could see the different depths of color in the water. The sky rattled my face. Somewhere in the distance was dusty, land-locked Tanner, and beyond that, Mexico. Up here, there was only Cade and me.

Us. All day. We held on the best we could to a huge inner tube as a small motorboat hurled us across the top of the waves. When we popped off, we hit the water like rocks skipping, falling underneath in a jumble of our own arms and legs.

And in the cloudy turquoise water, Cade grabbed ahold of me so I wouldn't get freaked out by all the fish. It took me a while to get used to the snorkel. I kept forgetting my nose was blocked and I could only use my mouth to breathe. Cade caught on fast, holding his breath and diving down to the coral below us to poke around, then spewing out the salt water as he surfaced.

Schools of tiny silver fish scattered around us and reformed on the other side like we weren't even there. Big yellow glazed fish glided by, their fins looking sharp enough to cut. Fish with underbites, fish with ridges, fish with huge tails. Their shadows danced on the sand of the seafloor. Off in the distance I spotted a huge one with an eye the size of a dinner plate. A barracuda, suspended, stared at me sideways. *It is more scared of you than you are of it*, I told myself. I wished that could be the case with people too. It was time to get back on the boat, I thought. Somewhere in the water, there are always sharks.

CADE

The sunset was crazy bright. I couldn't have ordered it up better. And right on cue, a pod of dolphins jumped out of the water and splashed back in, riding our wake back to shore.

The boat ground against the dock.

"I want to go back to the hotel," Jane whispered against my ear.

"We will."

"With *you*. Now."

"Oh."

I don't even know how we found our way there. We kept stopping to kiss each other, leaning against the sides of buildings, holding on to each other's elbows while walking along backward so our mouths could stay pressed together. At one point I scooped up Jane and ran with her on my back. We kissed in the lobby and in the elevator, and when the door opened on one of the floors, some uptight older couple looked horrified, which made us laugh.

We fell into the room, and I started to peel Jane's shirt off her.

"Ow, ow, ow," she said.

She was sunburned even worse than the day before.

"You're a lobster."

"I know." She pouted.

I grabbed the aloe we bought. "Lie down. I gotcha."

Jane glanced at me over her shoulder and lay down on her stomach on the bed. I gently eased her shorts off and undid the back of her bathing suit. She flinched and let out a little squeal as the cold aloe vera landed on her skin. I rubbed it as gently as I could across her shoulders, down her thighs. Then she rolled onto her back, and I leaned down to kiss her before rubbing the aloe across her stomach . . . and then all over. Jane reached up and took my shirt off over my head and pulled me down onto her, all slippery slick from the aloe. Her mouth met mine, everything I knew now—the full lower lip, her tongue, the little sounds she made that told me she liked what I was doing.

"Do you . . ."

"Yes."

JANE AND CADE

Cade kissed down the side of my neck, to my shoulder, tracing my collarbone with his fingers.

Fingers were ten points of heat on my back, Jane's hands wrapping around me, pulling me against her skin.

Skin on skin. When Cade's chest grazed mine, my back arched to meet him, and I pressed against him, breathing in time with his breathing.

Breathing her in, I ran my fingers through her hair, down her neck, up her bare arms.

His bare arms, strong, holding him over me, smooth chest. The world slowed down in the safety that radiated from him, even as my heart sped up. *What's your real name?* he whispered.

Whispered echoes of everywhere she'd been before me filled my head when she didn't answer me right away. There was still so much about her that I didn't know.

I didn't know why everything was unraveling. *Come on*, he said again, *tell me your name.* Why did it matter? Especially right now. I'm not that person anymore. "Jane" was the only version of me worth loving. How could he still not trust me?

How could she still not trust me? As long as I only knew "Jane," I wasn't in love with all of her. Maybe she didn't love *me*, just the idea of me, shelter, school, friends, a make-believe life. What happened to no lies, no secrets?

No secrets. The promise not to lie itself a lie. *I can't believe you still won't tell me*, Cade said, and abruptly got up and dressed. I pulled the sheets over me. But when Cade closed the door behind him, I was left a certain kind of naked no clothes can cover. I offered him everything. And he didn't want it. He didn't want me.

JANE

You would think that what happened in Mexico would have taught me to be good. But I am not good. Cade knew it. That's why he couldn't go through with it. He thought he was better than me—and he was. Or was he?

I got up and threw on my clothes. No. Not this time.

"Cade!" I called out to him as he opened the door to the stairwell at the far end of the hall. I jogged to catch up. "Stop."

By the time I got to the top of the stairs, he was already close to the bottom. I looked over the railing at him. He was framed by flights of stairs between us, squares inside squares, each getting smaller, and he was stuck in the smallest one.

"You don't get to just walk out on me!" I called down to him.

"Why? That's what you're going to do to me," he said.

"That's not true." I started down the stairs toward him, stopping when I was just one flight above.

Cade threw his arms in the air. "I'm supposed to believe you want to share the money? You want me to come find you . . . *someday*? I've told you about my mom. You've seen me beaten up by my dad, but you can't even tell me who you really are?"

"One thing doesn't have to do with the other. I meant what I said."

"Who knows what you mean?"

"Has anyone ever told you how judgmental you are? You think I'm this bad person . . ."

"I didn't say that . . ."

"You're no better than me! You took my money and lied about it. You *want* that cartel drug money!"

"Oh, come on now. Stop."

"No, you stop. You're a thief. You're no better than *anyone*."

"And you're a coward who latched on to a thug to get out of dodge. You're no different than someone like my mom."

Cade's words were a punch in the throat. I sat down on the steps. "And there it is—how you really feel."

"Shit. Jane. No." He rubbed his eyes and forehead and tugged at his hair. He started up the stairs toward me. His phone rang in his pocket, but he ignored it.

"I shouldn't have said that." Cade sat down next to me.

I didn't look at him. We sat in silence.

"I just can't wrap my head around it all sometimes, you know?" he finally said.

"It's not like I chose my life," I answered.

"But you *did*. You chose to go with Raff."

"I meant my *whole* life. My mom. The foster families. I mean, come on, Cade, stay with loser foster family . . . *or* . . . run off to a resort town in sunny Mexico. Spring break forever." I put my hands out like a scale. "What would *you* have done?"

I curled up against the railing and rested my chin on my knees. "I didn't see the underside of where all the money was coming from with Raff . . . until I was in too deep. My life felt like a crazy movie. Clubs. Fancy cars. Even the guns. Drugs. None of it seemed real."

Cade didn't answer. I fixed my eyes on his and challenged, "But the barn, I guess that wasn't real either, was it?"

"No. The barn was real," Cade said without hesitation.

His phone rang again. He pulled it out of his pocket. I looked over at the screen.

"It's Mattey. You should get it."

"He'll be fine."

"No. Look at your missed calls. He's called four times."

Cade picked up.

"Hey . . . wait. What? Mattey, slow down. . . . You're kidding me."

Concerned, I leaned in, trying to hear.

"Are you okay?" Cade asked. "Hold on, hold on . . . *when*? How are they? Where are you? . . . Are you serious? . . . For real? . . . We're on our way."

Cade hung up. He looked stunned.

"What? What is it?"

"Last night Mattey's house got broken into, torn apart . . . and then his sister Sophia . . . she was attacked."

My heart sank. "By who?"

"She was with Diego. Their car got stopped in the road. He got pulled out and beat up bad."

"Oh my God." It was my fault.

"They're both hurt real bad."

"Because of me?" I asked in a tight voice. "The passport?"

"Diego runs with a bad crowd. He probably owed somebody something. Don't jump to conclusions till we know more," Cade said, but I could tell he was thinking the same thing.

My heart was pounding. I was tied to everything going wrong in Tanner. The bridge. The bomb. The break-in. The beatings. If Tanner were a house, it was like I tossed a cigarette out the window and never worried about it smoldering near the foundation. I didn't pay attention to the early smell of smoke. Then, when I couldn't help but notice the smell, I still refused to believe anything was on fire. Only now, when the flames were visible, lapping at the walls, sucking out the oxygen, was I forced to admit my world was burning down. I never walk away in time. I run away too late. I knew this. I always knew. But it didn't stop me. I really wanted that house.

CADE

Door kicked in. Windows smashed into pieces you could slice a throat with. Drawers, cabinets, closets opened. Every belonging not where it belonged.

Mattey said their whole house was trashed.

That's how my head felt too, like someone went in and ransacked it.

I never drove faster. A ride never felt longer. We came to a screeching halt outside Tanner Memorial Hospital. I flew out of my truck. Jane hung back.

"I need a minute."

"I'm not leaving you alone out here. Come *on*."

"Where the hell have you been?" Jojo demanded when we rushed in. "Mattey called you, like, nine hundred times."

Jane approached Mattey cautiously. She tried to put a hand on his arm, but he shook it off and walked away. Jane faded back against the wall.

"How's Sophia?" I asked.

"We don't know yet. The doctors are with her. The police are talking to Diego right now. Where *were* you?"

"Doesn't matter. We're here now," I told her.

Right back at the hospital. Full circle. I could practically see Gunner sitting there with his dad in the ER waiting for word about his mother. But instead, this time it was Mr. and Mrs. Morales holding on to the girls and each other and crying.

"We were at a church thing when they broke in," Jojo said. "Who knows what might have happened otherwise?"

Mattey hadn't said a word to me yet.

"Can we see Sophia?" I asked.

"She's unconscious," Mrs. Morales answered.

"And Diego?" I asked.

"That good-for-nothing piece of . . . ," Dr. Morales hissed.

"*Basta, basta*," Mrs. Morales shushed him. "They both are alive. That's what we must focus on."

Mattey motioned for me to follow him around the corner, away from everyone.

"I *told* you we should have gone to the police right after the bomb," he said, fuming. "Now look at what happened."

We left with Tanner crumbling at the core, the families that held this town together, the good ones, coming undone. Dirt. Drugs. Booze. Blood.

We came back and it was the same.

Which made it that much worse.

JANE

I slipped into the lobby and out the other side while Cade was talking to Mattey, walking like I belonged down a hall where I definitely wasn't allowed. I needed to see what they did to Sophia. And then, when I found her room, I wished I hadn't. She was a mess of purple and red, bruises and cuts. She looked like a version of me when Cade found me. The machines beeped. She was unconscious.

I backed out and hurried around the corner, almost crashing into a nurse pushing a cart full of little bottles of medicine. "Sorry, sorry," I said, with my hands up, as I headed to *his* room. The *halcón*. Diego.

"Well, look who it is," he mumbled through puffy, cracked lips. "The girl everyone is looking for. Thanks for the makeover."

"What happened?" I whispered.

"You happened."

"Seriously." My heart did a weird skip thing, and my face and hands felt tingly and heavy.

"Oh, I'm serious."

A monitor hooked to him beeped high and steady.

"Please . . . tell me everything."

"You wanna know what happened? I'll tell you what happened. I'm driving with Sophia when my car tires get shot the hell up. Next thing I know I'm spinning out, the car comes to a stop, and I got my doors thrown open, a gun in my face, and me and Sophia, we're on the damn pavement."

Diego's eyes burned through the puffed slits of his bruised lids.

"And?" I made myself ask.

"And they said, 'You've been awfully quiet, boy. You got anything you wanna tell us? About a girl? A girl with real pretty blue eyes who maybe showed up here over the summer? A girl who asked for a new identity? One you gave her.'"

I froze.

"What did you say?"

"What do you think?"

"Did you tell them about me?"

"You shitting me right now? Do you think I would look like this if I'd talked? Do you think they would have gone after my girl if I'd talked?" Diego sputtered hoarsely. "But it doesn't matter anyway. It wasn't about *asking* me shit. It was about punishing me for not telling them. They already knew what they were looking for."

THE WOLF CUB

Bright blue eyes, my bull's-eye. The cell phone we took from Raff Santos when we killed him had been full of pictures of his girlfriend laughing, dancing, posing in a little white bikini.

When Alamo told me we hadn't heard from one of our loudest informants in Tanner in months, I knew he knew something. That kid, Diego, always had stories to tell us, a snippet overheard in his auto shop, something the sheriff was planning. He liked to perpetually pretend to have important information.

So when we asked specifically about the girl . . . to get silence? Weeks upon weeks. It was strange. He was protecting someone close to him.

A bird is only quiet when its own nest is in danger.

Watch his every move, I told my men. *Follow Diego. Take everything from every place he goes.*

I wondered why anyone thought they could out-strategize me. I am the bullfighter, the rock star who breaks the guitar and lights it on fire, the gladiator who wins fight after fight.

Reach into the dirt of Montera. You will find bullets. They will be rusty. Tells you how long the battles have been going on for. It was a way of life now, death. Was that so bad? Death does not have to be an abhorrent idea. The Aztecs, for example—I once read they viewed death as little more than an incident in the continuity between this life and the next, and human sacrifice was part of that process.

Every life that was owed to us, the people who needed our tunnels, they simply wanted a chance. I didn't decide what was wrong and right for them, what they were willing to sacrifice to get across. I only said, *This is what you owe us*. And I delivered. Drugs. Dreams. A promise. I was not the devil. I was a saint. *Santo Lobenzo* the powerful? The brutal? The wise? *El intelectual*.

I had my theory. And now I had my proof.

When my men broke into the house of Diego's girlfriend, they found sketch pads. Charcoal, ink, pencil . . . the notebooks they brought me were full of drawings that 100 percent matched Raff Santos's cell phone pictures. Someone was drawing portrait after portrait of the girl we needed, right there in Tanner.

I ripped out one of the sketches and issued an ultimatum.

"I want this girl by the end of the week."

CADE

I finally found Jane outside the hospital. She was facing the wall, holding herself up with one arm.

"Where were you? I've been looking for you everywhere."

"I—" Jane struggled to speak between sobs. "I snuck in to see Sophia and Diego."

I'd never seen her really cry like this. Tears, yes, shoulders shaking, can't breathe, no.

"It was *definitely* because of me, Cade. Lobenzo—the Wolf Cub—he knows I'm here in Tanner."

"We'll get help," I told her. My blood felt icy at the reality unfolding fast.

"I'm . . . ," she said between sobs. "I'm the worst person in the world. This is all my fault. All because I stayed."

I took Jane's face in my hands and roughly wiped the tears off her face. They needed to not be there. I wanted them gone. I pulled her close to me.

"I'm sorry about everything I said before, Jane. I didn't mean . . ."

"Me too."

I kissed her cheek. And then her lips were on mine. My mouth on hers. Her fingers in my hair. My hands on her the back of her head.

"What the *hell* are you doing?"

Mattey's voice sliced through.

My hands went heavy and dropped to my side as I turned to face him. Jane turned red and stared down at her feet.

"Mattey . . ." Jane's voice trailed away.

He shook his head.

"What are you doing, I mean, seriously?!"

"It's not what you think . . ." I started.

"Then what is it? Sophia has a broken nose, three cracked ribs . . . and . . ." Mattey's voice cracked.

"We didn't know what was happening back here."

"You do now. And you're here making out. For real?"

Jane reached out to try to take his hand. He shoved her arm away, hard.

"Hey now," I warned.

"You have no idea how bad it is. Sophia's brain is bleeding. She's in a *coma*," Mattey choked. "I'm *done* keeping this secret. I just told Jojo. She knows Jane isn't your cousin. She knows *everything*."

"And your parents?"

"They don't need this on top of worrying about Sophia right now. It's too much to even begin to explain to them. It's the police who need to know—immediately. Jojo and I are going, with or without you."

"It's *with* us," Jane quickly said. She looked at me. "We have to."

JANE

If I'd left Tanner when I was supposed to instead of running off to South Padre Island with Cade, I'd be long gone by now and maybe none of this would have happened. Although leaving Tanner when I was *supposed* to . . . would have meant never staying at all. Money or not, the second I stopped bleeding through the stitches I should have been on a bus toward somewhere fresh snow falls to cover the gray. Actually, I should have died in the cornfield. No, it would have been best if I'd been killed with Raff in Mexico. *Then* maybe none of this would be happening.

The ugliness had found me, hurting everyone who'd helped me. I would never forgive myself for what happened to Sophia. Mattey never would either. Or Jojo. How could I have been so selfish?

Mattey cleared his throat softly. Jojo had come out of the hospital to find us. Her eyes went from Cade to me and back again.

"All three of you lied to me." Jojo's eyes filled with tears. "And now everything I love about everything is going to be over. Jane, you know they're not going to let you stay in Tanner. Who knows if *any* of us can? Everything, school, home—it's never going to be the same. We don't even know if Sophia is going to wake up. My sister . . . could *die*."

"I'm so sorry, Jojo," I whispered.

"Let's go," she said. "I can't look at Sophia anymore or I'll burn something down."

"I never meant for—"

"I know," Jojo cut me off.

"Really?"

"Yeah, *really*. I'd do anything for the people I love. I would have hid you too, you know," Jojo said. "Then this would be my fault too. But it's not. And I'm glad for that. Because I don't know how I would live with myself."

CADE

We sat crammed together in the front of my truck, shoulder to shoulder, staring forward at the police station. When I texted Gunner, he wrote that his mom was on her way back from a specialist in Houston. Five hours away.

"I still say we should wait for the sheriff," I said.

"You've been saying that for too long. We don't have the luxury of time on our side right now," Mattey said.

"What's a few more hours?" I argued.

Jane answered instead. She sided with Mattey. "At this point, who knows? A few hours could mean more people hurt. That's not something I'm willing to risk."

"You sure?"

She nodded. "We have to."

I knew telling law enforcement was the right thing to do too. But my gut also screamed that inside this police station, it was the wrong group of people to tell. But we were stuck. They were our best bet because they were our only option.

"Fine. Let's do this," I said. Saying the words was like getting a bad piece of gristle in your steak, the meat all gray and tasteless, but you force the swallow and it goes down in a lump.

The cop working the desk looked annoyed as we walked in.

"And what can I do for y'all?"

"We need to . . ." I didn't know what to say. What did we need to do? How was I supposed to explain this?

"My sister is the one who got attacked last night," Jojo jumped in. "And her boyfriend. You had cops at the hospital interviewing them. Can we talk to someone? We have some important information."

"Oh yeah, about what?"

"The Lobenzo cartel," Jane said.

The guy squinted up at us. "For real?"

"Yes, for real," Jojo barked at him. "Get us someone in charge or something. Hurry."

"You kids better not be messing around."

The officer gave us a discerning look but picked up the phone.

"Yeah, hey, Captain . . . Listen, I got a couple of kids out here saying they got some cartel issue. . . . Yep, they say it has to do with the carjacking last night."

The police captain came out and ushered us into some sort of conference room along with a couple of other cops. Something about his face reminded me of someone, but I couldn't place it.

"This is Detective Jordan and Detective Erickson. They'll be helping gather some information," he told us.

We sat down at a long table next to a white dry-erase board where someone had drawn some stick figures doing obscene things. There was half a cold pizza sitting on a metal chair.

"So let me get this straight," the captain said after listening to our initial explanation. "You've been hiding this girl since June . . . from Grande's Gulf Cartel . . . *and* this new one out of Montera. And now, almost half a year later, you think they *just* caught on and are coming to get you?"

God dammit, these cops know how to make you feel stupid. The captain glanced down at his phone a few times and then back at each of us. He was a squirrely-looking guy with splotchy pink cheeks and beady eyes. *No, no. Don't go there*, I told myself. *Not every police officer is like the rat that ran off with your mother*. But still . . . I didn't like the way his eyes lingered on Jane. And then, right on cue, there it was.

The captain pointed at me. "You're Katie's kid, aren't you?"

My palms went all cold and sweaty. "What's it to you?"

"No need to git your panties in a bunch, boy. She married my baby brother is all."

"Yeah, well, she used to be married to my *dad*."

"I'll tell her you say hello next time I head on down their way. They bought a huge place on the water. Real nice."

The condescending smile on his face made me want to jump over the table at him. No wonder he looked familiar. He was related to the loser she ran off with. What's the damn likelihood he'd be the one here with us? The whole police force was crooked. I knew coming to them was a mistake. We had to get out of this place.

"You three wait back out there in the lobby. You"—the captain pointed at Jane—"come with me."

"Where are you taking her?" I asked.

"I'm going to talk to you one at a time. Her first," he said.

"How about me first?" I said back.

"How about you go on out and sit yourself down, like I say?" he snapped at me.

"Don't treat me like *I* broke some law," I shot back. "We're here to *report* a crime, so I don't have to do a damn thing you say."

"Really? Because last I checked, harboring a fugitive *was* a crime."

"How is she a fugitive?"

"You said she took cartel money from Mexico. Smuggled it across international borders . . ."

"Cade?" Jane's eyes were wide and scared.

"This is bullshit," I argued. "Come on, Jane. Jojo, Mattey, let's get out of here."

I reached for Jane, but the detectives muscled between us as the captain steered her through the far door.

The click of the lock might as well have been the click of a gun to my head. I was helpless. Jane was on her own.

JANE

Everything was wrong.

"Everything will be fine," the police captain told me, guiding me down a narrow hall with his hand on the small of my back.

Warnings blared in my head.

"Where are we going?" I asked.

"I want to get some more info from you. You said you took money that belonged to the Grande cartel from your dead boyfriend and ran."

I nodded.

"And you think this other cartel . . . that they're after you because you have information about a tunnel they want?"

"That's right."

Something was not right about this man.

"Hang on. Stop there." He snapped a picture of me on his phone.

"What was that for?"

"Documenting things."

"With your cell phone?"

There was nothing normal about what was happening. I started to scan the hall for an exit. There was only one, at the far end.

The police captain's phone beeped. The second he looked down at it, I started racing toward the door. I heard him shout, "Hey, hey, stop." I threw my weight against the door and popped it open, but as I burst outside, he kicked my feet out from under me. I went down hard on the concrete steps. The captain pulled me up and threw me against the side of a cop car, cuffing my hands behind me.

"What are you doing?" I struggled as he shoved me into the car. I kicked at the door and the back of the seat. "Stop! Let me go!"

I started screaming as loud as I could. How could the other police officers not see what was going on? Wait, there was a cop standing back by the door. He angled a security camera away from the parking lot and stood there with his arms folded. They were in this together.

"Cade!" I yelled. "Cade! Help!"

I knew he was inside. I knew he couldn't hear me. But I yelled for him anyway, because I had no one else to yell for. The captain fired up the lights and sirens, drowning me out, and peeled out of the lot.

"Where are we going?" I asked as he merged onto the highway at the edge of Tanner.

"I'm taking you to see my boss."

"The police chief?"

"The Wolf Cub. Lobenzo."

CADE

There was no reason they should have taken Jane alone to the back like that. I stormed out of the police station, scouring the outside of the building for anything strange. That captain's brother is cartel. That means he is too.

Jojo and Mattey followed me out. Right then, a police cruiser pulled out of the back lot and disappeared around the corner. In the back window was the unmistakable flash of Jane's face and bright blue eyes.

"Get in!" I gestured to them. "Now!"

"What the hell is going on?" Jojo demanded.

"Jane is in that police car!"

"What? Why?"

"I have no idea. But that captain is crooked."

"You think every cop is," Mattey countered. "Are you sure?"

"You heard him. He's my mom's boyfriend's *brother*. That says it all. You wanna wait around and talk about it some more while Jane is frickin' being *taken*?"

Confused, but prompted by the urgency in my tone, Jojo and Mattey got into my truck. It took everything to not peel out in pursuit, but I was trying not to draw attention to myself. The cruiser merged onto the highway and then took the first exit. I wove through traffic to keep up.

"We need to call 9-1-1," Jojo said.

"Are you for real right now?" I said. "9-1-1? So *this* captain can respond to a call about himself? No way!"

"Well, what are we going to do then? Drive him off the road?"

"I don't know, but we have to at least see where they're taking her."

The only thing I could clearly focus on was keeping track of that police car. Left. Now right. Behind the bus.

Finally, the car slowed down along a quiet neighborhood street and backed into the driveway of a run-down house hidden behind a fence. I drove past, praying no one noticed us, and parked around the corner down the road a little ways, rolling over the grass and going right in between some trees so the truck was hidden at the edge of some woods.

"Who can we call to help then?" Mateo asked.

"We gotta go try and get her," I said.

"That's insane! There's no way we can do this alone," Jojo said.

"You saw what they can do." Mateo was dead set. "No way."

"You want to let Jane be the next Sophia?" I asked.

Mateo got a look I had never seen before. For every bit of fire in Jojo's eyes, his anger was ice. I knew what I was stoking when I said their older sister's name. But I still wasn't expecting what came out of his mouth next.

"I *always* go along with what you say. Don't tell how you got a black eye. Don't say I stitched you up. Keep a *girl* a secret in your barn. Not once, Cade, have I ever told you, *No, this is a bad idea*. And you've had some bad ideas. But this one is the worst."

"We don't have a choice." I tried to calm him down.

"There's always a choice. My dad said anyone who helps the cartel is no better than the cartel. He was right. We didn't go to the police the second we found Jane, and look at what happened. They started hunting us. They've nearly killed my sister."

Mattey's face was red, the truck all filled up with the raw edge of his voice.

"Sophia was with Diego," I cut him off.

"Oh, don't blame this on him!" Mattey leaned over Jojo to get right in my face. "Diego helped *Jane*. The person at the root of everything bad is Jane."

"Guys, we don't have time for this," Jojo interrupted from in between us, putting her hands up, trying to push us back toward our sides of the truck. "We have to decide what to do."

"You know what, I take it back," Mattey said. "This isn't because of her. It's because of you, Cade. Because of everything you asked me to do!"

"*You're* the one who said for her to stay here. I never said that. *You* did," I snapped back at him.

"Because she needed us. It was too late. We were in it. What were we going to do, kick her out on her own?"

"She'd been on her own a long time."

"Then you know what?" Mattey collapsed back against the seat. "Fine. It was a mistake. My bad. I'll own it. And I'll *fix* it. I'm calling the police now."

"You *can't*. That's who brought her here."

"I'm not calling that messed-up cop shop. I'm calling Gunner back. Even if his mom's still on the road, she can tell us who to go to."

"It'll be too late."

"Well, then it's too late," Mattey said.

"You're really gonna act like this is someone else's problem? Like you don't care?"

I could barely form the words, I was so furious. How could he be acting all holier-than-thou when Jane's life was literally at stake?

"Stop it!" Jojo yelled. "We're wasting time either way!"

"Wasting time like when he was sucking face with Jane in the hospital while Sophia's in the ER?" Mattey said.

"Wait . . . what?" Jojo looked from him to me in confusion. "You and Jane?"

"Yeah, Cade and Jane," Mattey said. "While our sister was getting attacked, they were on a weekend getaway."

"That's not how it happened!" I argued. "Mattey, this doesn't matter right now. We have to help Jane. I'm going after her. Are you in or out?"

"I *know* we have to help Jane. And that's why I'm out." Mattey flung open the door. "I'm out and calling for help—real help. Because we need it. We can't go in there alone."

I punched the steering wheel hard and then slumped into the seat. Mattey disappeared through the trees.

Jojo grabbed my arm. "He's right. We *have* to wait for police. It's a suicide mission to go in that house."

"Sounds like you made up your mind."

"Cade, come on."

"If you're not coming with me, go with Mattey."

"Fine."

Jojo turned to get out . . . and froze.

Click.

Click.

Guns. Cocked. At our heads. A man at each window, eyes hidden behind dark sunglasses.

"Get out and don't make a sound," the guy aiming at me said. "Now."

JANE

A run-down house. A shadowy dirt driveway. And a Mexican police car.

Those were the last things I saw before I got blindfolded.

"Don't make a noise," the police captain said as he tucked a gun under my chin. He knotted cloth over my eyes and taped my mouth shut before shoving me out of his car.

The handcuffs dug into my wrists as rough hands pushed me to the ground. I tried to kick, but whoever had me easily grabbed my legs and forced zip ties around my ankles. I was completely immobile, in police cuffs and practically hog-tied. Two sets of hands picked me up and dumped me into the trunk of the other car.

We drove and we drove.

Without sight, there were only noises.

The hiss of the highway was secondary to the shallow, jagged sound of my breathing. It didn't sound like being alive. It sounded like being scared of dying.

When the siren suddenly kicked on, I realized what was happening. We were going to speed easily under the steel arches of the Gateway

International Bridge, lights flashing, in a Mexican police car that would never get searched. The border patrol agents wouldn't know. Or, more likely, would, but would be paid not to care—or terrorized enough not to ask.

We were going back.

Back to Mexico.

Mile by mile, minute by minute, this was the countdown to the end of my small life. At least I had met Cade. At least I had known what high school, friendship, and laughter were like. I was sobbing. I couldn't stop. Why aren't we allowed to start over? The demons hold. The demons stay.

When the wheels on the road sizzled like water spilled on a stove, I knew we were on a sandy road, leaving the highway. We came to a stop, and I was hauled out. They sliced the ties to free my feet so I could walk, then pressed a gun to my back.

Every step was a clue under my feet. I was walking over cobblestone. They pushed me up a staircase, and I heard a series of bolts unlock and then the squeak of a heavy door opening. Music played inside, acoustic guitar. I heard the twinkle of water—a fountain.

We came to a stop. More voices. New voices. My dry tongue stuck to the inside of my mouth. I tasted blood on the corners of my lips from the struggle of getting tossed into the trunk. The men forced me to my knees. The floor was cold and smooth.

"Welcome to Lobenzo's humble home," said one of the men, pulling my blindfold off.

The room came into focus around me. Marble floor. Massive chandelier. Oil paintings of grotesque moments in history, shipwrecks, fox hunts, hangings, war. Water poured out of a wolf's mouth in a huge glass-tiled fountain. I was in the foyer of a mansion.

"They call me Alamo," said one of my captors. "You got a nick-name, *guapa*?"

He was younger than I expected, muscular and square, barely older than me, with hollow circles under his eyes. He reached down and yanked the duct tape off my mouth. It burned like my lips got torn off with it.

The other guy was greasy and obese, his shaved head slick with sweat. He was wearing expensive-looking sunglasses, and his earlobes were weighed down by diamond studs.

"This is my friend Pozolero," Alamo said. "He is the Soup Maker. Do you like soup?"

"Everyone likes soup," said the Soup Maker.

"Our friend Asesino is on his way."

I knew what that meant in Spanish. The Assassin.

"Nothing?" said Alamo.

The Soup Maker's beady eyes glimmered above his fat, pockmarked cheeks.

"Let's talk about what you did to my friend Ivan," he hissed, hooking his fingers into my hair and yanking hard. "Did you shoot him? No, no you didn't, did you? Someone else did. Tell us who."

"Come on, Azules. Start talking. We know you have information about the tunnel."

I looked back and forth into their eyes.

They were letting me see their faces.

That meant they were going to kill me once they had what they needed. I stopped crying. I stopped shaking. When you know for certain you are going to die, a coldness comes into your body. The fight leaves. Like carbon dioxide—the only thing to breathe when breathing is done.

"Too good to talk to us? That's okay, *Lobenzo* is here." Alamo motioned toward the marble staircase. "Why don't you talk to him instead?"

Lobenzo was outlined at the top of the spiral stairs, shorter and slighter than I had imagined, flanked by two sleek, gray dogs. He moved as if made of liquid, pouring forward to lean over me. His nose was slightly crooked, broken at some point in his life. And he had a long scar along his neck to his jawline. It didn't say *weak*. It said, *Go ahead and try to kill me. It doesn't work.*

Lobenzo's shiny black hair and smooth skin made him appear even younger than Alamo. He looked like he could be any one of Raff's friends, just another rich surfer kid in designer sneakers and a fancy hoodie. The structure of his face was almost delicate. He didn't look a day over eighteen. When he got close enough to cup my face in his hand, he smelled like soap and mint.

Lobenzo reminded me of a portrait you'd see in a museum of a historic explorer setting out to find a new trade route across the world, his eyes full of energy.

"Jackpot." Lobenzo smirked. "Jingle. Jangle. Look at those pretty blue eyes, Azules. We've been looking for you."

He made a low snorting sound, half laugh, half disgust—a warning. My eyes flitted from the guns he carried to the dogs. They growled, and that's when I realized they weren't dogs at all. They were wolves. They weren't leashed. They sat at his feet, every muscle at the ready for his command.

"Do you know about the Aztecs?" Lobenzo asked.

I shook my head no.

"I've been reading about them lately. They believed that a god offered himself as a sacrifice and was reborn as the sun. The god of fate . . . And just as he sacrificed himself, he needed human sacrifices of blood and hearts to satisfy the thirst he experienced from the heat. During sacrifices, the priests would lay the person on a sacred stone, cut him from stomach to throat, and remove his heart."

He paused so what he said next would sink in.

"You do not do what I say, and I will slice the hearts out of everyone you love. Do you understand?"

I knew he meant it.

"Defect or die," Lobenzo said. "I thought I made that very clear. Everything that was Grande's is now mine. Somehow people are failing to grasp that concept. Why don't you tell me about your boyfriend? A good place to start."

I opened my mouth to say something, closed it again.

"Go on," Lobenzo said. "Raff Santos . . ."

"Raff worked for Grande," I whispered. "He was going to come work for you instead. He didn't want to die. He *did* defect. But then Grande killed him."

I swallowed, tried to find my voice again.

Lobenzo gave me a cold stare. "You really expect me to believe that that is the extent of your involvement?"

"That's all I know."

Lobenzo kept his eyes fixed on mine. Time hovered on the edge of a cliff, crumbled and careened into an abyss.

"I think . . . you . . . are . . . lying," Lobenzo finally said, slowly, with a sickly musical lilt. "Try again. I think you should . . . tell me what you know . . . about Grande's *tunnel*."

I took a shredded breath and said, "If I tell you, you'll kill me."

"I am going to kill you anyway." Lobenzo looked amused by me.

"So why should I say anything at all then?"

Lobenzo paused.

"Are you really trying to play hardball with me?" Lobenzo reached into his pocket and pulled out his phone and opened his saved videos. He held it up to my face and hit play.

"These men tried to rat me out to the feds."

The video began with two men sitting restrained and shirtless up against a mud wall. I tried to look away, but the Soup Maker yanked my head in place and pinched open my eyes . . . as a chainsaw off camera started whirring.

"Have I made my point, Azules?" Lobenzo asked. "It is not a matter of *if* you die. It's *how*. Make me want to show you mercy."

CADE

Praying for mercy is a funny thing. You start saying, *Please, God, let me be okay, please, I'll be good for the rest of my life, let me stay alive*, as if striking a bargain will make it happen. *Please, God, don't let them hurt Jojo. Please, God, let me save Jane.* Like I have the power or right to ask for anything.

"Walk like everything is normal," one of the men said in a low growl. "Don't turn around and look at us. Don't talk to anyone, or we shoot you and them and anyone in between. Understood?"

Jojo and I got out of my truck and walked like they said, but there was no one on the street anyway. The men led us to the house where they took Jane, forcing us around to the back door. I didn't see the police car anymore. But there were two sets of tire tracks in the muddy driveway, surrounded by a series of footprints like there had been some sort of scuffle. My heart sank. They must have forced Jane into a different car and she was long gone.

"Get down on your knees and put your hands over your heads."

They frisked us both down, taking our phones and shoving them in their pockets before leading us into the house. All the shades were pulled down. Dust floated in shadowy corners. A lightbulb hung bare over the kitchen sink. The table had a broken leg propped up on cinder blocks. The men motioned for us to sit down on the floor, our backs against the sagging counter, and zip-tied our hands behind our backs and to the rusty handles of the cabinet doors. It smelled like mold.

"Why did you follow the police captain?" the first man demanded.

Jojo was too terrified to speak.

"We didn't," I said. "We don't know who you're talking about."

"*Mierda.*"

"It's true."

"We will see if you suddenly remember," he said. "Tell us when you want to talk. Or stay here and rot."

The two men walked into the other room. We heard a door close.

"Are they going to leave us here?" Jojo whispered. "Can you break the ties?"

"No. I don't know."

The men left us there for what felt like hours.

My mouth went dry.

Jojo's shoulder pressed to mine was the only thing keeping me from losing my mind. Finally they walked back in.

"Look, you can talk to *us*. Or we can call the Wolf Cub," the other man said.

Jojo sucked in a sharp breath of air beside me as the man pulled out his phone and dialed his boss. He spoke in a low Spanish rapid fire.

All I could think about was Mattey waiting for help somewhere on the other side of the woods, wherever he went. Please, please, let Gunner's mom have come through for us. Let the good guys be on their way. There have to be some good guys left somewhere, right?

Sí, sí, the man on the phone said. He nodded to his partner and flipped his phone to video chat. The image that came into focus simultaneously filled me with relief and terror.

It was Jane. Alive. But Lobenzo had her. And that was a death sentence.

Jane's face was streaked with blood and dirt. Her shirt was ripped.

"Say hello to your friends, Azules," a voice from off camera ordered.

"Cade? Jojo?" Jane's voice was desperate.

"Where are you? Where did they take you?" I said at the same time, my arms flying out like I could somehow grab her through the phone.

"So, Jane, about the tunnel . . . are you ready to share your insight?" the man on the other end of the phone asked, the off-camera voice I could only assume was Lobenzo.

"Or do we need to watch some more of my movies? Or maybe we could *make* a new movie with your friends in it?"

Jane's face trembled up and down with the tiny movements of the hand holding the phone on the other end. If she didn't give him anything, we died. If she gave him too much, we died. There had to be the exact right amount to leave him needing more.

"Let them go, or I won't tell," Jane whispered.

"*Tell* . . . or I'll have them killed," Lobenzo said. "It's funny how you think you can call the shots."

I lunged forward, as if I could help her through the phone, only to get cracked in the head by the barrel of a gun. I landed on the floor. The guy pulled me up and pushed the phone back into my and Jojo's faces.

I could hear Jojo breathing quickly in and out next to me. Her dark eyes were huge and round.

"Who dies first, Jane?" Lobenzo's voice threatened. "Your friend? Or your boyfriend?"

Jane instantly caved at the threat against us. "No! Please."

"Where is the tunnel then?"

"It's called the tunnel at the end of the light!"

"Oh, look, you remembered." Lobenzo's words dripped with victory. "You lie to me, Azules, you try to run, they die. One misstep by you. One phone call from me. Their hearts are ripped from their chests . . . like we talked about."

Jane wrenched her head to look back at me through the phone. Had she had made the wrong choice by saying what she did about the tunnel? How do you gamble with information? She was playing chicken, running barefoot toward a train.

JANE

The tunnel at the end of the light . . . The second Lobenzo had what he needed, I could see the end of our lives blinking like a beacon.

When that tiny phone screen filled up with the image of Lobenzo's men putting the gun in Cade's mouth, the air went out of the room. My ribs felt broken, and my heart clenched dry. Cade and Jojo were going to be killed, like me.

Lobenzo put his gun to my head, the barrel a cold circle on my temple.

"Start talking to me," Lobenzo said. "Tunnel at the end of the light. Where is it? Go."

I thought about icepicks and chainsaws. Go.

Car bombs. Gunner's mom. Sophia. Go.

The gun against my skin. Go—talk.

I had to speak. Now. But the second I told him where the tunnel was, I was dead.

"I was only there once. I can't remember," I said.

"I think you can."

"I think I can too," I said. "But not from here. I'm sorry. I can only find it by sight."

Maybe that would buy me a little more time before a bullet.

"If you're lying . . ." He thrust a finger in my face.

I somehow kept myself from flinching. "I swear. I can show you."

"Fine. Let's move," Lobenzo announced. *"Ándale."*

Lobenzo moved us with stealth and skill. A run-down pickup truck with three men crammed in the front seat led the lineup. Then an old sedan. Then his dark-tinted armored car with a driver and two bodyguards. Behind us, two guys on motorcycles intermittently passed us, flanking or falling behind, the roving watchmen. The spacing between the motorcade was carefully calculated, the weapons in the cars enough to take over a small country.

We hit the main highway until we reached the edge of the city and then left it quickly in our dusty wake. The smaller towns were sleeping unaware, not a light on during these overnight hours. The people who lived there would wake with the scrawny roosters, put on their coffee, and heat their tortillas. They wouldn't know evil had passed by their doorsteps.

Our driver stayed on the phone with the men in the truck leading the way. *Left*, I would say. *Left*, he would say. *Now right. Right. Follow this road past the used-car shop and the scrubby, over-chopped forest. Now stay on this one road for a while.*

Lobenzo rode in the backseat next to me like we were just two travelers heading somewhere together. He smiled at me, which made everything worse. How could men like him even know how to make the shape with their faces anymore? It didn't mean what a smile means. It was like how a farmer calls gently to a chicken so it will come to have its head hacked off.

I couldn't get over how young he was. Once, he was a baby, just like me or anyone, with chubby cheeks and tiny little silky feet. We all start out the same.

"What are you thinking, Azules?" he asked.

I stared straight ahead.

"I suggest you converse with me. I speak; you answer. Understood?"

"Yes," I whispered.

"So?" He leaned in.

"I was thinking about how you became . . . this. About what your family might think."

"Do you think they would be *disappointed* in me, Azules?" He smirked. "Let me tell you a story. My father used to tow old cars across the bridge from Texas. Mechanics in Montera would fix them. Buyers from all over Mexico came to get a good deal on a used car."

He paused. "What does this have to do with that, you wonder. It is because the war on drugs became a war on all of us. If border security makes easy money difficult, the cartels will get it another way. Suddenly it was easier for the cartels to abduct the local jeweler and demand a ransom than get cocaine across the border. It was faster cash to kidnap the city planner's children and threaten to kill them than build a tunnel to move marijuana."

Lobenzo shrugged and stretched. "People stopped coming to Montera to buy cars because they were afraid of the violence. So, just like the cartels, we had to find new ways to survive."

He leaned even closer. "Do you know about autoimmune diseases?"

I shook my head no. I didn't know what he was getting at.

Lobenzo lit a cigar, the rancid smoke filling the car. "It's when the human body attacks its own healthy cells because some message has gotten mixed. Montera was sick like that, the city attacking the city, the cartel turning on its own people and turning the streets into a festering sore."

Lobenzo blew the smoke in a loose cloud at my face.

"When facing disease, you must build your immunities, find your antidotes," he said. "Vaccines contain the very virus they aim to cure. I am turning attention back to the border. I will make trafficking more lucrative than feeding like vampires on each other. I became the cartel to *fix* the cartel. So . . . what would my family think? They would be *proud*."

The car slowed. And there it was, the white stucco pharmacy with the big red cross painted sloppily on the side, the one I dreamed about, called out in the night about, waking Cade, haunting me.

It may as well have been the marker of my grave.

CADE

After Lobenzo hung up the phone, every fiber of my body burned with frustration. Here I was with his guys, staring at their guns, completely helpless. I looked at them. They looked at me. The minutes added up. They were daring me to speak by holding the silence. When I didn't say a word, they tried to get under my skin.

"How long after she shows him the tunnel does he wait before he kills her?" The taller man spoke to his partner but kept his eyes on mine. They glinted.

"Maybe he already has," he added. "And what shall we do with this one?"

He ran his sausage fingers across Jojo's face, tilting it up toward him. Tears streamed down her cheeks as she silently trembled. I balled my fists, wrists tied at my back, while my jaw, my bones, clenched tight enough to shatter. One wrong move and we were dead.

Once my dad caught a rabid fox in a cage trap. In my head I was foaming and pacing like that, like my teeth had gone razor-sharp and I could slice myself from the inside out.

Jojo's eyes were closed. I closed mine too. It was better not to watch the sunlight fade and know that the hours were passing with no sign of help. How much longer before the men got word about what to do with us? I had to believe that as long as we were alive, Jane was alive.

Mattey had been right, but I wasn't wrong. We couldn't do this on our own, but we also couldn't have waited to try to save Jane. Sometimes by the time you see a snake, it's already bitten you.

I prayed he'd reached Gunner's mom.

I let my eyes flicker open. The tall man was picking his tooth. The other guy was playing with a pocketknife, flipping the blade open, clicking it shut. Flip. Click. Flip. Click. It was like listening to a timer count down.

The room was almost entirely dark now. I had to consider the possibility that no one believed Mattey. If the sheriff wasn't well enough to help, who else would?

A little red light danced across the fat man's head. What was it? I watched the wavering dot move across his skin. It seemed to be coming through the crooked shades.

Just then the window shattered.

A bullet sank into his face with a sick *fwoop* noise. The tall man slumped like he was bored and falling asleep, not dying. And then . . . he was dead.

Holy shit.

"Federal agents—don't move!"

The shouts came from outside.

Lobenzo's other guy slithered forward on his belly and started firing like crazy at the door. I leaned forward with all my might and yanked. The old cabinet door came off, and I rolled in front of Jojo, curling over her, using the cabinet door as a shield on my back to hide us from the spray of bullets.

Boom. Boom. They were trying to break down the door.

"Let me see your hands. Everyone put your hands in the air."

A group of agents had stormed in the back too.

"I said hands up! Over your head. Now!"

Lobenzo's guy was surrounded. He raised the gun in surrender.

I locked eyes with a guy in SWAT gear. He reached down and hauled Jojo and me up. We burst out into blinding police lights. A SWAT team surrounded the house. As people's faces started coming into focus, I spotted Mattey. He grabbed Jojo like he was never going to let go, and he looked at me like he was never going to forget that I almost got her killed.

JANE

I was nothing special.

There are tragedies every day.

That was what I told myself as we waited in the car for word from Lobenzo's first round of men heading into the pharmacy, the police cuffs still holding my arms at my back, a gun forever angled at my head.

The all-clear phone call came faster than I would have thought—Grande's guys gunned down, the first round of his guards in the tunnel butchered.

"Are you ready to see if you are right?" Lobenzo asked.

I put one foot in front of the other, following orders.

The pharmacy smelled like blood. Like the pool deck in Mexico. I gagged at the sight of the murdered men. Freshly glassed-over eyes stared back at me, saying, *There are no good and bad guys here. Death is death.*

"Keep moving."

Behind the counter, in a closet, Lobenzo's men had discovered a trapdoor. It opened to gaping darkness. Narrow rungs hung from wooden side supports. I couldn't see the bottom.

"Go."

I fumbled down with no hands for balance, banging my chin on a few of the rungs and falling the last few feet. I landed hard on my right ankle, wincing as it rolled beneath me.

The air changed immediately, damp and hard to breathe. Lobenzo inhaled like he was smelling a five-star meal, touched the walls like they were about to slip away through his fingers.

The tunnel seemed to breathe back, alive and reptilian. Sour and thick, the silence of being underground moved over us. We pushed forward down the throat, and I felt like a prisoner in a python that would take months to digest me. I would feel it finger to toe, artery to eyelid, death in the belly of the snaking tunnel.

Alamo and the Soup Maker doubled back from where they led the way.

"We found a panel with a ventilation system. Do you want us to turn it on?"

"Yes. We need oxygen."

"But if it alerts someone?"

"You kill them."

Lobenzo motioned for us to continue. His men moved ahead, and within a few minutes we heard a big fan fire up, pushing the thick air. The tunnel closed in the farther we went. It had started out like a rocky sewer pipe tall enough to stand in, but within minutes it dropped to about four feet high and only about two people wide. In some places we had to go single file.

"Clear!" Lobenzo's men would call out as they checked ahead for him.

Others brought up the rear, ducking backward, ready to fire at anyone coming up on us from behind.

Lobenzo glanced over at me. The spark in his eye was deeply unsettling. He did not have the flat gaze of Ivan or his other thugs. Lobenzo was vibrant, manic, with the wild energy of an utter sociopath.

"Do you know how much money this tunnel will make me?" he asked.

"No."

"Hundreds of millions. Millions of millions!"

Just then: *"Mira!"*

Where the tunnel widened, shouts echoed off the wet walls, then gunshots. We dropped to the ground, protected by Lobenzo's two guards, their bodies between ours and the flying bullets. One of Lobenzo's men in the front went down. They were yelling in Spanish and kept unloading their weapons on each other. I covered my head with my arms. And then silence. Two of Lobenzo's guys lay lifeless. Four of Grande's guys were dead, one slumped against the wall, one on his back, another face down, the last crumpled mid-step.

"Just business," Lobenzo said to me once his men motioned for us to proceed.

We stepped over the bodies. Lobenzo didn't even look to see who he had lost. The tunnel wound on. It looked like the inside of an old boxcar, repeating over and over. Rounding the next corner revealed walls reinforced with wood and a track that extended into the distance, lit with dim construction lights. Ventilation. Electricity. And rail tracks.

His men cheered and clapped.

"Now we are talking," Lobenzo exclaimed.

"Five hundred!" his guard announced.

"Since the start of the tunnel?" Lobenzo clarified the distance marker.

"Since the start."

Lobenzo looked over at me. "There are roughly five hundred steps in a quarter mile. Let's see how long the whole thing is. Your turn, Azules. You can keep count from here."

I didn't dare not to.

Five hundred and one, two, three . . .

We must imagine the spirit to be free from how life ends. I would vacate my body before it could hurt.

Six hundred . . .

As soon as it was proved that this was in fact Grande's master tunnel, I would jump out of my skin and send my soul into space so I wouldn't feel what they did.

Seven hundred ninety-seven, eight, nine . . . eight hundred.

I would be slaughtered like Raff.

One thousand five hundred and seventy-three.

The tunnel started sloping up, and at the end of the slight hill we came to an abrupt stop at a service elevator. Alamo gathered three men and got on the lift. We waited. Nothing. Then a whistle. All clear.

Lobenzo, his guards, and I were the last to get on.

The open planked elevator cranked and clicked us up. Dark, blasted-out stone shifted to light cement as we popped up in some sort of warehouse surrounded by giant cargo boxes.

My mouth fell open.

Stamped on the sides of the containers: *Maddison Electric*.

We were in the far reaches of Savannah's father's factory.

The light at the end of the tunnel. It made sense now. The light-bulb factory, the electric supply warehouse. The tunnel at the end of the light. A play on words . . . and completely accurate. Savannah's *father* was working with the cartels.

I could see Lobenzo drawing the same conclusions. His brow furrowed as his eyes flicked over the room and its contents. As he put the final pieces together, he started to chuckle.

"Of course. The richest man in Tanner, Texas. Garrett Maddison. The 'Mad Son.'"

His men climbed up on top of shipping containers to peer outside.

"It appears we are on the very edge of the property," Alamo reported. "The production facilities are a good half mile to mile away. There are oil wells to the west and more abandoned storage warehouses to the left and right of us. Absolutely no sign of anyone coming or going. This doesn't seem to be a functioning section of the plant."

"Secure the warehouse," Lobenzo ordered. "It's time to let the Mad Son know he answers to us now."

A thin, sallow man piped up. He looked like he belonged in an office, crunching numbers, not pacing the room with an automatic weapon slung over his shoulder.

"What is it, Asesino?"

The Assassin cleared his throat, eager to share information he had.

"He has a wife and a daughter. The daughter's name is Savannah."

Lobenzo rolled his hands together into fists, cracking his knuckles, locking eyes greedily with the Soup Maker.

"Well then, I want Savannah Maddison by midnight."

CADE

We had been rescued, but I was still a prisoner.

"I get why you want me to stay here, but I need to be with my friends," I said.

The Homeland Security Investigation guys ignored me. Trying to talk to them was nothing like talking to Sheriff Healey. She knew us, was one of us. From the hospital she'd called the feds helping her department look into the bridge murders. They'd been asking me the same questions for hours and refused to acknowledge any of mine. I walked over to our open front door and stared out across the porch to the fields. In the distance I could see the barn. All I wanted was to be back inside those crumbling walls with Jane.

My phone rang. Jojo.

"Hi. Are you okay?" I asked.

"I'm fine. Any word on Jane?"

"Nothing."

"Shit."

"Sophia?"

"The same."

"Where's Mattey?" I asked.

"He's right here. You know these guys aren't letting us go any-where. You wanna talk to him?"

"Uh, no. It's fine. Tell him . . . tell him thank you for me, okay? For getting us out of there in time."

"You sure you don't want to tell him that yourself?" Jojo asked and handed Mattey the phone.

"Hey."

"Hey."

"Thanks," I said.

"Okay."

"I mean it."

Mattey paused, swallowed. "I didn't leave because I don't care about Jane, you know. It's because I *do*."

"I know."

"Call as soon as you hear anything about her. Promise?"

"Of course."

I hung up.

My dad sat on the couch behind me, drumming his fingers on the side of an empty beer can. One down, the rest of the six-pack to go.

"They're not doing anything!" I muttered and kicked the leg of our sagging coffee table.

"Let it rest, boy. You heard the feds: ain't safe. They're on it. You made a big enough mess already. Let them do their jobs."

"We're investigating every possible lead." The HSI guy who pulled me out of the flophouse finally acknowledged me—Chuck, I think he said his name was.

"Really? Because it looks like you're babysitting me," I shot back.

"Looks like you need it. We've got some more questions for you."

Chuck was joined by another agent.

"So, let's go over this again," he said. "Jane told you she knows how Grande's guys smuggle stuff into the country."

"Yes."

"And she said Grande killed her boyfriend and his associates before they could disclose that information to a rival cartel?"

"Lobenzo's cartel. The Wolf Cub."

"You believe you heard Lobenzo himself speaking on the phone?"

"Yes."

"Have you heard him before?"

"No."

"Then can you be sure it's him?"

"I mean . . . I guess not. But that's who Jane said was coming after her."

"Because she knows where Grande's tunnel is."

"On the phone he told her to say where the tunnel was or he'd kill me and Jojo, and she said it's called the tunnel at the end of the light."

"And that was it."

"He hung up once he had what he needed."

The investigators sighed. We'd hit the same dead end again.

"I have a headache," my father interrupted. "Where are my meds, Cade? Are we out, or did you pick them up from the pharmacy?"

Two beers down, four to go. I shot him a disgusted look and . . . wait! Pharmacy!

"Hold on," I told investigators. "There is another thing I just remembered. Jane talked in her sleep. She had nightmares and would wake up saying something about a pharmacy."

"Wait, what?" Chuck's head shot up.

"Jane always had nightmares about some pharmacy. She told me once that it's where her boyfriend killed a bunch of people."

The men exchanged a look, and the other investigator stepped away and got on the phone.

"What?" I demanded. "Tell me."

"It's federal business," Chuck said.

"Please . . . ," I begged, my voice cracking.

He took pity on me.

"Look, kid, this could be nothing or it could be huge. A pharmacy outside of Montera has been on our radar for months now as the possible entrance to Grande's super tunnel. We've been trying to get Mexican police to cooperate."

"Do you think that's where Jane is?" I asked.

"It's certainly a possibility," Chuck answered.

The other guy hurried back over. "Uh, yeah, we've got a problem."

"What now?" Chuck asked.

"Some bigwig factory guy's daughter just got abducted."

"Geez. Do we think it's connected?"

"The timing would say so. Either way, we've got to pull some resources to address it."

"What's her name?"

"Savannah. Savannah Maddison has been abducted."

JANE

"**This warehouse is Mesoamerica,** and you're in my sacred ball game." Lobenzo spun in a circle, arms over his head, waiting for word about the Mad Son. And Savannah.

"We've discussed the Aztecs. What about the Maya? Did you know that historical anthropologists used to believe the Maya were a peaceful people dedicated to building and astronomy, stonework and stars?"

Lobenzo was like an encyclopedia. Information spewed out of him. A computer melting down.

"Azules." He kicked at me. "Let's chat more, you and me. Now, where were we?"

"Stonework and stars," I whispered.

"That's right. So it turns out that the Maya weren't peaceful at all. Recent advances in the interpretation of their stonework revealed they were actually a very violent, warmongering society. Capturing prisoners was a priority."

Lobenzo threw back his head and laughed. "Those prisoners would be ritually humiliated. Sometimes they would force them to reenact the battles on their ball courts. The losing prisoners would be *sacrificed*."

His face was inches from mine. I somehow managed not to flinch.

"What? That doesn't disturb you?" he asked. "Me either. Many of the societies applauded for advancing mankind practiced ritual human sacrifice. Carthaginians. Ancient Israelites. The Etruscans who lived in what is now Tuscany. Wine country. *Salud!* How do you like that?"

He traced a finger along the profile of my face. "Hawaiians. Mesopotamians. Egyptians. The Chinese. One historian claims the Celts would build a huge figure made of straw and wood and would throw animals and humans into it and make a burnt offering of the whole thing . . . the wicker man. But . . . *but* . . ."

Lobenzo held up one finger to make his point. "For every writer who claims the barbaric practices are proven in archaeology, there is another who says that perhaps bones and drawings could be explained another way. Human beings *want* to believe we are better than we are. But I can tell you, human sacrifice is still alive and well today."

He was trying to terrify me more. A cat playing with the mouse it will eat.

A flurry of motion at the entrance to the warehouse grabbed his attention.

Oh no.

They had her.

The Soup Maker and the Fortress hauled in Savannah. She sank to her knees as soon as they released their hold on either elbow.

"Welcome," Lobenzo called out, and she shrank away from the sound of his voice. "Say hello to your new roommate, Azules. . . . I said . . . say . . . hello!"

"Hello," I whispered as my mind screamed silently in terror for her, for us.

"Jane?" Savannah could hardly breathe as she struggled to make sense of what was happening.

"Defect or die," Lobenzo said softly. "Everything that was Grande's is now mine. Your father, the Mad Son, as he's known, is not quite understanding that concept. He has been overseeing the construction of Grande's new tunnel. Apparently, I need to send a stronger message that it is now *Lobenzo's* tunnel."

"My *father*?" Savannah dissolved into more choked sobs. She didn't believe it. Of course she didn't. Her world didn't have a place for this in it.

"Stop crying," Lobenzo ordered. "It's bothering me."

That made her cry harder.

"Enough," Lobenzo said.

She didn't stop. Lobenzo nodded to the Assassin. He grabbed one of Savannah's hands, which were taped behind her back.

"Nice manicure," he said before ripping off her pinky nail with his pocketknife pliers. Savannah shrieked.

I wanted to dive to help her and cower in the corner at once. My stomach rolled. This was nothing compared to what they were capable of.

"Next time I tell you to shut up, shut up," Lobenzo said.

Savannah curled into a fetal position and dry heaved.

This was not what we were meant to be, dark matter, our own antigravity, the reason solar systems fall apart and explode. Big or small, quiet or loud, either way we progress toward our endings. At some point we try to end, we *want* to end, because it is better than the uncertainty.

"Gentlemen." Lobenzo smacked his lips. "Who's in the mood for soup?"

Their laughter in response grated low, rocks against rocks.

"Let's find a way to teach the Mad Son how we will kill his daughter if he does not work with us in every way for the rest of his life."

He paced like a tiger in a cage. "I know! We'll make a movie. You know how I like to make movies."

Lobenzo looked over at me. "Azules . . . you can be the star!"

CADE

It went off like a lightbulb over my head. That was the irony of it. When the feds said Savannah was taken, it hit me as hard as a tackle on the field that knocks out your air.

The tunnel at the end of the light.

The name Jane had said over the phone to Lobenzo was more than just a name. It was a clue, a code. End of the light. Light factory.

Why else would Savannah be targeted? The tunnel must have an opening in her dad's factory. It all made sense. The men strung up on the bridge worked for Mr. Maddison. This was the reason Tanner was heating up. Turf war. Grande versus Lobenzo . . . They were fighting for a tunnel somewhere in Maddison Electric.

I was talking to the investigators like a crazy person who is trying to warn everyone the world is ending.

"Calm down, take a breath," Chuck said.

They started all over again with their questions. I tried to slow down what I was saying. I told them every detail Jane ever blurted out in her nightmare-packed sleep. And then my theory.

"Don't you *get* it? It's like a play on words. Instead of *light at the end of the tunnel*, it's *tunnel at the end of the light. Lights*. Maddison *Electric*."

"Worth looking into, I guess."

"You *guess*?"

When I slammed my fist against the table, my dad butted in and told me to take a beat. I stormed upstairs to my room for a second to collect myself. That's when I had an idea: the money. Maybe there was some sort of clue in that bag. I took a deep breath and grabbed the bag of bills. Funny how something goes from meaning everything to not mattering at all. If Jane disappeared or was killed, every dollar would be stained with her blood. Each dollar would be every mistake I had made, every bad decision. My mother left for money. The tunnel under the border. Money. The cartel's constant violence. All for money. Greed. Hell's furnace.

I hurried back down to the authorities congregated in my house like a bunch of useless politicians and threw the backpack down on our kitchen table.

"Jane took this from her boyfriend who got killed, Raff. It's Grande's money. Some of it's marked up."

"You've had this the *whole* time?" Chuck was pissed. "Kid, if you want us to be able to help, you have to be straight with us."

My dad's eyes bulged at the sight of the stacks of bills the agents started pulling out as he began to put two and two together.

"Are you shitting me right now?" he said. "That's what that guy I popped was after!"

"Is this it?" Chuck demanded. "Or do you have any other surprises for us?"

"This is it," I said. "Does it help?"

"Certainly doesn't hurt to follow the money trail. We'll see what we can find."

Chuck motioned for his agents to take the bag. He sighed. "Let's see if your light-factory theory has any meat."

He stepped outside and got back on the phone. When he finally came in again, he shook his head in frustration.

"Look, I made the call, but Garrett Maddison won't authorize us going into his facilities," he said.

"Wait . . . what? Who cares? Go anyway."

"I'm sorry. There's simply nothing we can do. Without Maddison playing ball, we need a search warrant."

"Why would you need a warrant? Why won't he let you search his house and factory or whatever you need to do? I mean, are you kidding me right now?"

"He doesn't want police, especially the feds, anywhere near him right now because he says the cartel is watching. He's doing what he thinks will get his daughter back alive."

"What about Jane though? What about getting *her* out alive?"

"Trust me. We've got my best guys on this. What I need from you is to stay right here. Don't go anywhere in case we need you, okay?"

"Like I have a choice."

"I mean it," Chuck pushed.

I stormed into the kitchen and punched the corner of the wall. Plaster crumbled onto the stained linoleum. Jane. The only thing that made my life worth living and I was going to fail her. Life would become hating myself for letting this happen. This wasn't supposed to be how it ended. I promised her sunlight. I said we had a future. Her story couldn't be a tragedy. The world couldn't be that brutal.

I heard the front door open and close as the bulk of the agents left. Only a couple stayed behind, guarding the front porch. Protecting me, they said. More like holding me hostage.

My phone rang. Jojo again.

"Hey."

"Just checking. Any word on—"

I cut her off. "I know where she is, and they're not doing anything about it!"

"You do? Wait, what do you mean? They have to. Where is she?"

"They need a warrant, and Savannah's dad won't let them in."

"Hold on," Jojo interrupted. "*Savannah's* dad? What are you talking about?"

"Savannah's been abducted too, Jojo. This all has to do with her father. There's a tunnel that comes out in his factory."

"Cade, are you sure?"

"Jojo, I'm telling you. I *know* I'm right. He was helping Grande. That's why his workers got killed on the bridge by the new cartel . . . Lobenzo. The Wolf Cub. And he has Jane *and* Savannah. Her dad's not letting police in because he's scared they'll kill her."

I heard Mattey in the background. "What's going on?"

"I'll tell you in a sec," Jojo said. "So wait, Cade, you think Jane is *in* the factory somewhere?"

"Savannah too, maybe. But these frickin' agents . . ." I couldn't breathe.

"No, no. It's okay," Jojo tried to reassure me. "This is good news. It's a step in the right direction . . . hang *on*, Mattey, I'll explain in a minute. . . . You have to trust them, right?"

"Yeah . . . right," I said hopelessly.

"Don't do anything crazy, Cade," she said. "Promise me you're not going there by yourself."

"Bye, Jojo."

I shoved the phone back in my pocket and walked back up to my room. There was certainly no way I could rescue Jane and Savannah on my own, but if I could get close enough to *prove* my theory—show them Lobenzo was in the warehouse, manage to take a picture, some video, something—the feds would *have* to step in.

There was no time to wait for a warrant. Jane's life was at stake, and somehow I was the only person in the world who seemed to understand that urgency. My heart was pounding out of my chest. I had to try *something*. I couldn't just stay here.

I snuck into my dad's bedroom and grabbed the gun from his nightstand, sliding it into my belt, and then slipped out my window and down the gutter pipe, creeping across the backyard to the cornfield, that same damn field where I first found Jane. I knew a shortcut to Maddison Electric, where I was convinced I would find her again.

JANE

Savannah was losing it. She was thrashing and yanking at her restraints, shaking her head around like it would somehow make the blindfold come off.

"Okay. Okay," she panted over and over.

There was no talking her off the edge. She had stopped answering me hours ago. I tried to tune her out.

How long until Lobenzo returned with his video camera rolling on whatever he had planned for us?

Maybe I was going crazy too.

Cade . . . are you out there? I guess it stays this way, you and me, a secret, I love you. I love you, Cade. Can you feel me sending you that before I go? I don't need anyone else to remember me but you.

"Are you hungry?"

Lobenzo was back.

"I'm offering you some bread. Do you want it or no?"

"May I have water?" I was parched.

"Pozolero, get her some water."

He handed Savannah the bread, but instead of eating it she knotted it up into a dirty, doughy ball in her fist, kneading and rolling it.

"Thank you," she whispered. "Please and thank you. I'm a good girl, you know."

Lobenzo held a rusted metal cup to my lips as I gulped the water. There was an eerie warmth in his midnight eyes. He liked seeing me grateful. He was relishing the power of bestowing benevolence upon me. Lobenzo wanted to be worshipped as much as he wanted to be feared.

Even after he walked away again, Savannah kept hyperventilating. I couldn't take her heavy breathing against my dark thoughts anymore. It was like a twisted beat that would fuel a contorted dance. I needed to do something to keep myself sane. I could sing. Singing is like dancing, when your body can't move. Maybe it would help Savannah. I started with regular songs from the radio, and when I ran out of those, I sang songs from little kid cartoons. Then I remembered the lullaby my mom used to sing.

"Hush, little baby, don't say a word, Momma's gonna buy you a mocking-bird. And if that mockingbird don't sing, Daddy's gonna buy you a diamond ring."

Savannah finally spoke. "Again," she said. So I sang it again.

"And if that diamond ring turns to brass, Daddy's gonna buy you a look-ing glass. And if that looking glass gets broke, Daddy's gonna buy you a billy goat."

I sang that lullaby four times in a row, in the shadows of the giant cargo containers. Alamo and Pozolero paced in the distance, almost in time with the melody, it seemed, the toy soldier and the troll under the bridge.

"Thank you," Savannah said.

"You want more?"

"No. You can stop now," she said.

"Keep breathing. You're going to be all right. The police will figure out we're here. They'll save you," I told her.

The lies were a lullaby for me.

"I don't believe this is happening. They have to be wrong about my dad."

"I don't think they are, Savannah."

"No, I don't either."

Tears rolled out from under her blindfold, and she huddled into herself, shoulders caved, knees drawn, crushed by the reality of her life unraveling.

"Stop talking!" Alamo barked over at us.

I dropped my voice to an almost inaudible whisper.

"And if that billy goat won't pull, Daddy's gonna buy you a cart and bull. And if that cart and bull fall down, you'll still be the prettiest little baby in town."

"You don't have to sing anymore," Savannah whispered back.

"It's not just for you," I replied.

My singing felt separate. I pretended it was my mother, if my mother had stayed that early version of herself, a ring of light like mothers are supposed to be for their children. Somewhere an angel opened her arms, and her song was a halo, and this song was that light.

CADE

"I knew it!" a voice rang out.

Jojo and Mattey were sitting on their bikes on the trail that ran alongside the dry creek from my fields to the train tracks.

"Cade, you can't seriously think you're going in there," Jojo said.

"I'm not an idiot. I'm not going to storm in there guns blazing," I said. "I just need to get some proof to show the feds I'm right about the factory. Don't try to stop me. Please go home, where it's safe. How did you even get away?"

"We were at the hospital with my parents," Jojo said. "Sophia woke up!"

"Oh my God. Thank God." Relief flooded over me.

"Once we saw she was okay, we snuck out while my parents were with her, because I had a feeling you'd be doing something like this."

I scanned their faces. "You told the cops on me, didn't you?"

Mattey shook his head no. "We just wanted to stop you from getting hurt."

"But . . . what the hell?" Jojo's voice caught. "Jane could be killed.

And they're *still* waiting around for some warrant? I think you're right, Cade . . . we have to do something."

I pointed to Mattey. "He's gonna rat us out and blow our cover."

"Come on, Cade," Mattey said. "All I've ever wanted is to do what would protect us all. We did it my way . . . and here we are. Now . . . fine. Let's try it yours."

"We want to help," Jojo said. "We *need* to help. This isn't just about Jane and Savannah. It's about what they did to Sophia too. Who knows what you were *both* thinking hiding Jane in a frickin' barn, but here we are. How about you hash out your feelings some other day when she's not two minutes from getting carved up by the cartel?"

Mattey and I looked at each other. He gave a little nod of acceptance. I did the same.

"We've gotta have each other's backs," I said. "By the time the feds get through the red tape it'll be too late."

"Let's go," Mattey said.

I jogged along beside them, and once the factory was in view they ditched the bikes.

"How are we going to get inside?" Jojo asked.

"I have an idea." I led them along the dry riverbed, hidden from sight by the crusted mud embankment, down to the pipe that ran under the highway. It had led me to Jane's bag of money. Let it lead me to Jane.

"Are we going *in* there?" Jojo asked.

"Trust me," I said. "It's going to take us right where we need to be."

"To the other side of the interstate?" Mattey was remembering our boats.

"To Maddison Electric."

He and Jojo tentatively stepped into the muddy water. "Are you sure?"

"Positive."

The noise of the cars passing overhead groaned through the tunnel as we sloshed underneath the highway. On the other side of the grate was Maddison Electric. Now we just had to get the grate off.

"Help me push."

We rattled and pushed the grate together as hard as we could. Nothing.

"Try this." Mattey fished a thick branch from the water. I wedged it at the bottom of the grate and cranked down on it as hard as I could while they pushed.

"It's getting loose! Don't stop now."

We pushed with every bit of strength we had, and just as the branch bent and splintered, the grate came loose with a whine. We lowered the heavy metal as quietly as we could to the ground. Sure enough, the storm drain opened up to a drainage ditch on the factory's property like I remembered noticing.

Out of breath and with hands stinging, we hunkered down, backs against the slimy curve of the pipe.

"Now what?" Mattey asked.

I peeked out the opening. Half of the building we were closest to was so old the roof was in pieces. Scaffolding stuck out against the sky.

"Let's try to get up on the roof? To see where they might be. And get a picture. We have to get a picture to show the feds."

"Look." Jojo pointed. A mountain of wires and trash reached almost to the top of the building at the far end of the lot. "Think we can climb up it?"

"It's our best bet."

I went first, running low, as fast as I could to the base of the heap.

Then Jojo.

Then Mattey.

It was tough to find steady footing. Boxes and cords slid and tangled around our feet, but the three of us managed to reach the top and step onto the roof. We crept like spiders across the web of splintered wood and flaps of tar paper to the center of the roof. I peered through a rotted hole. It was dark and quiet below. No sign of life. Jojo pointed to a broken skylight a little farther down, and we crawled across the slippery beams until we reached it. When we peeked inside there, two stories below, clear as day, were two cartel guys pacing, guns at their shoulders.

Mattey leaned over and snapped some pictures on his phone. He motioned for us to retreat. But we still had no sign of Jane or Savannah. It wasn't enough.

I pointed us ahead. He pointed us back. I pointed forward again, more insistent.

That's when the shots rang out.

No, no, no. We pushed ourselves backward toward the heap of garbage, trying to stay low. But when I kicked my legs over the edge of the roof to make the leap down, I realized the source of the gunfire was right below us. A guy armed with a massive black gun was starting toward us.

I scrambled back and grabbed a long cord from the top of the pile of debris. I quickly looped one end to a broken ventilation pipe jutting out of the side of the building and fed the other through the scaffolding into a dark hall of the warehouse below. It was our only option.

"Go down it! Hurry!"

Mattey took a deep breath and let his feet dangle for a moment before lowering himself down the cord hand over hand. Jojo followed. I kept an eye on the guy crossing the lot. He had reached the garbage pile and was starting to scramble up it.

That's when the cord snapped.

Jojo tumbled the last few feet down but managed to stand up.

I was trapped on the roof.

"Run!" I yelled down to Mattey and Jojo, then bolted across the beams of roof. I scrambled behind a cluster of smokestacks, reaching out for balance. My fingers wrapped around a bar. The rungs of a ladder! The smokestack had a ladder. I shimmied down it as fast as I could into the thin space between two buildings.

My head went to football, the heat of the game, the drills hardwired in my brain. Blood alley, head to head, one person tries to tackle you, then two try to slam you. This was my blood alley. I tore down that narrow alley faster than I'd ever run across a football field and slid across the gravel as I took the corner. I scrambled on my hands and knees toward an old delivery truck, pulling myself under the belly, where I hunkered down behind the wheels.

I could see the pipe we came through in the distance. We had to get back there.

When there was no sign of movement, I took a deep breath and ran for it, praying that Mattey and Jojo had gotten out of the empty room in the warehouse below and had already made it back through. But when I came out the other side of the highway, there was only dirt and dry blades of grass, the sound of my own breath.

I was alone.

My heart hammered.

They weren't there.

All of my friends were trapped inside Maddison Electric, along with the pictures I needed to prove it to anyone who could help me.

I lay with my face in the mud. Every second that passed was a countdown to the end of Jane. Savannah. Mattey. Jojo. And that was the end of everything.

An engine rumbled. I cautiously peeked over the edge of the embankment and saw . . . my truck?

Behind the wheel was my dad, about to turn down the road leading to the main entrance.

"Stop!" I jumped up and waved him over to the side, running to the truck and frantically filling him in.

"Dad! Mattey and Jojo are inside. The cartel is there. I was right. I *know* they have Jane and Savannah."

"Boy, you are out of your damn mind, sneaking off." He jumped out. "I told the feds you had to have come here on your own."

"If you think I'm gonna wait for them, you're out of *your* damn mind!"

"I said I *told* the feds. I didn't say I was gonna wait for them. You're my *son*, for God's sake—you think I'm not gonna come after you?"

I stopped pacing and turned to face my dad. He returned my gaze in a steady way I hadn't seen in who knows how long.

"Cartel ran off with the woman I love. They're not gonna get my boy." He spun around and started pulling out every gun he owned from the back of the truck. "Mattey. Jojo. Savannah. Jane. All those kids are in there? Let's go get 'em out."

"How?"

My dad snorted. "I called in some reinforcements."

While it was no surprise Tanner had plenty of people with an ax to grind with the cartel, I didn't expect that when my Dad said, *Let's go get them*, they would say, *Sign me up* without a second thought. But this was a testament to their anger, sure and steady—a line of cars was pulling in behind our truck, filled with the people who had become symbols of the cartel's deadly reach in this tiny town.

First were the old postmaster's two sons. Next, Lola's sister Brenna, her cousin, and his best friend. Then my dad's old buddy Tommy Mack, whose company cleaned up more corpses and crime scenes because of the cartels than anyone should in a lifetime, including the one in our house. Two of his guys had hopped in the back of the truck with him, because why not? Enough was enough. And then there was the Moraleses' neighbor whose cousin, the doctor, got killed, along with a bunch of guys I didn't even recognize. People's brothers. Neighbors.

This wasn't just about me rescuing my friends. It was about Tanner saving itself.

I looked at the factory. The smokestacks seemed to puff an almost violet haze. I looked back at everyone gathering in the field, silent and focused like a tribe heading to war. People made phone calls. Our reinforcements had reinforcements. We were a vigilante military parade. What search warrant? Tanner doesn't wait around. We protect our own. No one else will.

Lola's sister stepped up. Brenna served three tours of duty, two in Iraq, one in Afghanistan, worked private security now, and had access to some serious guns. She naturally took charge, splitting everyone into search parties and making sure each group had enough firepower and manpower.

I led them to the pipe under the highway. My dad went ahead of me. Brenna and Tommy Mack covered my back, weapons drawn, protecting me as I showed everyone the way in. We crept single file back through the pipe. Low. Silent. My heart had never pounded harder. Brenna led our group around the left side of the building. Tommy Mack's crew headed to the right in a long loop to come in the back.

Brenna's arm went up. We froze against the side of the wall. She pointed to her eyes and then up. We looked where she told us. A man stood on the roof, facing away, on guard. He started to turn, finishing his scan of the area.

Go, go, Brenna gestured for us to cut across the alley and hide under the roof's overhang so the guard couldn't see us, and we ducked beneath the shadow of the corrugated metal without a second to spare.

I dug my heels into the crumbling cinder blocks and pulled myself up to a narrow window. I could only get a good enough hold on the windowsill to do a quick chin-up and glance inside, but what I saw was enough: the two men I had spotted from the roof leaning against a storage container, guns against their shoulders, and what looked like more men in the far corner.

We had people on all four sides of the building. Our group continued forward until we got to a supply entrance. Everyone looked at Brenna. She nodded and crossed herself.

"Here we go," my dad muttered, and kicked down the door.

JANE

Gunfire broke out far away. Then it got closer. It had to be Grande's guys, surrounding us and taking back their territory. I willed myself to die in a cartel shootout instead of the murder Lobenzo had planned for me.

"*Mira!*" Alamo spotted a group of intruders.

He ducked into the shadows as another group of people burst through a side door. A spray of bullets erupted. Savannah screamed. I rolled over on my shoulder.

"Get lower," I yelled.

Savannah tipped over sideways too, and I kicked my legs to slide to her. The gunfire didn't slow. It was the wild, continuous spray of serious automatic weapons. I flattened myself out the best I could. Alamo unloaded his gun in an arc in front of him, but it was no match for the firepower coming at him.

The carbon clouds from the shoot-out seemed to take on a purple hue as a group approached, guarding in a tight unit, heading purposefully for us. As they got closer and I began to make out faces, the fear that Grande's retaliation would be unleashed on us dissolved into disbelief.

"Jane!" the people were yelling. "Savannah!"

One voice rang out clear above the others, and I shrieked his name in response.

"Cade!"

A voice can pull you toward it at warp speed. A voice can bring you to your knees.

"Get the girls out of here!" Lobenzo yelled, and someone hauled us to our feet and uncuffed us from the shipping container.

"Move!" Lobenzo shouted.

Lobenzo's men came from the dark corridors of crates and containers behind us, from the walls themselves, it seemed. Their rapid gunfire choked out in hard-edged g's: *g-g-g-g-g-g*. And then other sounds, different guns. *Ka-ka-ka. Pop, pop.* Everything was just noises to me. I couldn't conceive that bullets were actually raining in every direction.

I had to get to Cade. I had to . . . but Lobenzo had me at gunpoint. Moving in absolutely the opposite direction of where your body is screaming to go is like running with bones that have gone to jelly, the weird slow motion of an astronaut bouncing around a shuttle. The gun forced me toward the elevator. The entrance hissed smoke, and we all started coughing. A strange, purplish cloud seeped out, a cloud from hell, like the breath of a devil sucking us back into the tunnel.

LOBENZO

Purple smoke clouded the air. I tried to clear the space in front of me with my arms. A peasant uprising doesn't take down a king. The village burns. Heads on stakes mark the misstep of ever believing good holds a candle to greed. Greed is my gasoline, and this inferno was blazing. I pushed ahead. What was it, this smoke? I could barely see.

Like heaven, hell is a kingdom, and the devil reigns there as God. There should be no question who has the upper hand in the corners and crevices of this revolting small town, USA.

The fact that we were under siege not by the feds but by a scattered amateur army should have been laughable. But their numbers—and their guns—were a surprise. Surprises must be met with surprises. I would disappear back through the tunnel with the girls. It would be like we were never here. They would fight ghosts. I was an apparition. And I would haunt this town. I would claim its sad streets and stagnating businesses. I would steal its children and control its leaders. Every step I was forced to take back down that tunnel was a life I would own. *I will be back*, I promised. *I will be the locusts and the plague, the ocean waves that close in over your heads.*

This tunnel was lost. Everything we had been working for, finished. But I would come back stronger with my pack of wolves to take Tanner down. You do not cross the Wolf Cub. I fight fire with more fire.

"Burn the warehouse behind us," I choked out. "Burn it to the ground, and make sure they're all trapped inside."

JANE

The elevator sank us back into a deeper level of hell, back to how it was always going to end: my blood on their hands. This was the life I built. This was the death I would meet.

Each minute that passed might as well have been a mile between Tanner and us. We were disappearing back to Mexico, too many steps ahead to be stopped. Lobenzo and his men ran, and we ran with them, our breaths heavy, the uneven rhythm a rhythm of its own, jagged with our hurried footsteps and the tunnel's own clicks and hisses. My eyes burned. The smoke thickened. I couldn't get a breath in.

The lights flickered. The fans whispered the dank air down the tunnel.

Savannah choked. Even Lobenzo succumbed to a dry, hacking cough as he continued to push us forward into the violet smoke. It streamed past us, back into the warehouse. What was it? Some sort of gas leak? A chemical from the factory?

"Keep moving!" Lobenzo shouted. "Or I'll shoot you right here."

A massive boom rang out overhead from the direction of the

warehouse. A low rumble rolled through the tunnel. Rocks and soil rained down on us. I dove out of the way, grabbing Savannah.

When we sat up . . . we were alone, a wall of dirt and stone separating us from Lobenzo and his men. But before we could even begin to hope, another explosion shook the tunnel even harder. The purple smoke persisted, and a frightening heat coursed through the limited air. *Boom, boom, boom.* Three more explosions overhead. The wooden support beams creaked and snapped, tumbling in spears around us, cutting me off from Savannah.

We were going to be buried alive.

CADE

With only empty rope and chains to tell me Jane and Savannah had ever been there, I wondered if I imagined them across the warehouse, ghosts in a strange purple smoke seeping from the elevator across the room. My father's voice cut through the throbbing of my own pulse in my head. He was yelling at me to get down.

Lobenzo's men had stopped shooting at us, instead turning their attention to huge petroleum tanks stored against the wall and spraying them with bullets. Bullets rang out. Sparks flew.

And then a massive blast as one of the tanks blew up in the hail of gunfire.

Searing heat shot through the air, stinging my skin, making my eyes burn. Flames raced out and up the walls. The room pulsed with the blast.

My father reached me, pulled me up, and tried to drag me to the doors. "We need to get out now!"

My leg was going numb, my left arm hanging. It felt like a fire poker was shoved through me. Brenna and Tommy Mack raced to gather our group and get us out.

"What about Jojo and Mattey?" I hollered. "We can't leave without them."

Sirens wailed outside.

"The feds are here," my dad said. "You're gonna have to leave it to them. You need help, Cade. You're shot. Keep moving."

More huge booms tore from behind us as gas tank after gas tank started going off like bombs.

"Get down!"

Heat hit our backs.

Then we were blown off our feet and onto the ground.

The air rippled.

Where was color? Where was sound?

Everything went out of focus. A high-pitched ring was the first noise I heard when I could hear again, followed by muffled voices.

Through the blur, a line of men and women ran toward us. Uniforms, weapons.

The head HSI guy, Agent Chuck, was screaming at us to get out.

Feds were everywhere. Armored vehicles, police cars, fire engines, ambulances.

"Jojo and Mattey never came out!" I shouted. "We have to go back! Lobenzo took Jane and Savannah! The entrance to the tunnel—it's in there. I told you! I told you!"

"We *know*!" Chuck yelled, forcibly dragging me behind police lines. "We found the entrance by the pharmacy on the other side of the border. Mexican cops and our guys pumped colored smoke through from that end to see where it popped up here. Sure enough, it started pouring out from Maddison's warehouse here. See? Look!"

I looked up at the sky to see a plume of deep purple intertwined with the thick black smoke from the explosions.

"Seeing that purple smoke. That was our just cause to storm Maddison Electric without a warrant. But you damn fools took it on yourselves first! You didn't give us that chance!"

Another tank blasted into a fireball of toxic orange, and we all hit the dirt.

I used the moment of confusion to wrench myself to my feet and take off running, lopsided and crooked, barely able to function on my shot-up leg. But I had to get back in there, to the tunnel, to rescue my friends, to save Jane.

"Stop him!" I heard Chuck yell.

I dropped to my stomach and crawled out of sight. I kept pushing back toward the inferno that housed the entrance to the tunnel. But there was no getting back inside the burning building. Flames danced up the wooden beams and fanned out across the debris ahead me.

I couldn't catch my breath. I collapsed to the ground. *No. Get back up. Now. Do it.* Face in the dirt, my gaze fell to the sideways horizon. The dry riverbed, cracked and muddy, came into focus. The ground was uneven and angled down in a weird sinkhole, like it had caved in . . . like it had caved in on a *tunnel!* A burst of energy brought me back up to my feet, and I scrambled toward that gaping hole in the ground.

"Cade!" I heard a voice call out from the smoke.

It was Jojo and, beside her, Mattey. They emerged from the flames, and we collapsed against each other in a split-second embrace. There was no time to talk. They were alive. They were here. That was all that mattered.

"Mattey, get everyone down here to dig. I found the tunnel!"

He took off running. Jojo and I started picking through the rubble.

"Jane!" we screamed. "Savannah!"

I was scratching at the dirt like an animal, my hands rubbed bloody and raw. I wouldn't stop. Not until I found her.

JANE

The blood around me was the blood that should be in me. The red was how I was ending.

I stared beyond it to the thin and thick blades of grass, either fighting or giving in to the push of the wind off the dry riverbed. The dirt was spiked with broken pilings, splintered, reaching. I tried to reach my own arms up, to pull myself out of the rubble. I had to get to Savannah. I had to show Cade I was still here.

The wind moves and moves nowhere. I could smell everything burning overhead.

Taking on the cartel. What we did was like trying to uproot a river, yanking the current from the mud, silt from the rocks. Together we wrenched and raised all that flows and tangles, spinning or winding, above the ground. Streams flowed sideways, crashing into downpours, the thunder of a sky forced into thinner air, a surface sliced from earth, trees dangling on the edges. All sense of space in space now, black, weightless, lost.

The riverbed was dry, the crater enormous. It was the only thing visible from this quiet orbit, schools of minnows reflecting, shimmering like stars. Reeds and weeds freeze with no oxygen, dry into spears.

"Jane!"

Dust and dirt crumbled overhead, and bright sky blinded. In pieces there is peace.

The river becomes ice and rock. It either shatters or is the island.

I tried to say something.

Cade's hands reached down.

I reached up.

He pulled me into him.

Like the first day I met him.

Ten, nine, eight . . . Counting would move us backward, and we would spin and tumble and emerge squeaky-clean to last June, before all this began, before all our strands snapped and threads tangled. It was time to start again.

"Krista," I whispered to him. "My name is Krista."

"Krista," Cade repeated, as if saying hello to me for the first time. "We made it, Krista. I promise. I'm here."

CADE

It was like pulling her out of a shallow grave.

The feds caught up to me, surrounded me, and then descended into the hole, searching for signs of Lobenzo. They slid Savannah onto a stretcher, placed oxygen over her mouth.

But I grabbed Jane . . . Krista. I grabbed Krista, and even though I could barely walk, I carried her like she was about to disappear. She was bleeding and broken, like the day I first met her. She never asked me to save her that day. And I never knew she would save me every day since in so many small ways.

Home is her.

My world left perfectly askew, blown apart and put back together. I could have been run over, standing there on the tracks, but instead I jumped on this train, hauled myself in, never looked back. A couple of kids took on the wolf.

Lobenzo. His body's burning somewhere in that tunnel.

"We're going to be safe now."

She was fading. I wouldn't let that happen. We were going to be all right. We were going to be all right. I repeated it with each step I took toward the ambulances.

I remembered how once I saw a group of little sparrows take on a red-tailed hawk. The hawk flew at them singular and solo, disrupting their shape, and as they scattered, he made his strike.

But then the sparrows swung in a sharp turn together. They became one big bird, with all their beating wings and stabbing beaks moving in unison. And they came back at that hawk, and they drove him away. The flock can be a hawk to the hawk.

KRISTA

Cade's voice brought me back. My eyes flickered open to the flashing lights, the faces that promised me protection. I registered each person. The boy I love. My friends. My only family.

No matter where we would have to go now to be safe, to move on, to rebuild, home was us. And we would certainly need that in the months to come. Hospitals. News cameras. Courtrooms. Testimony. Witness protection. The fallout from an accidental war.

Life as we knew it in Tanner, Texas, would be over now. But the life we would know instead glimmered hope.

The horizon shifted in and out of focus as we picked our way to safety, uneven steps on uneven ground.

The ground beneath us can be dry or dead.

Or the ground beneath us can be carved out. A way out. Toward something better.

There is the earth you stand on. And then there is what you unearth—tunnels to the darkest places that lead you out into the brightest sun.

We fought through the storm and made it to land.

Cade is the shore. Unconditional. Jojo, Mattey, the way we learned to love. We are the gravity that holds us to the earth. We are the beginning of the light.

ACKNOWLEDGMENTS

To the team at Razorbill, I'm so incredibly lucky to go on this journey with you. You are forward-thinking, edgy, and relevant, and create the perfect balance between commercial and literary. From cover art to edits to marketing, I'm so proud and grateful to bring my debut novel to life with you.

Jess. My editor. My superhero. Do people know about all your powers? You turned my story into a book. You're destined for an incredible career and I'm beyond lucky to have gotten to work with you on *Hide with Me*. My writing is forever changed for the better because of you.

Tamar, you are a secret bolt of lightning. When you called and said that you missed your train stop because you were reading my manuscript, I knew I had just won the literary agent lottery. Thank you for loving my story, selling my story, and making my dream come true.

Jarrod, my husband, my backbone. Thank you for believing in me, pushing me, and picking up the pieces of Boni bombs as I tried to juggle it all. You gave me Texas. You gave me Cade. And you helped me discover that I even had a Lobenzo in me. This story would not exist without you.

Mom and Bap, you showed me the world and filled it with wonder. From the stories you read to me, to the ones you told me . . . thank you for the great gift of imagination. You are the roots I draw from and stars I reach for. Everything I achieve is because of you.

Dev, my little brother. From the first stories I told you about Stinky the lizard, to our radio stations, to all of our crazy games, you inspired so much of the childhood creativity that turned me into "me." Thank you for reading early drafts, and for your invaluable feedback and unconditional support.

Aimee, you (somehow) made it through my time-traveling lifeguard book. I love you for that and for your unwavering support. You keep me laughing. You keep me striving. You keep me sane.

Lisa. Thank you for Rome. From the first drafts of *Keystone* to last drafts of *Fallow* you've helped me craft every story that fills my heart. I am beyond grateful. There's a lifetime of collaboration on books and filmmaking ahead for us. A friend like you is what empires are made of.

Chris, there are three things we always need to do: eat, drink, and go to the bathroom. Thanks for always taking care of me. You can't write a book without a big brother having your back.

Dominique, my YA writing partner, the best discovery of the century. What if? Find it! Thank you for brainstorms, brainstorms, brainstorms. Your passion and knowledge have been an incredible blessing. Tour bus filled with unicorns and coffee, here we come!

Tuki. You've always known my heart. *His Eyes Shine of the Sea* was my first "novel" and you were my first fan. Thank you for encouraging me to follow my dreams. Budu, the stories we spun to get out of trouble is probably where it all began. Kakima, Norkaku, both master storytellers, I wish you were here to celebrate.

Mom Holbrook, you never blow smoke, so I know when I'm on fire! You make me believe in my worth and challenge me to up my game. Dad Holbrook, there's nothing more encouraging than when you announce "that's my daughter-in-law!!!" always with a million exclamation points.

My early readers and best cheerleaders, your critiques, feedback, and excitement made this happen: Misty, for reading my book in a day (at work, sshh). Christine, my "person." Julie, my perfect combo. Marcia, for asking all the right questions. Martina, you always knew I wanted to be an author, and knew better than me I should go for it. Thank you for reading every story and idea I send your way. Islay, thank you for teaching me that "sometimes you have to throw up your art and make this ugly thing, to make way for the great thing."

Steven Cramer. You said once a poem is simply words that never danced together before. This book is full of dances you helped me find.

Justin. A long time ago you pulled the raw honesty from the sticky angst. Thank you for celebrating every success (including kindertransport and wheelchairs rolling down the stairs).

Mrs. Gray—for your creative writing unit back in fifth grade. Getting to read aloud to the class and have them lean forward and say, "what's next?" all excited and vested in my stories, is what made me "want to be an author when I grow up."

"Agent Chuck"—you know who you are. Thank you for the true accounts of border conflicts, violence, and cartel takedowns. Thank you for the purple smoke that inspired it all.

Jase, the little love of my life, everything I do is for you. If I wasn't pregnant in the pool house, taking a little break from news, I never would have had time to pursue my passion and finish this book. You've taught me what matters in every possible way.